Our Destiny Unfolds

Constandina

Frey Dreams Publications

Editor, Nicole Mullaney

Cover Design, Frey Dreams Publications

ISBN 978-1-951185-41-1 (ebook)

ISBN 978-1-951185-42-8 (paperback)

Frey Dreams Publications

https://authorconstandina.carrd.co/

Dedication

For Jiddo, Riad.

Testimonials

"Thank you so much for the opportunity to read your great book. I really enjoyed Davina and Roger's story."

AJ Campbell
Author of *The Wrong Key*

"A tale of fates formed in a world of friendships, heartache, lost love, and manipulation. Constandina gives us a glimpse into a culture where marriages are arranged, but not necessarily beneficial. As anticipated, she doesn't disappoint in giving us the whole perspective, a happy ending, and a twist you won't see coming to get there."

Annie Mick
Author of *Manipulation 101*

Prologue

♥

*L*ight cuts through the blinds as I lay still with my hand on my belly. His arm wraps around me and for a moment, I feel only joy. This life is not mine anymore—it's ours.

A phone rings, he stirs, groggy. "Hello?"

He slips out of bed, heading to the bathroom. Muffled voices echo down the hall, but I don't linger because I'm starving. In the kitchen, I picture our child: laughing, running down the hallway. It's everything I've ever wanted and more.

When I return, he's pacing. Pale. "What happened? Is it your mom? Your Dad?"

He stops, looking at me. "I've got to go. This... this was a mistake."

"You don't mean that. You love me, I know you do."

"I can't, Jen. My wife is pregnant."

My chest tightens. "You said she lost the baby."

"She did. But now I'm going to be a father."

His eyes light up. That joy is not for me. Blurting, I say, "I'm pregnant, too."

He stiffens. "What?"

"Surprise!"

Sinking to the bed, he grunts, "How long have you known?"

"A while."

"What do you mean a while?"

"I wanted to make sure before I told you."

He looks up. "This was only a fling, Jen!"

"You don't mean that."

"I do." He stands. "I'm sorry I've got to go."

Tears fall fast. "You do what you have to do, but I'm having this baby."

He steps in close, eyes blazing. "You think you can trap me?" He grabs me too hard and I kiss him, but he jerks back. "Stop. It's over. Get rid of it."

"No. You knew I've been trying to have a child for a long time."

"You're nothing more than a fling! You agreed, and now this." He laughs, bitter. Storming out, he shouts, "You're on your own!"

The next morning, a black limo idles outside my house. For a second, hope flickers. Maybe he changed his mind. But when I open the door, my blood runs cold.

"What are you doing here?"

He smirks. "Surprised to see me, Jen?"

My hands tremble and my heart beats fast, knowing this is not good.

"Please," he says, motioning to the car. "Allow me to drive you to work."

"I don't need a ride."

"I insist." He flashes a wide, callous smile.

Reluctantly, I climb in. He follows, sitting close. His presence feels like a storm waiting to break. "What can I do for you?"

"You could tell me what you're doing with my son. He's married."

I scoff. "You're one to talk. What was her name? Laquesha. How's she doing?"

He leans in. Voice low. "Watch your tone, Jen. You should know better."

"Should I?"

He chuckles, dry and sharp. "I knew your parents, they were good people. Be mature. Water?"

I take the bottle, sip fast, too nervous to say no. "What did he tell you?"

"Everything. I'm his father. Of course, I know."

"I'm not getting rid of it."

"You already did."

I blink. "What?"

"That water I gave you," he says, "had some medicine to take care of the problem. You drank more than enough. Feeling sick yet?"

My stomach clenches, not from the water, but him, from what he's done—what they did to me. Cramping starts. Dread floods in.

"I'm taking you to the hospital," he continues. "You'll need care. Don't worry, I'll pay." His eyes narrow. "Stay away from my son."

At the hospital, I'm rushed inside. He doesn't stay. The doctor sighs and I fall to the floor. All my dreams, gone. Ripped away by power and cruelty.

But I won't forget.

And one day, I will have my revenge.

One

♥

Davina

Standing at the kitchen counter while Dad whips up our meal, and Mom plans the flowers for an upcoming event, I stare at the envelope in my hand. The bold letters and slanted writing emphasize importance.

And it is important.

It would decide my future. Either I'm accepted or rejected.

Now, as I hold the envelope, all my doubts flood back. My eyes fix on the green trees standing tall outside the window, attempting to ignore the contents in my hand. Because of the summer heat, the trees don't shade us much, like they do in the winter.

Brummana, the town in Lebanon we live in, is 20 KM east of Beirut. Brummana is a world unto itself, known for its beautiful natural surroundings and referred to as the Green Town. But to me, it's home.

Or at least it should feel that way—

I'm nervous. What if this was another rejection? And if so, what would be my next step?

The sunlight illuminates the kitchen. My nerves hammer into me, striking like a boulder of bricks. The sharp edges of the envelope still tremble in my hands, digging into my skin. My mind whirls with countless possibilities, while my heart yearns for one answer.

Taking a deep breath, I finally open it and read:

Roadwood University

October 1

Dear Davina Dwain,

It is with great pleasure that I inform you that you have been officially accepted to Roadwood University for the upcoming academic year. After careful consideration, we believe that you will thrive in our distinguished academic environment and contribute to the rich legacy of our university.

Roadwood University, founded and led by me, Mrs. Elena Roadwood, has always been dedicated to fostering a community of excellence, innovation, and tradition. We pride ourselves on providing an elite education, offering over one hundred majors in a variety of fields. Our commitment to maintaining the highest standards of academic and personal development is something I hold dear.

Please find enclosed the information necessary to complete your enrollment and confirm your place in the fall semester. Kindly return the required forms by October 5th to secure your position within our community.

I look forward to welcoming you to Roadwood University and witnessing the contributions you will make to our distinguished legacy.

Warm regards,

Mrs. Elena Roadwood

Founder and Dean of Roadwood University

Joy floods my heart as I leap into the air, excited to begin a journey I wasn't sure would happen to me.

And just like that, it begins...

On October 13th, I walk onto campus for the first time.

Roadwood University sits high on the mountain of Adma. The campus is surrounded by green so vibrant it makes Brummana look plain in comparison. Approaching the gates, excitement stirs within me.

Everything about this place is designed to impress—from the cream-colored walls and mahogany-framed windows to the silver and gold lockers gleaming in the sunlight. It is stunning but intimidating, making me feel like an outsider.

The people here are even more overwhelming. Students casually wander by in their designer clothes and shiny sports cars radiating privilege. Professors carry themselves with quiet authority, their brass-plaque parking spots a symbol of their status.

Strolling through the grounds, I feel like I don't belong. But this is the beginning of something new: an adventure. Making my way down the concrete hallway towards the dean's office, my thoughts turn inward, replaying the choices that brought me here.

Taking a year off wasn't an easy decision. For so long, I thought I didn't deserve this kind of life, as if happiness and success weren't meant for me. But now, walking through these halls, I want nothing more than to be a university student. Reaching the waiting room, I smile, with this acceptance, I believe I can be so much more.

The space is brightly lit and sterile. The only sound is the ticking of the clock on the wall, though my heartbeat seems to echo louder in my ears. I lift my gaze and my eyes lock onto a boy about my height, five-feet, eleven-inches. He looks like every girl's fantasy, dressed in an elegant suit. His dirty blond hair is tousled as if he just ran his fingers through it. He stands by the dean's office, his striking greenish-blue eyes holding mine.

We exchange a quick smile, and a spark of electricity pulses through my body. I'm so caught up in the moment I don't realize how close I've gotten until I collide with him. My bag slips from my hands, scattering its contents across the floor.

"Easy there, klutz." He catches my arm just as I've hit the ground.

"Sorry." Embarrassed, I scramble to gather my things.

"Here, let me," he offers, kneeling beside me.

His deep voice washes over me, sending a magnetic pull through my entire body, while he extends his hand toward me. His gaze steady as our eyes glimpse a quick look at each other. We suddenly find ourselves locked in a powerful stare. Slowly, we raise up off the floor.

Clearing his throat, he asks, "First day?"

I giggle. "Is it that obvious?"

"Kinda, yeah."

Placing a lock of hair behind my ear, I nod. "It is." Playfully, I hit his arm.

He smirks. "Well then, welcome to Roadwood."

"Why thank you, kind sir."

"Some things to know about Roadwood: the professors are generous, the guys are hot," he claims stretching his arms out, as he takes off his suit jacket. "And, the ladies, well—I'm still discovering, myself."

"Is that so?" I give him a crooked smile.

"It is. I'm Roger, and you are?"

"Davina. But you can call me Klutz for short."

He grins. "So, what's your major?" He looks around and leans in as if he's trying to tell me a secret.

"I don't know yet. But I'm glad Roadwood accepted me."

"Why, what happened?"

I shrug unsure if I want to open up to a total stranger, even if he is hot. "I took a year off."

He gives me a half smile, and butterflies start fluttering in my stomach. "Sounds like a conversation we can have over dinner, perhaps?"

"Smooth." I giggle. "Yeah, sure."

"Great. I'm glad you're here."

"Glad? Has it been that bad?"

He chuckles. "Nah, just being polite." I bite my lip nervously, as he angles towards me, our mouths a few millimeters apart. His lips dance on my cheek, leaving an imprint. "Nice meeting you, Davina."

I take a deep breath releasing the tension throughout my body from his kiss on my cheek.

Reaching out, he asks, "Can I see your phone?" I hand it over without question and watch as he adds his number in my contacts. Grinning, he hands it back. "Stay in touch, Klutz." He glides his fingers onto the place his lips had just been.

My eyes widen and my skin ignites.

The dean opens the door, clearing her throat. "If I'm not interrupting anything," she begins, "I'd like us to get started, Mr. Hoards."

We chuckle, glancing in her direction. He turns and I watch while he walks into her office, without peeking back at me. Tingles roam throughout my body starting from the spot his hand left my cheek. I rub the side of my face where his lips were stamped.

Before the door closes, Roger takes a seat in front of the dean's desk, his posture relaxed. Just before his eyes leave mine, he speaks my name, "Davina."

My eyes remain locked on the door as it shuts, my mind taking inventory of everything I'm feeling, from the moment we met, to the kiss on my cheek, and the emotional tornado in my stomach.

The intensity of this moment will be engraved in my memory for all my life. Klutz, the endearing way the word fell from his lips was like the sound of the waves crashing against the shore in pleasurable gasps of ecstasy.

Beating heart. Sweaty palms. Is that what I should feel when I meet someone I like?

A parade of people walk outside the door of the dean's office. I try to distract myself by casually sitting in the chair waiting for my meeting.

After a few minutes, Roger opens the door and taps my shoulder. "See you around." I nod, staring after him, secretly wanting him to come back to chat more.

The dean giggles beside me, embarrassment washing over me and my cheeks flushing knowing I've been caught daydreaming.

"He's cute, isn't he?" she teases, clearly having picked up on my instant crush on Roger.

I couldn't help but blush even more, managing to stammer out a response without thinking. "Yeah—very, very, cute."

She ushers me into her office, and I sit opposite her. Her next words catch me off guard. "So, he's your type, then?" She arches her eyebrows. "Someone you'd take home to meet Mom and Dad?"

I freeze.

I'm not used to being so transparent about my feelings. I definitely wasn't expecting the dean to bring up the idea of introducing someone to my parents. The question hangs in the air, unanswered, as I attempt to collect my thoughts.

"My parents mentioned you have a sense of humor," I tell her, trying to avoid the query.

"I do? Yeah, maybe. Your father and I studied together and when your mother came into his life, she was in mine too. When I got married, your mother was my maid of honor, so, they know me well. I get how they may say I have a sense of humor. Thank you for the compliment."

I look closely at her, curious about my parents' friend, but I couldn't stop thinking about what she said about Roger. My parents and I never talk about boys in that way, and that was kind of—surprising. I hope this won't be a thing. She doesn't seem like a typical dean. Mrs. Elena has a certain style to her that I find both professional and unique. Her office looks different from any other office I've been to before.

The room glows with bright colors, decorated with vases from China, pictures from Italy, and chairs from Spain and England. It's like stepping into a worldly café instead of a stuffy dean's office.

That fact helps to put me at ease as I settle into one of the comfortable chairs. Along with the welcome note, she gave me a handbook. I thumb through it quickly, taking in the information about classes, resources, and campus activities.

As I read, the dean began to share her own experiences as a university student, offering advice and encouragement. I could tell she genuinely cared about helping me succeed and making the most of my time here.

Feeling more comfortable in her office, I start to open up and ask questions, grateful she patiently answered each one.

"In case you need anything specific, please don't hesitate to ask. Based on what your parents told me, you had a hard time looking for a university."

I clear my throat as I rubbed the back of my head. "Yeah, it was rough. But—I am happy you accepted me here..."

"No problem. I know you haven't filled out the major form, which I'm hoping you will do once you're sure of what you want to study. The beauty about Roadwood is that we give you a year to decide–take any courses you want and then choose a major. Students usually take the whole year to decide, but some choose halfway through. Don't rush it; just enjoy and have fun. I've assigned you an advisor, someone who's down to earth and helps all his students get wherever they need to end up."

"I'm interested in finding a roommate or a dorm room, for my late-night studies at the university, if possible?"

She places her hand on her lips, tapping them before speaking. "Unfortunately, none are available, but if anything changes, I'll have your name in my file for housing and let you know when I find a place for you. Sounds good?"

"I guess, thanks." I stand up, taking my stuff with me to leave. "Thank you very much, Mrs. Elena."

"Welcome to Roadwood, Davina. We're lucky to have you." She gestures to her door, and I walk out.

My meeting was nothing like I expected, from the warm welcome to the colorful décor, everything felt inviting and even comfortable. I had envisioned a formal environment, but she left me feeling optimistic about my time at university.

I can do this!

Two

♥

Roger

I run my hand through my hair, groaning in frustration. "Okay, Jiddo, yeah, I get it... I get it, okay!" Hanging up the phone in defeat as I sit in my black matte BMW 330i, I can't help but think about my life, being born into a wealthy family.

My parents are successful in business. All my friends thought I had it easy because I'm rich and have everything handed to me on a silver platter. But they were always busy with work, leaving me with nannies and tutors for most of my childhood. Not even having time for each other, and I often heard them arguing behind closed doors.

As a child, I didn't fully understand what was going on, but when I grew older, it became clear that they only stayed together for my sake, and while I appreciate their effort, it always left me feeling like I was walking on eggshells around them, like something was missing. Now, I still crave genuine love and connection, something my parents seem incapable of providing.

A text chimes on my phone.

LEXI

Why haven't you answered my calls, Roger?

Great! Clenching my teeth, I slip my phone in my pocket without responding.

Lexi and I never went to the same school, but we lived in the same neighborhood. I was in love with her once, at least I thought it was love. She's stunning. Long blonde hair. Big red lips. A rack guys would drool over. She was the visual epitome of the perfect girlfriend.

From the start, we appeared to have a strong connection, and everyone saw us as a power couple. But as our relationship progressed, she became too clingy to the point where she made me anxious and tongue-tied, when I know a future with her is not something I want.

We were destined for failure from the start, just like my parents' marriage. Eventually, I broke things off with her, convinced it was better to end things, but she never let go. She's still adamant we are meant to be, and no one else could have me. Lexi has destroyed every relationship I tried to have with a girl, which drove me to hate her more every day. Unfortunately, my parents love Lexi and me together, always pushing for dates between us.

This gave me reasons to move out of my family house. It never felt like a home. But still, having my own flat weighed on my parents' shoulders, too. This place is for me. When I'm supposedly staying longer in university, I'm here, letting loose and enjoying myself with my friends.

In truth, I would stay there most days, to escape, or the nights my parents were out doing their own thing, which was very lonely at home in a giant mansion. For me, the way to handle my life was to drink and mess around.

But I'm tired of being alone.

Heaving a sigh, I reluctantly step out of the car, leaving behind my troubles and responsibilities of being in the Hoards family.

I make my way to Mrs. Elena's office. Mind racing from my last conversation with Jiddo. He's the most feared politician in Lebanon and my grandfather. He informed me I'd be following in his footsteps, something that was set for me before I was even born.

Who does that?

Leaning against the wall, I try to find peace in the familiar surroundings. The polished hallways and the hushed murmurs of others waiting provide temporary refuge from the ceaseless whirlwind of my thoughts.

Standing there, in a suit my mom forced me to wear to keep up appearances, I scan the room. My eyes locks with a spectacular beauty. Long, black, shining hair, braided to one side, cascading over her shoulder and a smile that lights up the room.

She has to be new here, that much is clear by the way she's searching, lacking the experience of being in university. My eyes trail all over her as she bumps into me and I gasp, she's fire making my skin ignite.

"Easy there, Klutz," I tease as she scrambles to pick up her things. Kneeling to help, our eyes meet, briefly, and I stare into her beautiful hazel eyes. There's something about her, catching my attention in an instant.

"Sorry," she utters.

Her voice slams into me making everything else fade into the background. "Let me."

Holding out my hand for her, she takes it. Slowly, we raise up off the floor. I clear my throat. "First day?"

She giggles. "Is it that obvious?"

I like her laugh. "Kinda, yeah."

She places a lock of hair behind her ear. "It is," she jokes, playfully hitting my arm.

I chuckle, feeling at ease around her. "Well then, welcome to Roadwood."

"Why thank you, kind sir."

"Some things to know about Roadwood: the professors are generous, the guys are hot," I claim showing off my body physique by removing my suit jacket and holding it. "And, the ladies, well—I'm still discovering, myself."

"Is that so?" she asks, shaking my hand as my eyes continue scanning her from head to toe.

Damn, what a girl.

"It is. I'm Roger, and you are?"

"Davina. But you can call me Klutz for short."

My stomach tightens at her playful words. Glancing around quickly, I make sure no one's watching, especially not the ones who could expose me. The last thing I need is to be outed right now. My reputation as the wealthy guy who parties hard, having been with almost every girl on campus, is not something I want her to know if I can help it. Some of the guys can't stand me for it. A few women aren't too fond of me either.

And, I don't want to see Lexi, especially now.

"So, what's your major?"

She peers at me with beautiful hazel eyes. "I don't know yet. But I'm glad Roadwood accepted me."

"Why, what happened?"

"I took a year off."

Took a year off? To do what? God she's so beautiful! "Sounds like a conversation we can have over dinner, perhaps?"

What the hell did I just ask her...? I haven't gone on an actual date with anyone since Lexi.

"Smooth," she giggles. "Yeah sure."

Relax. Deep breaths. Slow down. Say something smart. "I'm glad you're here though."

"Glad? Has it been that bad?"

"Nah, just being polite." I've got to pull myself together before I lose my cool in front of her.

She bites her lip, as I angle towards her. My lips dance on her cheek, leaving an imprint. Her face is soft, like fluffy cotton. She makes me feel something, I don't know what.

Reaching out, I ask, "Can I see your phone?" She gives it to me and I add my number in her contacts.

Maybe she could be the one to make me believe in love again? We'll see... I'm drawn to her, like we have some sort of connection.

"Stay in touch, Klutz." I trace my finger along the spot where my lips had touched her cheek. The attraction between us sparks like igniting fire, but I don't want to rush anything.

When Mrs. Elena interrupts us, I reluctantly walk away, thinking about Davina. There's something special about her, making me want to see her again. She agreed to dinner so maybe...

Before the door shuts, Mrs. Elena smiles, glancing at Davina before turning to me. I sit in the chair in front of her desk. Looking up, I meet Davina's eyes one last time and say her name: "Davina."

Mrs. Elena walks into her office and closes the door, breaking my connection with Davina and my straying thoughts.

"So, we need to talk," she begins.

"What?"

She makes her way around her desk and sits down, my eyes remaining on Mrs. Elena, waiting for her to speak. "Your father informed me that you will be joining your grandfather in politics."

I roll my head backwards and all around, trying to make sense of what she's saying, but I totally zone out. My mind is still on Davina. What is she like? Is she single? Maybe she is because she blushed at my touch and agreed to dinner.

"So, I fixed your schedule for that," she informs me.

As always, I wonder why I bother with planning my life if it is already organized for me.

Back to the conversation with Mrs. Elena, I try to focus on what I need to know before walking out of her office. "See you next week, Roger."

I open the door and tap Davina's shoulder before I leave. "See you around," I emphasize.

She nods as I depart, wanting to stay and chat with her more, but I have to get to class, or I'll be answering to my wardens at home about my grades and class attendance.

Three

Davina

My stomach grumbles, food beckoning me, so I make my way down the halls of Roadwood and out into the courtyard. Finally, I find the cafeteria, a building all on its own connected with a walkway to the gym and the library. Journeying through the many chairs and tables scattered around the yard, I stroll to the counter.

A familiar face approaches me as I set eyes on him. "Roger."

"Klutz." He winks. "Care to join me for a bite to eat? It may not be dinner, but…"

I nod and he grins, ushering me to his table, placing his hand on the small of my back. Electric bolts fire throughout my entire body at his simple touch. It's as if I were gliding to the table because I don't feel the ground after his hand meets with me.

We make it to our seats before he informs me, "There are all kinds of foods, whatever you're into you'll find it here."

I plop onto the chair in front of me. My neck tilts to the back, looking up at his chin, following his movements as he sits next to me. I place my hands in my lap, fingers curling slightly, trying to ground myself. My head lowers avoiding eye contact.

I got used to my shyness when I was in school, so being here with Roger, I don't know how to act. When our eyes meet, he asks, "What would you like?"

"Surprise me," I said, hoping he'd do the thinking.

"Yes Ma'am." He jumps off the chair and I roll my head following his body, moving around the courtyard, making his way to the counter.

A while later, he returns and sets two trays in front of us, taking the seat next to me. One tray has a burger with fries, and another holds roast chicken with white rice and a green salad.

"Wow. They both look great I don't know what is more appetizing."

"Well, since it's your first day, all first day-ers have the burger."

"Is that so?" I quirk my brow.

"Yeah."

I nod, following his advice, and taking a bite of the burger.

"So, how's your day so far?"

"It's better now than when it started." Licking my lips nervously, I pop a chip in my mouth.

He clears his throat. "I wanted to ask about the year off thing."

I glance away, feeling a bit awkward. "It's kinda a long story, and I don't think we have enough time for that now."

"Oh, so you want to see me again?" A playful smirk tugs at his lips.

"Erm, no, I didn't mean it that way," I stammer, my cheeks flushing.

He leans back, raising an eyebrow. "Oh, so you don't want to see me again."

"No, I mean yes, I mean no..." I trail off, flustered and tripping over my words.

"I'm joking," he says with a grin, his voice warm and teasing. "Fine, you can tell me this weekend."

"What's happening this weekend?"

Snickering, he reveals, "Party at my place."

"A party?"

He clears his throat and goes back to his normal tone. "I'm hosting a party for the new students. Would you like to come?" he questions, smiling.

His eyes lock onto mine before he examines me from head to toe. "Davina?" He runs his hand through his short, curly, ash brunette hair.

Clearing my throat, I try to focus on his words. "Yes?" I bite the inside of my cheek.

"Interested?"

"I'm going to have to think about it. You see, I just started university and this weekend I may want to stay in and read, or maybe get acquainted with the handbook," I joke, playfully hitting his arm.

"That's not happening." He smirks, reaching out for my hand.

Giving him mine, I smile, feeling the pressure of his, grounding me for a moment. My fingers tingle as I pull away. "Fine, but is there like a dress code or something?"

He laughs. "No, but you don't need a dress code to be beautiful."

My cheeks redden, and our eyes meet, the gaze between us growing heavier, drawing us closer without either of us realizing it.

At that instant, I forget about the university and the people. Everything around us fades away, leaving only the two of us. Just me and him. Each breath between us deepens the connection.

Our eyes locked in silent conversation...

Until he stammers, "I mean—you look good."

Great, trance over.

"Thanks." I smile back, pulling my hand away.

Students around us move in and out of the cafeteria, and I watch them with a pang of loneliness. But then, again, that's why I'm here – to start fresh. To meet new people, like Roger. Turning my attention back to my lunch, I take a bite of the burger. It's juicy and delicious, just as Roger promised it would be.

While I'm eating, I notice Roger still staring at me. Self-conscious, I ask, "What are you looking at?"

He shrugs. "Just admiring the view."

I blush, not sure how to respond.

"Seriously, come to my party, Davina."

"I'll consider it," I say, tucking a lock of hair behind my ear.

"You do that."

When we finish eating, he stands and reaches for my hand. Looking up at him, I give him mine and he lifts me up off the chair. "Thank you for lunch," I tell him.

He gives me a crooked smile. "I'm glad I ran into you again."

Leaning in, he kisses my cheek, and I feel them warming up with a blush. It was such a simple gesture, yet it made my heart flutter. He waves goodbye as he leaves.

Walking out of the cafeteria, I couldn't stop smiling, excited about my crush. Turning towards the parking lot, I suddenly remember I didn't drive.

Taking a year off meant spending the money I could have used to buy one. According to the terms of my agreement with my parents, I had to commit to a year of university studies before maybe getting my own car, just maybe.

But today, I find myself catching the bus home.

Opening the front door releases the smell of freshly made cookies coming from the kitchen. The scent floats through the air, like rain on a summer's day. Mom and Dad should still be at work and working in Lebanon is like working in any other country. They both have a 9-5 job, which meant I see them in the evenings.

So why does it smell like cookies?

I walk into the kitchen and find Mom there. My eyes widen in surprise. I would have thought she was still at work, since her commute would take a long time from the flower shop she owns in Beirut.

"Why are you home early, Mom?"

She takes me in a hug, beaming. "I came home early to ask about your day."

"Right..." I stand with my hand on my hip, pretending to believe her. Uh huh.

"Well, how was it?" she asks as she hands me a plate with a cookie on it.

I sample the cookie melting in my mouth. The moist cookie dough with chocolate chips is the best treat to come home to.

"Well, if you must know," I start, taking another bite, "Mrs. Elena is nice."

Cleaning up, I rinse the plate before putting it in the dishwasher and following my Mom to the living room, where, to my surprise, Dad is home too. He owns a restaurant in Brummana and tends to work late. He greets me with a hug, holding a bouquet of red roses.

"Dad."

"Honey." He grins, handing me the roses. "These are for you."

"Thanks, I'll put them in a vase on my dresser."

Mom nudges Dad out of the room. "Go make us dinner. Davina and I need to chat."

"Fine, I know when I'm not needed. I'll take those and put them in your room."

"Thanks, Dad."

"So, Davina. Anything else happen today?" She bumps my arm.

I pull up my hair and tie it in a ponytail. "Eh, no…"

"I can see it on your face. Who is he?" She points to my cheeks, tapping on the pink spots.

"Who is who?" I try to get her to stop.

She smiles, excitedly. "Mrs. Elena told us you were settling nicely, met a nice young man too."

I sigh. "Course she did, okay, yeah. I met someone."

"What's he like?"

"He's cute." Flushed, I say, "Mom, I'm not going to give you any more details. For now, he's cute."

"Well, okay." Crossing her hands in front of her chest, she pouts. She usually does that to get her way, and sometimes she does, manipulating me into doing what she wants, but it gets old.

"Mom, I love you so much. I just don't want to make a big deal out of nothing. Okay?"

She sighs, turning to me, and taking my hand in hers. "I know honey, but I only want to see you happy."

"I am happy."

We hug before I make my way to my bedroom. Dropping my bag on the floor, I lay on my bed, facing the ceiling, staring at the white wall. What if I accepted his invitation? What harm would that do? My breath thickens and my heart drums in my chest, as I begin texting, nervous about what to say or how I'll sound.

> It's Davina. Thanks for the invitation. I don't think I'll make it, maybe another time.

I press send before I can take back my refusal instantly questioning if I did the right thing. My heart pounds like a freight train making its way to its destination while I wait, hoping for an immediate reply but I don't get anything, and disappointment slams into me. I would've loved to have one of those continuous conversations where we'd stay up all night talking to each other.

Staring at my phone I wait and wait. Finally, I place it in my drawer, attempting to ignore it. Guess I got too excited for nothing.

This waiting for him to reply has gotten my brain into debacles. Maybe, I blew it with him? Roger was sweet and even good looking. Why am I so eager to say no to him? I mean isn't this the reason why I came to university? To experience everything that comes with it.

Moments later, a text chimes. The sound echoes in my ears as I quickly reach into the drawer and pull my phone out. His name gives me goosebumps all over my body.

ROGER

You break my heart.

His message catches me off guard. I had no idea he felt the same way I did, when we locked eyes, when we touched hands, even with the cheek thing. A rush of energy stirs in my stomach, and I immediately regret what I told him. What about starting new? I like him, even if it's fast. What about living like there's no tomorrow? Nothing like this has ever happened to me—not during my year away, not in school.

So, I'm going to do this.

Fine.

ROGER

Is that a, yes?

That's a yes.

Emotions flood in all at once. Thoughts and words make no coherent sentences, at least not loud enough for me to hear. The memory of when he kissed my cheek comes to the mind, a rushing wave crashed into me as if I was the shore with no stopping it at the entrance of the bay.

Now... what will I wear to the party?

Browsing through my closet, I frown. My clothes are outdated. I'm in dire need of a fashion run. But do I want to do so much for someone who may not be anything more than just a friend?

It's just a party.

In the bathroom, my mind spins. Brushing my teeth, I wonder about my first. Will Roger do the honors, or should I, not that I mind. Then again, I don't want to look desperate.

Pushing my worries aside, I slip into my PJs, trying to quiet my racing thoughts in hopes of getting some sleep.

Four

Roger

I'd never been to lunch with a girl who loves simple foods, but Davina looked really excited to dig in, and I love that. My eyes took in every detail of her: those captivating hazel eyes, the soft curve of her pink lips, the elegant line of her neck.

Even her t-shirt-covered chest held my gaze for a few moments before tracing downward to her waist, wrapped in a pink dress, with a blue belt and blue trainers.

Davina's getting to me. This shouldn't be happening.

Her hand on me sent a tingling sensation erupting throughout my body. God, everything about her is sexy as hell.

What is she doing to me?

She needs to come to my party this weekend, but she's making it so difficult. I want to make her feel welcome, introduce her to people, anyone but Lexi, but some friends—and preferably not guys.

What am I saying? I can't think like this, my family would have my head. Oh—God.

Before heading back to the mansion, I stop at my flat to unwind and shake off the tension lingering between Davina and me. Messages went out to a few people about the party this weekend, reminding them to prepare all the essentials like last year's first party for the first years, but there's still more to be done.

But no matter how busy I keep myself, Davina remains on my mind. Do I want a relationship right away? I just ended things with Lexi, but Davina is rare, and I don't want to miss my chance. Hopefully, I'll kiss her at the party.

As I'm about to write a list of things I need to do for the party, my phone pings, interrupting me and I frown.

MOTHER

> Honey, we arranged a business dinner. You need to attend. Wear a suit.

FATHER

> Don't be late.

> Whatever. Yeah, I'll be there.

When Lexi and I broke up, my parents had a field day of emotions. They love Lexi, everything about her and her family made sense to them. She's the ideal, wealthy, beautiful girl, the typical

Lebanese edition to our family. It would make us look good at events, parties, and political gatherings because she's someone others envied. She oozed money, beauty, and class. Glowed every time she entered a room with all eyes on her. Unfortunately, she's the one my parents would have chosen for me.

However, this is my life.

If I could force my heart to choose the easier path, I'd stay with Lexi because we have history, but we grew apart. I moved on enjoying myself easily forgetting her making it clear she's not the one for me. She never let go, constantly coming to my house, telling my parents we're meant to be.

She's fucking crazy which annoys the heck out of me.

Unlocking the door to my parents' house, I clench my jaw, anticipating what may come. Walking into the kitchen, I find mom telling the workers to prepare things. "Clean the China because we have guests coming over." She stops and stares at me, before moving over and hugging me. "Roger! Son how are you?" she asks, kissing me on my cheek, and immediately rubbing off the lipstick she left with her hand.

Reaching up, I swipe my face where my mother kissed. "I'm good, Mother, but I'm hungry."

She smiles. "Of course, you are. Here, have some soup." She pours me a bowl of vegetable soup. Not wanting to argue, I take it with me and dump it down the toilet, before going to see Dad. She knows I hate vegetable soup. Yuck!

"Dad," I call out as I enter the study. "You here?"

"Hi, Son!" He steps towards me, taking me in a hug. "Glad you could make it."

"Yeah, sure."

"Roger, we have an important announcement to make, but most importantly, Mr. and Mrs. Barnes will be coming to dinner with their daughter."

"Lexi is coming?"

"Yes, Roger. You two are meant for each other."

"Whatever." I sigh helplessly, losing hope for Davina and me. "I'll be in my room. I'm exhausted," I lie.

Walking to my bedroom, I sit on my bed, glancing at our pictures from times we were a real family even behind closed doors. Life made more sense. When Mom baked cookies, Dad cooked barbeque ribeye steaks, and I, I was happy, smiling, and thrilled to be with them. I remember dragging them out of bed to go to the beach.

While thinking, I notice I have a missed text.

UNKNOWN NUMBER

It's Davina. Thanks for the invitation. I don't think I'll make it, maybe another time.

No! No! No! This can't be happening!

She has to be there. So, I text her back.

You break my heart.

That message sounded a bit desperate. Because I am, I need something new and maybe she could be it.

DAVINA

Fine.

Is that a, yes?

DAVINA

That's a yes.

Was I that convincing? She may have felt the connection between us.

Exhausted, I stumble onto my bed. With a heavy sigh, I kick off my shoes and sink into the comfort of the sheets. My eyes shut.

Taking a deep breath, I let go of the stress and lie there as my muscles slowly unwind. The quiet of the room interrupted only by the soft rustle of the curtains as a breeze blows in from the open window.

My mind drifts off and I fall asleep.

The next day, I'm woken up to an alarm clock I don't remember setting the night before. The cleaning lady enters my room without knocking almost right after.

"Morning," I tell her, as I slowly stumble out of bed. "What time is it?"

"7 AM, sir. Shall I come later?"

"No, it's fine. Where are my parents?"

"Breakfast."

"Okay, thanks." I slip on shorts, and a t-shirt.

Walking downstairs, I prepare for the anger I assume to find for skipping dinner, instead, they seem surprisingly calm. "Morning," I greet them, slumping onto the chair in front of a long dining table.

"Glad to see you awake, Roger," Dad cheered, taking a sip of what I assume is coffee in his mug, the smell reaching my nostrils. He takes a bite from what looks like a bagel sandwich.

My parents try their hardest to do things the non-Lebanese way and it gets annoying at times. We never have bagels at home. This is a first.

"You missed an eventful night," Mom claims.

"What happened?" I ask, not sure I want to know.

"Well, we had a great dinner. Speaking of, is it true you're planning another party here this weekend?" Mom takes a bite of the almost burnt toast.

"Yes, why?"

"I'll have the cleaners prepare a few bedrooms; in case you're going to have anyone sleep over." She giggles, looking at Dad like they've got a secret. It leaves me uneasy—I seriously don't want to find out they did something behind my back.

"Thanks. I'll see you later then." I drink a bit of the coffee and get up to leave.

"Before you go, son," Dad begins, "you know the rules. Your Mom and I have things to do this weekend, and we'd like things pristine when we come back."

"Like always," I concede as I depart, taking my keys and bag with me, making my way to my car.

Climbing inside, I drive towards the coast, my mind racing with my feelings and worries. The streets of Beirut are crowded and chaotic, but as I approach the beach, the bustle of the city begins to fade away.

Living in Brummana, life is slow and less messy, but Beirut is another story.

Arriving, I park my car. The sound of the waves crashing against the shore is a welcome relief from everything happening in my life right now. Stepping out, I pull my shoes off and feel the cool sand between my toes.

In the distance, the laughter of children playing on the shore, and the sound of seagulls calling to one another makes way to my ears. The sun climbs higher in the sky, brightening the horizon, and the clouds shimmer with the early light.

Sitting there, lost in thought, I watch the day settle in. My worries and concerns that plagued me all week fade away with each wave. The rhythm of the water is peaceful and the beauty of the world around me remains constant. Yet, in the middle of the serenity, Davina's face slides into my mind.

Will this go anywhere, or am I wasting our time?

Five

Davina

The week ended with enthusiasm and hope. The opportunity to make friends at the party stood in front of me like a blank canvas waiting to be filled with vibrant colors and lively memories. Tonight is my chance to let loose, to forget about my studies and responsibilities for just a little while, and to simply enjoy the moment.

I was never invited to parties in high school, so I don't really know what to wear. Walking to my closet, I pick out a beautiful flowery pink top with white jeans and white sandals. I braid my hair to the left side and apply pink lipstick.

Mom and Dad didn't like the idea of me going out, but I told them everyone was going, and I need to meet people. Of course, I can't blame them for their hesitation, it is a party at a boy's house after all.

I glide to the door, hoping I won't get another speech about my ice cream, as Dad likes to call it, oh—bugger. Of course he's standing by the door.

"Davina," Dad begins, "remember..."

I interrupt, "Yes, Dad. I know."

"Boys want that precious ice cream you have."

"My ice cream, Dad. I know they all like ice cream and I have the best flavor. Got it."

Mom laughs. She holds out her camera and takes a couple pictures of me, having me pose.

"Enough, Mom. It's just a party."

Mom chuckles. "Okay, so, I will lend you my car, on one condition—"

"—No drinking and driving. I know. Got it, anything else?" I groan.

"Nope." She smiles. "You're good. Have fun."

"Bye guys, love you."

I make my way outside, into Mom's black Beamer. Turning the radio on, I sing along as I drive to Roger's house. His house is close to mine, since we live in the same Metn area of Brummana, but it's a bit on the lower side where all the elite and rich people live. Apparently, his dad owns all the banks in Lebanon and is a well-known influential person.

The drive to his house goes quickly, missing all the busy streets. I pass my old school, remembering my high school days before I took a year off to travel. The biggest reason for my year off was because one girl made my life a living hell in school and I needed time to mentally heal. She would bully me and take advantage of me. It was as if I was her emotional punching bag for no apparent reason. I wish I knew why she hated me, but I never had the guts to ask. Here's hoping I will never see her again because I don't know how I would cope.

Finally arriving at Roger's place, my heart races with eagerness and a tinge of uneasiness. Cars are parked haphazardly along the street and in every available space. I spot a small opening beside the gate and make my way towards it, pushing Mom's Beamer into the tight spot.

With a deep breath, I pocket my phone and keys after locking the car, hoping it would be safe there. Music blares from the stereos outside as I make my way towards the house, and flashing lights illuminate the dark sky. Approaching the door, I feel my palms sweating and my heart beating faster, unsure of what to expect.

I knock on the door and wait for someone to answer. But no one comes. So, I try the doorknob, and to my surprise, find it open. The sound of thumping music grows louder as I make my way through the hallway.

Photos hang all over the walls; pictures of Roger with friends and family, some from his childhood playing ball, some by the beach and many places I can't identify, as well as others from recent events. The photos were overlapping and crooked, but they all seemed to capture happy moments frozen in time. The pictures tell us a story of his time growing up with his family and what his friends mean to him.

Reaching the end of the hall, I step into a kitchen leading to the back of the house, which looks like a pool area, with a DJ stand and a lot of college students all around.

To my predicament, I see a lot of people I don't know, again feeling a bit out of place.

Suddenly, an arm wraps around my waist. Startled, Roger steps closer. I breathe a sigh of relief discreetly checking him out. He's wearing a black shirt, black baggy jeans, and sneakers. His hair is styled in a messy but attractive way, and his hazel eyes sparkle as he smiles at me.

He gives me a hug, greeting me. "Hey."

Blushing, I try to contain myself, but I can't. "Hey," I reply, almost out of breath as I bite my lip nervously looking into his beautiful eyes; mesmerized I'm in his presence and I'm actually here.

He takes my hand in his, guiding me through the many people, waving hi to almost everyone, some appearing almost too drunk to function.

We reach a bench beside the pool and sit, smiling at each other. Leaning in, he kisses my cheek. I look around to see more people arrive at the party. Some are dancing to the loud music, while others are hanging out by the pool.

"I'm so glad you came," he tells me, kissing my cheek another time.

"Thanks for the invite."

"'Course." He nudges my arm, getting my attention. "How's university so far, since you're here one week now?"

"It's hard! I had no idea I had to memorize so many theories in the first week."

"You seem pretty smart, you'll get there."

"Do I?"

"Well, yeah, you're not the typical university party girl."

"Is that a compliment?" I shrug, unsure if that was rude or not. And if it was, it wasn't cool.

"Well, it should be."

Rolling my eyes at his comment, I scan the crowd. A few seconds later, he turns to me and asks, "So, wanna tell me about your year off?"

This question always gets to me. Looking at him, he seems genuine, like really interested in knowing what happened to me but was I ready to tell him everything? Like exactly what went down in school. Why I took that trip?

I don't know him well enough, but am I not ready to hash it out with anyone yet, or am I too scared to be judged? I don't know. It all piles up into the many things I regret in my life. Even though, it wasn't exactly a bad thing, it was like I was running away from facing things head on...

I take a deep breath, pulling myself together, preparing to say something that makes sense. I'm trying to gather my courage, fidgeting in my seat, playing with my fingers in my lap.

It's now or never...

"I did it because I never thought I was worthy of a university life."

"What do you mean?"

"I had a hard time in school. I was always bullied, and it got to me. I wanted a break from society's expectations and people, and when I got back to try and get things on track, I was rejected. So, when Roadwood said yes, which I think is because my parents know the dean, I jumped at the opportunity to be a university student."

He takes my hand in his and caresses it, comforting me. I needed that, and I think I still do. "I'm sorry you went through all that." He glances at me with a soft smile. "At least you got to do your own thing for a while."

"Yeah. You see, Dad's a chef, and I love baking with him. But I also love Mom's job because she's a florist. Honestly, I wasn't sure if I wanted to follow either of their jobs or something else entirely because I'm not sure what I want to do."

"I don't know what to say," he says, his voice quiet.

"You don't have to say anything," I reply, trying to sound reassuring but feeling a little awkward.

"I guess you're lucky," he mutters, gazing away.

"How am I lucky?" I ask, narrowing my eyes slightly.

"You don't have your life planned out for you," he says with a faint shrug, his tone tinged with envy.

"Maybe you're lucky. Haven't you thought of that?" I counter, leaning forward, my voice challenging.

This conversation is getting pretty intense, so I cough uncomfortably.

"Drink?"

"That sounds good."

"You look beautiful, by the way."

Smiling, I whisper, "Thanks."

"I'll be right back." He jumps up and walks away.

My eyes dart around the party, landing on a skinny girl with straight, long blonde hair...

Oh, my God—Lexi.

What the hell is she doing here?

Lexi. Is. Here.

At Roger's house.

At his party.

My heart beats hard in my chest as if I'm about to faint. I can't believe she's here. A growing panic rises inside me.

She can't see me. Oh my god!

"Breathe, Davina. You got this," I speak to myself, hoping she doesn't notice me or even recognizes me. "She's not able to hurt you anymore. You're stronger than this. Stay calm!"

She's wearing a mini red dress with red pumps. Our eyes meet. Shit!

Her gaze is so crippling. My body sags. Out of the corner of my eye, Roger rushes towards me. Thank God.

"I'm back," Roger announces, handing me the drink.

Forcing my gaze away from Lexi, I mumble, "Thanks." Taking a sip with my eyes plastered on him, my side glance remains on her. "What's this?"

"Vodka and coke. I didn't ask you what you would like to drink so I chose mine," he explains, shrugging.

Smiling, I take another gulp with my eyes closed. When I open them, they land on Lexi again. "Roger?"

"Yeah?" he prompts while drinking his vodka.

His hand lands on mine, and we still. Goosebumps roam through my body, radiating purely with happiness and joy. But Lexi won't stop glaring at me.

"How do you know Lexi?" I hint without pointing at her.

Turning to look around to see what I'm talking about; he gasps loud, rolling his eyes. "Oh, fucking hell! Who the hell invited her?"

I stop drinking, concentrating on them at the same time, observing back and forth, between the two. "Well?"

He breathes in deep. "Do you remember your big mistakes that won't go away?" he asks, grimacing.

"Maybe."

"For me, that's her."

My stomach flutters with nerves, taking in a deep breath I let go of who she was to me in school, because I'm no longer that girl—I'm different.

"Oh." I place the drink on the table, grab his arm, and drag him to the dancefloor.

"What are you doing?" he asks, confused.

"Well, if Lexi wants to look at me, let's give her something to look at."

He chuckles and pulls me closer to him. "You mean like this?" He gasps, his breath dancing on my lips.

I lick mine in anticipation of an almost kiss, instead he places his head on my neck and breathes deep, tickling the sensitive skin. My eyes skim through the crowd, but she's nowhere to be found. "It worked."

"Was that some ploy to get closer to me or were you making Lexi jealous?" he asks, causing me to blush.

Playfully, I push him off me. He laughs and takes my hand as he leads me back to the bench. "A bit of both, I guess."

"You're funny."

"So, you and Lexi dated?" I lean in closer, anxious, wondering how he and her were ever an item. They don't match. They're so different–he's cute and sweet and she's a bully.

He smiles. "You amaze me, Davina."

"How? And don't change the subject." I slap his arm.

Roger nods. "Yes, we dated. She didn't go to my high school though, but she lives in my neighborhood. Wait... how do you know Lexi?"

"We went to school together."

Roger sighs. "Really. Okay... So, Lexi and I drifted apart. I wanted to explore college life, and she didn't."

Compassionate, I nod. "That's tough. Was it a mutual decision to break up?"

Roger shakes his head. "No, but we both knew it was for the best."

"It doesn't sound like she's okay with you moving on."

Roger smiles weakly. "Yeah, but I believe we're better off as friends," he tried to say but looked away. "Can we change the subject, and talk about you or your exes?"

"Exes? As if I had any..."

"What?" He arches his eyebrow.

"I've never dated anyone," I admit, removing my hand from his.

He notices. "I'm sorry. I—I'm sorry I didn't mean to make you feel uncomfortable."

"You say sorry a lot, don't you?"

We laugh.

"Touché!" He grins at me.

The music stops abruptly, interrupting our conversation. Roger stands, searching for the source of the music problem. At the same time, I spot Lexi holding the wire in her hand. Everyone halts what they're doing to witness the fight unfold but I don't want to watch.

In high school, as long as she stayed out of my way, I was fine. But here, I don't want to deal with her. I graduated and left that school, along with everyone in it, including her.

Taking that as my cue to leave, I escape. Roger and Lexi's shouting grows more intense. It's unpleasant being caught in the middle of their argument. Finally, I manage to reach the front door, when a hand lands on my shoulder making me screech, and I spin around.

"Sorry." Roger frowns. "Let me walk you to your car."

Silence moves along with us as we walk outside. "We can talk about it if you want."

"It's nothing," he claims, hiding his emotions.

"Roger. Please," I plead, taking his hand in mine, and drawing him closer. "Open up to me."

He places a hand behind my back, and the other hand around my waist, grabbing me in a passionate embrace. "It's okay, Davina. I'd rather concentrate all my attention on you."

Under the clear moonlight, we stand by Mom's Beamer. Before I have time to think, his lips press firmly to mine: my first kiss. It's raw, full of intensity and power, catching me completely off guard.

For a moment, I forget everything and everyone. All my nerves and doubts dissolve beneath the stars, the world around us fading into the background, leaving only our connection. When we break apart, I gasp for breath, my heart racing, and my cheeks flushed with electricity.

The cool breeze of the night air brings me back to reality as we continue to hold each other, our eyes meeting in a shared silence. I could stay in this moment forever, feeling safe and seen in a way I never have before.

"Thank you," I tell him, unsure what to say.

He laughs. "That was a first."

"What was?"

"Being thanked for kissing someone."

"That was my first kiss."

His eyes dart open. "You're kidding."

"It was perfect."

He smiles, making my stomach twist. "Just like you."

I can't stop licking my lips, so I go in for another action-packed kiss, one that lasts for a few minutes. We move, still kissing, to a bench beside the cars.

We can't stop.

I'm completely mesmerized by the way his lips move against mine and I'm hooked.

Hooked on him.

Six

Roger

The weekend finally arrived. It wasn't any ordinary weekend; it was the perfect opportunity for me to make a move and get closer to Davina. Perhaps, if everything went well, I would even kiss her.

The DJ is busy setting up his equipment which gives me hope this night will be unforgettable.

Before diving in, I spare a glance at my appearance in the mirror. After all the running around and preparations, I want to guarantee I look my best.

With a quick adjustment, I smooth out any wrinkles on my black button-up shirt, dark, baggy jeans and my favorite pair of sneakers, a combination of class and comfort reflecting my personal style.

"You look great, Davina will like the outfit," I proclaim, giving myself a pep-talk.

Grabbing my phone, I check to see if Davina texted me, but no such luck. She's probably getting ready and will be here soon. The DJ starts playing some music and my friends begin dancing. It's still early, but the party is already heating up.

Finally, I spot Davina walking in, gorgeous, radiant. Striding towards her, my heart skips a beat. Wrapping an arm around her waist, I pull her close. She startles, then turns, warm and familiar against me, and breathes a soft sigh of relief.

Still grinning, my hand finds hers, and I guide her through the crowd, waving at a few drunk friends on the way. We reach a bench beside the pool and sit, smiling at each other.

"I'm so glad you came." I brush my lips on her cheek once again, for some reason knowing I need to take it slow with her.

"Thanks for the invite."

Nudging her arm to get her attention, I ask questions, talk, and smile at her beauty. I'm lucky to be in her presence, will my parents approve? I don't know, but my heart is eager.

Suddenly, I spot Lexi across the party, wearing the mini red dress I loved when we used to date. I remember fucking her in that exact dress. Knocking back my drink, the vodka burns trailing down my throat.

What the hell is she doing here?

I sure as hell didn't invite her, and she's not wanted. I can't help staring, until Davina pulls me back. My hand finds hers, my voice dropping, cautious, hoping she didn't catch me glaring.

"How do you know Lexi?" she finally asks.

Fuck. I'm not ready for this. What am I supposed to say? That my life's been mapped out, and anyone outside my parents' plans isn't acceptable?

"Oh, fucking hell! Who invited her?" I spit, lying, even though I know exactly who did. Why can't they leave it alone? Why do they have to ruin everything?

Tonight was going great—until now.

I breathe deep, lean in like I might kiss Davina, but rest my head on her shoulder instead, breathing her in, her scent soft and addictive. I want to kiss her. I really do. But not because Lexi is watching. Then it hits me, how the fuck does Davina know Lexi? How did I miss it? Davina called Lexi by name—not the blonde like most girls before.

Lexi always lurked whenever I went out with someone new. We grew up next door, but our lives were split, private school for her, local school for me, thanks to my parents trying to force some Lebanese tradition down my throat.

My heart pounds, flashing back to the day we broke up. She threw everything she could find at me. I still have the chipped tooth to prove it. Fuck Lexi. I'm not letting her screw this up. Davina looks so beautiful, thinking of me, not judging, and I want to kiss her. I shift, trying to pull the focus back to her.

The music stops, interrupting our conversation. I stand to see the source of the music problem and low and behold: Lexi.

"Damn it," I shout, glaring at her. "Why are you here?"

"Does it matter? It's a party," she says, coming close to me I remove her from my space and push her backwards. "I can't believe you're with her. Do you know what they call her? The frigid queen. The one who doesn't give it up so easily. You're going to have a hard time getting into her panties, Roger," she shouts. "Besides, I know how to get you hard big boy."

Clearing my throat, I clench my fists, uncomfortable. She's ruining it for me and Davina. "Lexi, we broke up," I insist while my eyes search for Davina, but she's nowhere to be found.

"And, what if I want us back together again—"

"I don't give a fuck what you want!" I grab her arm and pull her indoors. "Get out of my house, Lexi! I don't love you anymore. Stop trying to get me back."

She glares at me before storming off in anger.

I remain stiff but watch Lexi as she gets her stuff to leave. Out of the corner of my eye, I catch sight of Davina walking to the front door, so I run to her. It's now or never. Finally, I reach, placing a hand on her and she screeches, spinning around.

"Sorry." I give her a half smile. "Let me walk you to your car."

Silence moves with us as we make our way to her car. "We can talk about it if you want," she offers, glancing at me.

"It's nothing."

"Roger. Please," she pleads, taking my hand in hers, drawing me closer. I place a hand behind her back, and the other hand around her waist, grabbing her in a passionate embrace, desperate to have her close and seal out the rest of the world. "Open up to me."

"It's okay, Davina. I'd rather concentrate all my attention on you."

Should I, do it? Should I kiss her? What about everything else? What will happen to me, to my family, to life—oh fuck it!

My lips plaster against hers in a most sensational kiss. She gasps, hesitating for a moment before kissing me back. We kiss under the stars, raw and unrestrained, charged with emotion.

The cool breeze brings us back to reality as we continue to hold each other, gazing into each other's eyes. She takes a deep breath when I reluctantly release her, and we finally break apart.

"Thank you," she murmurs.

I laugh. Like really laugh.

My heart pounds, my blood pumping a thousand gallons a minute. My emotions are running wild.

This girl. Thanking me.

She blushes revealing, "That was my first kiss."

Shock engulfs me and I'm not able to stop the visible reaction on my face. Were the guys stupid enough not to look at her? What idiot would not want to kiss her?

Without hesitation, she leans in for another kiss, pulling me deeper. The connection between us intensifies, as our lips lock in a passionate embrace, only making me want more. Time stands still, the electricity coursing between us.

We instinctively shift, moving to a more comfortable position on a bench beside her car. Our bodies are close; our hands intertwined, as we continue to share this heated moment. The world around us fades into the background bringing us closer together.

Her lips captivate me. The way they slide against mine sends shivers down my spine. Every touch, every movement is filled with desire. An undeniable chemistry.

Time slips away as we lose ourselves in the pleasure of the moment. Our kiss exceeds boundaries, leaving a permanent mark, and igniting a fire within me. We finally break apart, catching our breath. Reluctantly, I help her to her car; not that she needs any help. She kisses me another time, before I watch her drive off.

All I can think about is our kiss—and what could I do about my parents? Maybe this won't last like the rest of them. Why worry now? Turning around, I step towards the house, Lexi appearing from behind her car.

"So, did you fuck her?" she asks.

"No." I glare at her.

"Roger... Let's try again. I know I messed up and was clingy, but I can change. I know you want me; I can feel your energy craving my touch."

Clasping my fists, I try to keep my cool, breathing in and out not letting her get to me, but it's hard. She always knew what I liked and how I wanted to be spoken to.

"You want to fuck me, don't you?" She places her hand inside my jeans and on my now, hardness. "Hmmm, you got a boner, don't you baby? It wants me, doesn't it..."

The truth is my body wanted her and I hated her for it. Her hand reached for me, but I turn away, flipping her around and shoving her against her car.

"Yes, baby, just like that," she moans, assuming I'm about to give her exactly what she craves.

Amid her escalating desire, I grind my teeth in frustration. "Why are you pushing us all of a sudden?" She isn't what I want and she knows it.

"We were always meant to be. I was just giving you time to realize it," she claims, glancing back at me. "Why aren't you touching me?"

The memory of Davina's electrifying kisses floods my mind. In that split second, I understand the significance of the connection we shared. It's a jolt of clarity coursing through my veins.

Realization hits me like a punch to the gut. "You're jealous, aren't you?"

She scoffs. "Why would I be jealous?"

Gently turning her around to face me, and locking my eyes onto hers, I let out a low growl, laced with determination.

"Stay away from me and Davina."

A surge of strength disperses in me knowing I made the right decision. I set my boundaries with Lexi. I'm not going to fuck things up with Davina. Everything will be different this time.

I'll make sure of it.

Seven

Davina

After the party, I feel a billion emotions with Roger's kiss lingering on my lips. I try not to lick them to keep him on me a little longer. Driving home, a song ballad enters my ears and exits my mouth. My voice rises as the piano music gets louder, my entire being swaying to the music, happy.

Pulling into the community parking lot, I see it's crowded again and find a spot to park my car, my mind drifting back to the party. My emotions feel foreign. On one hand, relief fills me at the end of the night. I let go of my insecurities and allow myself to enjoy the company of the people around me, including Roger.

But on the other hand, there was a nagging voice reminding me of Lexi. She's his ex, she could ruin this for us knowing our history... Shutting the radio off, my mind races, questioning everything.

What if he didn't feel the same way?

As I'm reaching for my phone, a sudden chime pierces the air, sharp and insistent. My heart skips a beat. The sound cuts through the silence of the car, setting my nerves on edge.

Gripping the steering wheel tighter, I force my attention back to parking Mom's car. The phone buzzes again in my pocket. It could be nothing. Or it could be Roger. The thought makes my stomach twist.

My fingers fumble with the phone. Sweat forms on my palms, the pressure increases. My pulse quickens, adrenaline fuels my actions. Finally, I unlock the screen and read the notification: a text from Roger. A wave of conflicting emotions washes over me—a sense of anxiety at the thought of engaging with him.

We had an incredible night, to say the least, but I'm not sure I'm ready to open my heart to love. Memories of the old days still bring me back to what Lexi did to me, one of the reasons I hesitate, the thought of her making me wonder if I can feel normal again—or if I'm not worthy of that kind of happiness.

With trepidation, I turn my attention to the screen. Taking a deep breath, I brace myself for whatever happens. The scenarios flooding my mind still leave me uncertain.

What if the text says he's going back to Lexi?

A single thought resonates within me: *Davina, just read the text. You won't know until you do.*

No amount of speculation or fear could truly prepare me for the contents of the text. With trembling fingers, I tap on the message, the screen illuminating as I read.

ROGER

> Klutz, that was one amazing, unbelievable electric kiss.

Reading his words brings a smile to my face and makes my mind wander to the future. Standing in a church in front of our friends and families, we kiss, signaling our love for one another and the priest says, "I now pronounce you Mr. and Mrs. Hoards."

Okay, that's a bit too unrealistic, but it could happen, couldn't it?

I take a deep breath and compose my response, my fingers trembling as I type out a message, trusting I don't say the wrong thing.

I'm nervous, but I have hope. The night was good, including me and him, his party, the kiss, and our feelings, while the bad is only one thing, Lexi. She was the real issue—her problem with me was obvious, but the negative tension between him and Lexi was apparent too.

What's her deal? I get she's still in love with him, but he moved on, shouldn't she?

Before second-guessing myself, I press send.

> Ha-ha, Klutz? I had a lot of fun too.

ROGER

> That kiss was one of the best I've ever had.
> And, yes, your nickname is Klutz.

My heart skips a beat. Another reason I like where this is going. I don't know if it's my nickname or the fact that he liked our kiss. I loved it, and having never been kissed, for me, it felt like something out of a fairytale.

> I like the nickname—especially coming from you.

ROGER

> So, what are your plans tomorrow?

> Not much. Chilling, I guess. Why, do you have anything in mind?

ROGER

> Yeah, I do. How about we go to the park or something?

> Hmmm, sounds tempting. Are you that eager to kiss me again?

ROGER

> Maybe, so?

> Okay.

ROGER

> I'll pick you up, Klutz. Until then, sweet
> dreams.

Walking to the front door, my heart explodes with emotional euphoria. He wants to see me. And maybe, kiss some more. I'd love to do that too. I can't stop touching my lips where his lips just were. I've been biting my lower lip at the memory of his on mine.

Who would ask for anything better? I surely wouldn't.

Slowly, I unlock the door and step into the living room. The moonlight filters through the window, casting long shadows across the room. Dad lay snoring on the couch, his hand still clutching the TV remote. I tip-toe across the carpet, trying not to wake him.

"Davina! You're finally home," Dad exclaims, his eyes widening in surprise.

I smile. "You know you don't have to wait up for me, right?"

"I know, but... things like this are not easy to handle. You've never been out to any party before, and I wanted to be available in case you needed me." My heart softens. I give him a big hug, thanking him for being there for me as he always does when I need him and even if I don't need him, he'd be there for me.

He turns the TV off and together we make our way to my parents' bedroom so I can wish him goodnight. Before I walk into my bedroom, Dad calls out to me, his voice tinged with sadness, "Davina?"

I turn to face him. "Yes, Dad?"

He pulls me into a bear hug that seems to last forever. "I love you," he says, his voice thick with emotion.

"I love you too, Dad." Tears well up in my eyes. It's not often I see that kind of emotion from Dad. "Thanks for being amazing."

"You too," he rasps, his voice barely above a whisper. "Night, sweetheart."

"Night." I turn away, my heart full.

Checking my phone once more, I scroll through the messages with a smile on my face. Roger and I had a wonderful time, and I couldn't help but want more out of this—whatever this will be. Sleep takes over me and I drift off, thinking of being in his arms.

The next morning, golden sunlight filters through my blinds, waking me with a gentle nudge. It's the kind of morning that always makes me feel alive. The world feels full of possibilities—and maybe, just maybe, one of them is him.

I glance at my phone and pick it up. An early morning message glares back at me through the screen. His name is plastered across it.

ROGER

> I couldn't sleep. Even though I had to. Are you ready? I'll be there soon. Better yet, look out your window.

Smiling at his eagerness to meet, I jump out of bed and head to the window. There he is, standing outside near his shiny black

Beamer, dressed in jeans and a fitted black shirt. He looks so good—almost too good, like he's something I could eat.

Yummy!

Waving at him from the window, I show I'm still in my PJs. He smiles and texts me.

ROGER

You know, you could come out just like that.

Not happening. I'll be a few minutes. Where are we going?

ROGER

Wherever I want. Now, hurry up, Klutz. Chop, chop! We don't have all day.

Coming.

ROGER

Ooo, I could entertain that.

Again, not happening.

ROGER

Ha, ha, hurry up already.

Hurrying to find something casual in my closet, I grab a pair of white jeans and a yellow crop top. I slip into white sneakers and quickly tie my hair into a ponytail. After rushing into the bathroom, I brush my teeth and swipe on black eyeliner and rosy, pink lip gloss.

Grabbing my bag from last night, already packed with everything I need, I head for the door. It's Saturday, which means both my parents are at work, leaving me completely alone—and free.

Walking outside, I find him waiting by the car. He opens the door for me with a warm smile and helps me in, sneaking a quick peck on my cheek before I can react. Blushing, I slide into the seat and fumble with my seat belt, my heart racing just a little faster.

"You ready?" he asks as he slides into the driver's seat and puts the car into gear.

"Yeah, but I'm still wondering—where are we going?"

"To my favorite spot," Roger replies, taking my hand in his. His touch is warm, inviting. I twirl my fingers in his and he smiles. "You'll love it."

"Will I?" I tease, raising a brow.

"You will, Davina. Trust me."

The drive to Beirut is calm and soothing, the steady beat of my heart almost like music in my ears. The silence in the car feels natural, yet I can't help but fidget, unsure of what to say. Nervousness twists in my stomach, even as my thoughts betray me—I can't stop imagining pulling him close and kissing him.

Is it bad to fall so fast? Because I think I already have, and the thought terrifies me.

We arrive at the beach, the rhythmic crash of waves against the shore providing a soothing backdrop to my racing thoughts.

"What do you think?" he asks, reaching for my hand as he helps me out of the car.

"Breathtaking," I whisper, the word slipping out.

I can't stop biting my lip, and he notices. "If you keep doing that, you're going to force me to kiss you," he teases, his voice low and warm.

"Force you? As if!" I shoot back, trying to sound bold, though my heart skips a beat.

He pulls me closer, his arm brushing against mine as we walk side by side toward the shore. "I'm just playing, Davina," he says with a small smile. "But... I do want to kiss you."

My breath hitches. "What are you waiting for, then?"

"Permission."

He turns me to face him. We lock eyes, his image instantly capturing my attention. He lowers his head and places his soft lips on mine as I lick him and kiss him back. I am breathless as we continue to kiss each other, his hands skimming my sides and mine around his neck. We break away for a second, both almost out of air.

"Well, that happened," I blurt out.

"It did." He grins.

We sit at the shore and stare at the water. The waves playing a soulful song as we revel in each other, with no words passing, just nudges, kisses, and caresses. He takes my face in his hands and kisses me some more. We fall to the sand and soon he's on top of me, his body grinding onto mine, and I'm in awe, hooked.

But then, a lightbulb flashes in my mind, snapping me back to reality. This is happening too fast. We need to stop.

I gently nudge him off. "I'm..."

"I'm sorry, Davina. I didn't mean to—"

"No, it's not you, Roger. It's just, I—"

"No need to explain," he interrupts. "I get it."

I need to break the ice that just formed around our chat. The kiss was electrifying but I'm not ready for more. Not yet anyway. My fingers trace small patterns in the sand, trying to ground myself. The heat between us still lingers, but the reality of what just happened hits me all at once, I'm rushing into something I'm not prepared for.

"Roger, listen," I begin to say, but he turns to me and looks deep into my eyes as if trying to tell me a secret.

"Don't explain yourself, Davina, I shouldn't have done that," he insists, his voice apologetic.

"No, but you don't get it. I'm trying to tell you something. During the year away, I never thought of guys in any way except as friends, because I was scared. But—when I met you..."

"Everything changed?" he asks, a slight smile tugging at the corner of his lips.

"Yeah, something like that. It's like an alarm in my body that's constantly ringing—for you."

"Well, I'm flattered, Davina," he says with a grin. "It's nice that you think of me like that."

"Among other things," I tease, playfully hitting his arm.

"The way your touch sends ripples throughout my body is insane. I'm going to only kiss you again. Am I allowed Klutz?"

"Okay," I agree, biting my lip.

Instantly, his mouth meets mine, and we continue to devour each other, our kisses so deep, we nearly leave ourselves breathless.

"I better get you back home before anyone notices you're missing," he says.

"Now that's headline news," I giggle, shaking my head. "Thank you."

"For what?" he asks, his brow raised, curious.

"For this," I reply with a soft smile. "I had fun."

"Yeah, Davina, me too," he says, his voice sincere.

We arrive at my house, and I climb out of the car. He walks me to my door, a playful grin still lingering on his face.

"Honestly, Klutz, this was entertaining. I'm glad we did this."

"Yeah, me too," I reply with a smile, not wanting to say goodbye.

"So, what are you doing next week?"

"University," I say, raising an eyebrow. "Unless you're planning to bail for some reason, Roger."

"Right, university..." He hums to himself. "Well, how about lunch at the cafeteria on Wednesday?"

A wide smile spreads across my face. "It's a date."

"Yes, it is," he says, giving me a slight chuckle before he jogs back to his car. I watch him go, my heart fluttering.

I can't wait for Wednesday. But for now, I need to focus, get back to my books and study for university, or risk falling behind.

Eight

Roger

After my date with Davina, I slipped back into old habits—ignoring the wrecked house, slouching on the couch, replaying the night in my head. Her lips. Her neck. Her body. She left me breathless and aching for more.

Frustrated, I dragged myself upstairs, stepping over the aftermath of the party. Cleaning could wait—my parents wouldn't be back until Monday anyway.

I flopped onto my bed, hard and restless, debating whether to take care of it myself or hit the shower. Davina's body flashed behind my eyes, and damn, it would've been easy—

Until my phone buzzes.

Jiddo.

"Hello, Roger. I hope you'll attend Sunday lunch. We have things to discuss," he says.

I sigh. "Sure, Jiddo."

He hangs up without another word.

I stare at my phone, frustration sinking into something heavier. Davina fades. Reality doesn't. Sleep finally drags me under.

Sunday morning arrives with misery, knowing all too well it's family day. The usual mess of the house was still present, so I called a cleaning crew to come and do what needed to be done. The sunlight streams through the windows, stabbing at my eyes. The clatter of supplies and muted voices fills the air as the crew rushes to tidy up before my parents see the mess.

But the sound of clacking heels to marble makes way to the living room. Great! I'm too late. My mother is already here, standing in the doorway with her hands on her hips. She doesn't have to say anything; the disappointment in her eyes says it all.

"Have you forgotten your promise to me, Roger?" she challenges, tapping my shoulder with sharp, deliberate movements. Her voice is calm, but there's an edge to it, the kind that makes my stomach twist.

"No, Mother," I reply quickly, sitting up straighter. "I haven't, but I didn't know you were going to be back so soon." I rub the back of my neck, avoiding her gaze. "Had I known, I would have hired help last night."

She raises an eyebrow, crossing her arms. "Funny," she says dryly, her tone heavy with skepticism. "Come along. We're going to your grandfather's for lunch."

"Do I have to?" I groan slouching as I stand.

"Yes," she snaps, her voice leaving no room for argument. "And don't forget to brush your teeth."

Making my way to my bedroom, I change my shirt and put my jeans on. Then, I go into the bathroom and brush my teeth. "Ready," I call, though my tone betrays anything but enthusiasm.

The drive to Jiddo's remains silent thick enough to cut with a knife. Jiddo, a prominent politician and a power in his own right, is never far from my mind especially with all the expectations he has for me. We pull up to his mansion, a sprawling estate that oozes luxury and influence.

It sits in the heart of Beirut, towering over the skyline with its white walls and red-tiled roof. The entrance is guarded by an ornate wrought iron gate, leading to a cobblestone driveway. The lush gardens and fountains surrounding the estate are bathed in sunlight, and the air smells of jasmine.

At the gate, the guards signal that we're family, and allowed to park on the mansion grounds. We follow the butler through the halls, the familiar grandeur of the place making everything feel both impressive and suffocating.

I've always known my grandfather to be a powerful man, respected and feared. I followed in his footsteps, even getting involved in university politics, but now it feels like it is too much. Dad's not the one in line for this life, he doesn't deal with politics: I am.

"Welcome, family," Jiddo says, standing at the dining table, waiting for us to join him.

"Hi, Jiddo," I reply, pulling him into a hug. "What's so important we need to have lunch together?"

"My boy," he starts, his voice firm but warm, "it's Sunday. It's family day. And in my household, you're part of the Hoards family, which means lunch on a Sunday is an obligation, not a choice."

Father and mother sit next to each other at the long dining table made of some kind of wood imported from Spain—or something like that. There are eight wooden chairs, which feels a bit unsettling because I'm really hoping no one else is invited. The table is set for an entire group.

When I see Lexi walking in with her family, my heart drops to the pit of my stomach. Fuck. She greets my grandfather with a big smile, shakes my parents' hands, and makes her way to me. I notice my grandfather watching us, so I give her a friendly hug to keep things from getting awkward. She sits next to me, and her hand lands on my thigh.

Leaning into me, she whispers, "Hello, soon-to-be hubby."

"Hell no!" I shriek, and suddenly, all eyes are on me.

"Roger, is everything all right, dear?" Mom asks, her voice full of concern. I quickly nod.

"You'll have to behave, Roger, honey," Lexi spits out, her tone dripping with venom.

There's silence at the table, then my grandfather stands to address us.

"I'd like us all to raise our glasses to our future children," he says, glancing at me and Lexi. "These two, even though still young, have a wonderful life ahead of them. Roger will join me in politics, and you, Lexi..." He glares at her. "You will become a Hoards, and you will raise Roger's kids."

I spit out my drink in shock. The fuck! Hell no!

"Roger? Are you okay, son?" my father asks, knowing full well I'm not okay.

"No, I'm not fucking okay!" I rant staring at everyone knowing all too well what this means for me after my outburst.

"Oh, hush honey, you're fine," Lexi replies on my behalf. "He's just in utter shock that you're okay with us being together. I'm so excited and happy to be part of your family."

"But we're not together, Lexi," I say firmly, glaring at her. "We agreed. I mean, you should have told your family. Mine knew, but apparently, they have an odd sense of humor."

Lexi shrugs a mischievous twinkle in her eye. "What can I say? Your family is growing on me."

Staring at them, longing to get away, I try to fight my way out. "This is not happening! I'm not going to agree to this."

Jiddo gives me a long, scrutinizing look, clearly unimpressed by the chaos, raising his glass again looking at everyone except me. "To us, Hoards and Barnes, to a whirlwind romance and a financial benefit for all."

I think I'm going to be sick.

"To us," they all say in unison, but I don't join in the celebration. My glass remains firmly on the table by the plate. My heart's not in it. It will never be.

What about Davina? What will happen to us? I really wanted to get to know her, be with her, maybe try for a happy life, but now that's never going to happen. Ever.

Lunch carried on for a couple of hours, and I spent the entire time fighting off Lexi's advances. To be honest, I want to punish her for letting this happen. My heart aches.

I want to see Davina, talk to her, touch her, kiss her. Not this. This will ruin us. My stupid commitment, a promise to people who are supposed to be my family but have become my enemies because of their expectations.

Clearing my throat, I stand. "May I be excused?" I ask politely.

"Yes, you kids can go while us adults discuss the next steps. Lexi, be sure to have everything ready for the wedding. It will be held here at my mansion, and I'll take care of the rest. Get a cake, a dress, and Roger, make sure you have your groomsmen and everything ready. Lexi, you know what to do with the bridesmaids. Understand kids?"

We nod, and I turn, Lexi trotting along behind me. When I reach my car, I grab her and pull her close, fuming. "This will never happen. I'll make sure of it. I need to figure out what to do, but you and I are over. We'll never be together. Do you understand me?"

She laughs, yanking her hand away. "Oh, you silly boy. Do you think you can get rid of me that easily?"

"Lexi, you and I are finished!" I seethe, glaring.

"Oh, honey, I'll never let you go. No one can have you—not even Davina. Toodles." Grinning like she already won, she blows me a kiss before spinning on her heel. She gets into her car and drives off.

Standing there, staring at the sky, I wonder, will I ever be happy?

Nine

♥

Davina

Sunday morning. Birds chirp outside my window, pulling me from sleep.

I roll out of bed and stretch, feeling refreshed for once. Every bedroom has its own bathroom, pale blue walls and all, and I'm grateful for the privacy. I make a beeline for the sink, splash some water on my face, and flick off the silver faucet.

Stepping back into my room, the cool tile underfoot, I head toward the kitchen, stomach already growling.

I find my parents in the living room. Dad enjoying his coffee, Mom flipping through a magazine on the couch across from him.

Mom looks up and smiles. "Good morning, Davina,"

"Morning, Mom. Morning, Dad." I grab an apple from the fruit bowl on the coffee table.

"How was the party?" Dad asks, curious.

"It was great. I had so much fun, apart from Lexi crashing." I frown, rolling my eyes at the memory of how stupid she looked standing there with the wire in her hand.

"Lexi, as in your bully from school?" Dad asks, his eyebrows drawn down in concern. I nod, looking away. "How did it feel seeing her after all this time?"

I shrug off the emotions from the party. Everything I ever went through in school was because of her, but I never knew why she hated me so much. I never asked. I thought it was because I was different, taller, maybe even more attractive, but that couldn't be it. To her, and to everyone in school, she was stunning, and still is.

The way she would torture and torment me in school, my stomach would knot so tight I could barely eat lunch. My hands would shake every time I saw her coming down the hallway, my throat tight with dread.

Stepping into my high school bathroom, I walked into a stall and locked the door behind me to change because the locker room was full. Everyone else got dressed quickly, but I took my time — I always felt self-conscious.

Suddenly, Lexi pulled the fire alarm, and in the panic, I rushed outside in just my underwear and bra, thinking it was a real emergency. She was already there, standing with the boys and girls from our class, laughing.

They all pointed, sneering, calling me names. "FRIGID QUEEN! FATTY! LOSER!"

Lexi threw her milk carton at my face making me gasp and shouted, "Cover yourself, fatty. Ew, you look so ugly — no one wants to see that body of yours."

A tear slips down my cheek as I try to shake off the memory. It would go on for days, and no one did anything to stop it. Not because they didn't want to, but because they couldn't. Her family was powerful, and no one could speak badly of them without fear of consequences. I thought I was free of her and everyone from school.

But now, a year later, here she is... still. Why can't I get rid of her?

I step up and give him a hug. "Thanks for being there for me, Dad. I appreciate it."

His arms tighten around me, comforting me. "Of course, Davina. So, care to tell us how you spent your Saturday?"

My Mom leans in, her curiosity practically bubbling over.

"Erm, so—Roger came and took me to the beach," I reply trying to avoid eye contact.

"And?" Mom asks, probing for more.

I can feel the pressure building, but I want to keep it simple.

"We had fun. That's all you guys are getting."

Mom sighs a loud gasp. "Fine..."

We sit together and eat breakfast, chatting and laughing. It's times like these that make me realize how lucky I am to have such loving parents.

"So, what are your plans for today?" Dad asks, placing the newspaper on the coffee table.

"Studying mostly. Why? What? What's up?"

Mom's smile widens, as if it could light up a dark valley with its intensity. "Well, we have a surprise."

"A surprise? What is it?"

Dad laughs. "It won't be a surprise if we tell you, Davina."

"You'll have to join me in the kitchen for the big reveal," Mom suggests, beaming.

"Okay." Curious, I follow her.

My eyes widen as we step into our modern kitchen, decorated with black and white cabinets and all the latest appliances. Mom and I love experimenting with different ingredients, and the granite countertops make food preparation a breeze.

But right now, I can't believe my eyes, staring as they lay out various items on the kitchen table, surprising me with my very own baking material. They set down mixing bowls in different sizes, measuring cups and spoons, whisks, spatulas, and rolling pins.

"No way!" I explode with joy and contentment.

I've always loved baking. The way flour, sugar, eggs, and butter come together to create something delicious and beautiful has always fascinated me. I would spend hours watching baking shows on TV and scrolling through specialty baking books, dreaming of the day when I could make my own cakes, cookies, and pastries.

Baking sheets and pans of all shapes and sizes, including cake pans, muffin tins, and loaf pans cover the counter. I spot cooling racks, a set of pastry bags and tips, as well as a kitchen scale and thermometer. They thought of everything.

I'm beyond ecstatic hugging both my parents tightly. "This is incredible. What is all this for?"

"Well, we remember how you loved baking when you were a kid, and decided to surprise you with your own set since you weren't around last year for your birthday. This is your gift," Mom answers.

"Thank you. I promise to make you the best cakes, cookies, and pastries you've ever tasted."

With my new bakeware and baking tools anything is possible. I can't wait to get started on my first creation. And, with the support of my parents, I know I'll be able to do something truly special. I feel like I could conquer the world one cake at a time.

Immediately, I know what I want to make first—a chocolate cake. I always dreamed of making a delicious, moist, chocolate cake which melts in your mouth and heats up your heart with love from scratch. I'm more than ready to take on the challenge.

I quickly get to work, pulling out my new supplies and ingredients.

"Look at her go," Dad exclaims.

"I believe we better get out of the way," Mom jokes.

"While you do that, I'll get back to it." I walk over, hugging them again. "Thank you!"

It's not long before my first cake is baked and frosted. I step back to admire my handiwork. Pride washes over me. It's perfect - moist, chocolatey, and beautifully decorated. I can't wait to share it with Mom and Dad. I hope it tastes just as good.

As we all sit down to enjoy a slice of cake, I'm suddenly overwhelmed, grateful for my parents and their generosity. "Thanks guys, this means a lot."

"You're welcome honey," Dad responds, as he takes a big bite. "This is tremendously delicious."

"It sure is," Mom confirms, swallowing the piece of cake.

Life couldn't get any better than this!

Ten

♥

Roger

Davina and I had an amazing time at the beach. But I shouldn't lead her on to think there could be anything between us. Or could there be secretly? I don't know, maybe it's selfish, but I don't want to let her go.

Jiddo is adamant that I marry Lexi. The whole thing is a nightmare.

Desperately, I type out a text, hoping it will distract me from the chaos of my life. A life I'm living with people who should love me for who I am, not for what they expect me to be or do.

> Hey Klutz, are we still on for our date on Wednesday?

Hopefully, she says yes. I really like her. And our kisses, I can't stop thinking about them. I was blown away, causing all these emotions I never thought I could feel. Ever since I broke up with Lexi, I was floating along with random women, doing whatever I could not to feel alone.

Lexi and I should have stayed friends, we never made sense as a couple. Yes, she's hot and fuckable, but I don't love her, and I don't think I ever did. Sitting at home, flipping through my books, all I can think about is what if I had been born in another life, another family.

Would I be forced into this torment?

Monday morning comes too quickly. I barely slept the night before. Yet, I didn't work on my political science paper that's due today, so I scramble to grab my things and rush to find a classmate who I know can help with my mess. I spot him in the library and sit down next to him.

"Is this seat taken?" I ask, glancing at him.

He smirks and leans back in his chair. "You know it's not. Let me guess, you didn't do the homework for today?"

"Nope," I say, rubbing my face.

"Well, you're in luck," he says with a grin. "I can help you. For a price."

"Does money always have to be a thing between us?" I ask, raising an eyebrow.

He shrugs. "No, but it's more fun this way."

I sigh and ask, "How much do you want this time?"

"$100," he says, holding up his hand.

I stare at him, shocked. "You're kidding."

"Nope," he replies, smirking again.

I pull out my wad of bills and hand him the money, knowing there's no other way around it.

"Nice doing business with you, Mr. Hoards," he says with a grin.

"Can't say the same about you, Mr. Scimitar," I reply, rolling my eyes. "Hopefully, I get a better grade than last time."

"Yeah, you will." He sighs and gets back to work. Then, he turns to me and asks, "So, what's going on between you and Lexi?"

"Nothing, why?" I ask, hoping he leaves it where the conversation should end. I don't need to explain myself to anyone about my family issues.

"She said you guys got engaged yesterday."

"What?" My eyebrows hit my hairline.

"That's what she's telling everyone," he says, leaning in slightly.

"I can't believe her," I grumble, feeling a twinge of annoyance. "We just had a family lunch. Her parents and mine are friends and she joined. I can't get rid of her, but I wouldn't say engaged."

In her sexy pink mini and blue heels, she strides up to us. "What would you call it then?" Lexi asks, her tone challenging.

Glancing up at her, I frown, I don't want to make a scene. "It was just lunch with our parents because they've been friends a long time," I state, trying to sound confident.

She drags her teeth over her bottom lip, as she leans down. Charlie's eyes lock onto her. She doesn't bother me anymore, because when Davina's face appears in my mind, I can stay grounded.

"Well, if that's the case, why did your parents call mine this morning to say we're joining them for dinner tonight?" Lexi asks, raising an eyebrow.

"Lexi, stop daydreaming," I reply, trying to focus.

"I can't, you're all I think about," she claims, her voice soft but intense.

"Lexi!" I snap, a little frustrated.

"Oh, Roger, you think it's easy to resist me?" she asks with a teasing smile.

"I know it is," I insist, staying firm.

"Really? I'd like to see you try," she challenges, her eyes narrowing slightly.

She moves closer and just before she sits on my lap, Charlie shoves her away and she falls to the floor. Lexi grunts loud as if pissed. I nudge Charlie in thanks, even though he doesn't even glance in my direction, appearing as though he did it for some other reason. He gets up quickly, taking his things with him, while she stands and walks back to sit next to me.

She whispers in my ear, taunting me. "Should I pet it for you?"

"Lexi, we're in university," I remind her, my tone strained. "And, by the way, don't you have class now?"

"Oh right, I do," she says with a smirk, almost as if she forgot.

She leans further into me, attempting to kiss me, but I push her away, refusing to kiss her back. Spinning on her heel, she stalks off, obviously irritated.

Charlie makes his way back to me, laughing, and I snap, "Shut up, Charlie."

"I can give you your paper in class later," he offers, glancing at me with a casual shrug.

"Yeah, great," I reply, trying to sound uninterested.

Wishing for a distraction to ease my frustrated state, my prayers are answered, when I see my Klutz walking into the library and purposefully collide with her. Her books fall all over the floor.

"Davina," I say.

I help her, taking her hand and pulling her up off the floor. Leaning down, I gather her belongings and hand them to her.

"You good?" I ask, glancing at her.

"Yeah, sorry I never texted you back. As you can see, I've been swamped," she tells me, apologizing.

"No worries. Are you free to chat now?"

"Busy," she says, gesturing to the books in her arms. "Can we meet at lunch?"

"Sure," I agree, sighing. "See you later." I lean in and kiss her cheek before walking off to my next class.

Eleven

Davina

After spending Sunday baking, I was exhausted. My parents tasted the samples, and I shared my cookies, cakes, and cupcakes with the neighborhood. The reviews were great, and one woman even hired me to bake her son's tenth birthday cake. The evening was spent catching up on reading and homework before I fell into bed, quickly drifting into sleep.

Monday arrives, too fast.

I struggled to stay awake during my morning classes, especially when the professor just read from the textbook, while someone copied every word onto the whiteboard for us to write in our notebooks.

It makes me wonder how he ever became a professor.

I head to the library to get some work done, losing track of time. When I finally glance at the clock, I'm shocked to see it's already time for lunch. In a hurry, I pack up, forgetting one of my notebooks, and rush to the cafeteria to meet Roger.

Arriving out of breath, I spot him at a table alone and walk over. "Is this seat taken?"

He meets my eyes and smiles. "Now it is."

"I'm so sor—"

"Don't worry. What would you like to eat?"

"Something light, I had a big breakfast," I inform him as I place my stuff on the table.

"Sure." He nods as he stands up to go get us something to eat.

While the sun streams into the cafeteria, casting a warm glow over the tables and chairs, I look around; everyone was deep in their own conversations or studying. That's when a tall, dark-haired man walks in. Heads turn, and people stop mid-sentence, all eyes on him. He has a casual swagger to his step, dressed in jeans, a red shirt, and red shoes. His broad shoulders and muscular frame fill out his clothes as he moves.

Scanning the room, his intense blue eyes meet mine. My heart rate quickens, watching him stride over to my table, his long hair flowing behind him like a wave.

"Your notebook." He hands it to me, flashing a dazzling smile.

"Thanks," I whisper.

"I'll see you around," he says and turns to walk away.

"Wait," I call as I stand to stop him, not sure whether to thank him or not.

"What?"

"Join us, if you want?"

"No thanks." Without another word he walks out.

Roger arrives with our trays and places them on the table. "Ooh, yum," I exclaim, eyeing the delicious-looking salad with mozzarella cheese. "Thank you." I take a forkful savoring the flavors.

"So," Roger begins.

"So?" I probe, hoping he didn't notice the guy who gave me the notebook. From the way he looked at me, it left me feeling uneasy. He was an attractive guy, but that's it and I don't want Roger to get the wrong idea. Roger is the one I like.

"About our date," Roger prods.

My heart skips a beat. "Date, what date?" I ask, trying to stay cool.

He pauses, staring at me, confused. "We agreed to go out, didn't we?"

My face lights up with excitement. "That sounds amazing. But I thought this was a date."

He chuckles. "No, this is cafeteria food. And I'd love to spend time with you. We can head to an Italian restaurant after university on Wednesday."

I nod already picturing the delicious pasta and wine I would be enjoying sitting across from him. "Should I bring clothes to change into?"

"You can wear whatever makes you feel comfortable. Since it's a cozy place, we can keep it casual."

"Sure." I nod.

After finishing our lunch, Roger and I exchange goodbyes, and I head off to my next class: Calculus.

Dread washes over me as I make my way to the lecture hall. The thought of spending the next hour and a half doing math problems makes my stomach churn.

Shivers run down my spine, but not in a good way as the guy from earlier sits down next to me, leering at me. There's something about the way he looks at me that leaves me uneasy.

Just as I'm about to turn my attention to the front of the lecture hall, the professor's voice interrupts my thoughts. "If you're done ogling each other, I'd like to begin."

The entire room bursts into laughter.

My face turns red with embarrassment as the eyes of my classmates turn towards me and my seatmate. I quickly look away from the guy next to me and focus on the professor's lecture, trying to shake off the awkwardness of the moment.

"Thank you," she says, and I nod my head while he chuckles at my predicament. "Let's get back to Calculus."

"Stupid," I whisper to myself.

He nudges his arm to me. "Don't worry, you can stare, and I'll tell you when to look away."

"Oh, shut it," I shriek at him; unaware I said that so loud.

"Care to enlighten me, Miss—"

"Dwain. My name is Davina Dwain, and no Miss. I was only informing my fellow classmate."

"Charlie Scimitar, Ma'am," he supplies.

"Whose name is Charlie, that he's got to quit while he's ahead."

"Should he though?" she taunts, and he laughs.

"Well, I believe you should get better acquainted with each other, Miss Dwain and Mr. Scimitar," she lectures, turning to face the rest of the class. "The person who you're sitting next to will be your study-buddy the entire semester."

"Huh?" I question, wide-eyed.

He laughs, reaching his hand out to touch mine. "Well, nice to meet you."

"Is it though? It's like you're already trying to make my life hard."

Leaning in, he whispers in my ear, as I breathe in deep, "I did no such thing." Shuffling away, he looks forward.

My eyes plaster to his, releasing the breath I was holding. "You did."

Out of nowhere, he places his hand on my knee, and I swiftly whack it off. "What's wrong?" he grills, sounding genuine.

I huff, "Who gave you the right to touch me?"

He chuckles. "Your body movement did."

I gulp hard, trying to gather my composure. "No, I didn't, so don't touch me again."

He places his hands up in surrender. "Can I lick you?"

"Ugh," I grunt, in a whispered tone. Getting up, I move my chair away from him.

Throughout most of the lecture, I become increasingly anxious about the thought of working with Charlie on any project. I need to talk to the professor about changing.

Class finally ends, so I gather my things and make my way to the front. As the last of the students file out, I approach the professor. "Can we speak for a moment?"

She looks up at me, curious and motions for me to take a seat. "What now, Davina?" she asks, folding her hands on the desk in front of her.

"Can I have another partner?"

She furrows her brow and leans back in her chair. "No."

I hesitate before pushing, not wanting to come off as rude or difficult. "Please?"

She nods thoughtfully, mocking me. "I see. No. Now be gone and have a nice day."

"How can I have a nice day, if you won't adhere to my request?" But as I try to ask again, Charlie walks by and furrows his brows at me.

"I said it once and I'll say it again," she begins, her head tilted to the side. "This is a class of many talents. That young man has a talent with numbers, and you'd be so lucky as to be paired up with him. Don't you think?"

I shrug, defeated as I make my way out of the class, bumping into Charlie on the way out. "Great." I huff in annoyance.

"You don't like me much, do you?" he asks, playfully nudging me as we walk, side by side through the hallway. There are so many people around, but I couldn't keep my eyes off him. He is a good-looking jerk. I feel like slapping that smug look off his face.

We reach an empty corridor, standing alone when we stop. I glare at him, trying to get my point heard, but I didn't realize I was up against the wall. He places one hand on the wall and leans in closer, running his other hand up and down my arm, making me uncomfortable.

"I don't know you enough not to like you, but since we're on the topic, nope. I don't."

His hand traces my stomach, making circles trying to tickle me. A sense of uneasiness washes over me. His hand isn't on my skin, but my fabric is so thin, it might as well be my skin he's touching. My heart pounds in my chest, while my breathing picks up its pace.

However, I stand temporarily frozen. He's not my type and my heart already feels for Roger. Why does this guy even bother trying?

"Like you said, you don't know me." He leans in and tries to kiss my lips, but I turn my head, giving him my cheek. "I want to eat you."

Planting my hands on his chest, I try to push him off me, and gasp out loud, "Stop."

"Why?" he whispers again in my ear. "You like this don't you?" he asks as he trails his finger from my stomach up over my chest and stops where my nipple perks out.

Gasping, I shove him away. "No." I move from the wall to the door. "So, stop trying."

He laughs. "See you around, Davina." He walks away, disappearing into the crowd of students.

Stupid. Stupid. Stupid.

After a long day at university, my mind is spinning. It's hard, and I'm not enjoying myself. I don't want to be here; this was a mistake. I feel like I could be doing something more with my life than wasting time in this place.

My parents never went to university: they built businesses instead. Dad pours his soul into every dish, while Mom breathes life into her art with each bouquet she designs. I can't help but wonder if I'm wasting my time following a path that's not really mine.

Lost in thought and barely noticing where I'm going, I almost collide with someone. I quickly stuff the paperwork into my bag, then glare at the person I bumped into.

"Well. Well. Well. If it isn't the frigid fucking queen," Lexi mocks, her tone dripping with sarcasm.

Blinking in surprise, I stand there speechless, heart pumping fast, unable to move.

She crosses her arms in front of her chest. "Did you follow me? Are you obsessed with me?"

"I—I—" My voice does not make way to my lips.

She approaches me, taunting. "Are you still scared of me, Davina?"

"No, yes, no, yes," I say panicking not able to meet her gaze. "Please, Lexi, I, we, I... We're not in high school anymore."

"Yeah," she says, rolling her eyes at me. "You matured." Her expression hardens. "Listen here, frigid girl!"

I gulp, unable to breathe. This is the first time we're alone, without anyone close by to help or stop her, not that anyone did any of that before, but still. I feel my throat constricting and I'm about to faint.

She snaps her voice laced with venom. "Looks like your year away, did you good, didn't it?"

"What did I ever do to you?" I challenge, tilting my head.

"You exist and I hate you," she hisses, her lips curling into a sly grin.

"Yeah, but what did I do?" I ask, staring at her. I want to know what I did to hurt her this much, to make her hate me, or—do whatever she did in high school.

"I don't need a reason to hate you, frigid queen." Her response is laced with malice. "You shouldn't have come back. Now, I'm going to make your life a living hell."

"Whatever," I retort, rolling my eyes as I turn to walk away, refusing to let her see the irritation bubbling inside me.

My heart pounds as I climb into Dad's Merc, hands trembling on the steering wheel. Fumbling with the keys, I finally start the engine. As I drive away, relief washes over me. Lexi confronted me, throwing verbal punches, but somehow, I didn't break down. I'm surprised I didn't cry, but glad I kept my weakness hidden. Even without defending myself, I'm relieved I confronted her.

I arrive home to find an empty house, Mom and Dad likely still at work.

Hungry, I make a sandwich, before changing into my PJs, and sitting at my desk to tackle my university homework. One thing's clear: if I'm paired with an ogre, I'll need to prove to my teacher I'm good enough to work with someone else.

My phone rings, just as I'm about to get into bed. Mom flashes across the screen. I answer, happy to hear her voice. "Hey, Mom. What's up?"

"I'm going to be late again tonight, honey," she says, apologetic. "Just wanted to check in and see how you're doing."

"Everything is fine, Mom."

She hesitates. "Listen, Davina, I need to talk to you about something." My heart sinks as I wait to hear what she has to say. "Dad and I are having some problems. We've decided to take a break from each other for a while."

"What do you mean you're having problems?"

"It's something between your father and I, we don't want you to worry about it. I will be staying late at the shop like we talked about earlier. But Dad's staying at his sister's for a while."

I try to keep my voice steady. "Is there anything I can do to help?"

"No, honey. We'll work things out eventually."

After we hang up, I feel drained and a little sad. Mom and Dad have sacrificed so much for me, and it's hard to see them go through this, whatever this is. As of now, I don't know what they have between each other and I'm sure when the time is right, they will tell me what I should know, but I wish there was something I could do to help.

My chest tightens and I text Dad.

> Dad, I love you. No matter what you decide, know that I love you and I'm here for you.

It's a small gesture, but it's all I can think of doing. He doesn't respond to my text, but I hope it would at least let him know I care. Despite all the challenges and responsibilities in my life, I'm determined to stay focused on my academics.

Besides, I am still looking forward to my date with Roger, at least I still hope it is happening.

Twelve

❤

Roger

I'm dreading dinner tonight with Lexi and her family. The thought alone makes my stomach churn. I've made it clear that there is no "us." There never will be. I'd rather be anywhere else, preferably on a real date with Davina, learning more about her and losing myself in her warmth. But instead, I'm stuck here, bound by family obligations that feel more like chains.

What's worse, Jiddo has already taken things too far. He's spoken to the minister, locked in his house as the venue, and even arranged for caterers. All without asking me. As if my consent doesn't matter. It's like I'm not even a person in this; I'm just a pawn in their grand game of politics and power.

Everything is happening so fast, spinning out of control, and I can't seem to stop it. Every decision is being made for me, my life dictated by people who claim they love me. But this isn't love. Love wouldn't force me into something this suffocating.

I grip the steering wheel tightly driving to dinner. No matter how many times I tell myself I'll find a way out, the walls keep closing in. And the worst part? Lexi thrives in this chaos. She wants this, pretending it's all for love, but I know better. She's as calculated as Jiddo, and together they're orchestrating my life.

I'm screwed!

Parking outside my house, I stare at the glowing light in the dining room. My reflection in the car window looks just as trapped as I feel. With a deep breath, I step out, ready to face another evening of pretending to be someone I'm not.

As I make my way to the door, my phone rings, drawing me back into my car. I glance at the screen and answer, bringing the phone to my ear.

"Hey," I say, unlocking the car door. "What's up, Charlie?" my voice crackles through the line. "I'm getting ready for dinner," I add, sighing.

"Wednesday," Charlie says bluntly, his tone suggesting he's building up to something.

"What about it?" I ask, already bracing for whatever I've forgotten.

"The elections," he replies, pausing for dramatic effect.

"Okay," I respond quickly, relieved it's nothing too heavy.

"Well," he says, the sound of a smile in his voice. "I've finished your speech."

"Can we meet later so I can read it?" I ask, trying to keep it low-key.

"Yeah, sure," Charlie says with an easy chuckle.

Placing my phone in my back pocket, I walk into the house, trying to plaster on a fake grin. Not too forced. Just enough to appear genuine. Walking around, I greet everyone, exchanging quick hellos, until I reach Lexi. Her bitter smirk greets me like a slap to the face, as if I've already done something wrong.

"Hi," I say softly, leaning in for a polite hug.

She hugs me back, her grip a touch too firm, and whispers in my ear, "We need to talk."

"Sure," I reply, nodding, "but after dinner."

"No," she snaps, her voice firm. "Now."

I hesitate but nod again, frustrated. Together, we excuse ourselves. Her gaze feels like a drill on my back as I lead her upstairs to my bedroom.

Once inside, she closes the door behind her with deliberate force and turns to stare into my eyes. I begin undressing casually, pulling at my shirt and stepping out of my shoes. She's seen me like this before, so I don't bother hiding it. All I want is to get into more comfortable clothes, but her gaze remains charged with tension.

"What did I do now?" I ask, exasperated, as I pull on a fresh T-shirt.

"It's about Davina," Lexi says, her arms crossed and her tone accusatory.

I pause and glance at her, trying not to react. "What about Davina?"

"Did you have lunch with her in the cafeteria?"

"Yeah, we're friends," I reply, keeping my voice steady.

She narrows her eyes, stepping closer. "Looks like more than friends from what I was told."

"Who told you that?" I ask, rolling my eyes.

"You don't know them, Hun," she retorts, smirking.

I sigh and shrug. "What do you want?"

"Are you dating her?"

"No," I say firmly, wanting her to stay away from Davina.

"Are you lying to me?" she presses, her voice dropping to a dangerous whisper.

"No," I repeat, meeting her gaze head-on.

Her eyes narrow further, and her voice turns icy. "Don't make me angry, Roger. You don't want to see me angry—"

"Shut up, Lexi," I cut her off sharply. "We're not together."

She tilts her head, a mocking smile curling her lips. "Oh, but honey bun, we're engaged."

"Like hell," I fire back.

"Oh, but we are," she says sweetly, almost sing-song. "Your Jiddo has prepared everything for us. Isn't that amazing?"

I walk up to her, anger coursing through me, and nudge her backward. "Never."

She stumbles slightly but recovers with a laugh. "Poor baby," she coos mockingly. "You think you have a way out."

She gallops out of my room in a skip, her steps light and carefree, making her way toward the dining room. I trudge behind her, trying to keep my cool, when suddenly, my arm is grabbed and shoved to the side.

"Jiddo," I say, looking up to meet his stern gaze.

"What is this I hear about another girl?" he demands, his voice low but commanding.

"It's nothing. We're only friends," I reply quickly, hoping he'll let it go.

"It better be nothing, Roger. You don't want to ruin your future with Lexi," he warns.

Gulping, I manage to say, "I—"

"Don't bother. I know you don't like Lexi. Your father never liked your mother, but look how good that turned out," he interrupts.

"Jiddo, can I talk to you about something?" I ask, my voice quiet, uncertain if I want to hear his response.

"No. We're going to have dinner, then, you will go up and prepare for your speech. I'll be there for the elections. You need to win," he commands, his gaze unyielding.

"But it's a university function. You don't need to be there," I protest, trying to push back.

"I do. You're my investment," he states firmly, as if that settles everything.

Dinner goes by fast. I'm not concentrating on anything except my date with Davina that clashes with my speech for the elections. Maybe I could rearrange another date? Or maybe I should cancel it all together.

Charlie arrives in his car, and I climb in. He hands me the paper, and I read it out loud. The light from the car lamp illuminates the pages.

"Hello, Roadwood! My name is Roger Hoards, and I'm running for your student body president because I believe in us—the students. We're more than just a university; we're a community."

"Keep going," Charlie encourages.

I take a deep breath and continue the speech. "A community that deserves a voice, a leadership that listens, and a change that improves our everyday experience. I promise to fight for better resources, fair representation, and most importantly, for each of you to feel heard. This isn't about me; it's about us, together, we'll make Roadwood a place we're proud of."

"So, what do you think?" Charlie asks, watching me closely.

"I love it, thanks," I reply, feeling a bit of relief.

"Yeah, so I made it so that people will see you," Charlie adds with a smile, trying to lighten the mood.

"Yeah." I sigh.

"Why do you sound defeated?"

"I'm just overwhelmed with everything," I admit, running a hand through my hair.

"Don't worry. You'll do great," Charlie reassures me.

"Thanks again, Charlie," I say, feeling a little better.

We wave goodbye, and Charlie drives off. I watch him leave, then make my way toward my home. But instead of walking in, I turn and walk toward my car. I can't breathe in this life anymore. It's suffocating. I need space. Freedom.

Maybe I should let go of Davina. This world is not for her, and I don't want her to be part of it. She's too innocent, kind and bubbly while I am surrounded by dull, manipulative and duties. Yet, having her in my world makes everything feel right. Better. So much more blazing.

How can I choose between her and my family?

Eventually, I end up at my flat. I barely remember how I got here. My legs feel like metal as I climb the stairs to my door. Walking inside, I fall into bed, hoping sleep will bring clarity or, at the very least, quiet my mind.

Thirteen

♥

Davina

Wednesday arrives so fast, although my days at university have been drowning me in work. I barely have time to breathe, let alone think about anything else. But despite the chaos, there's one thing that keeps me going, my date with Roger today. I've been looking forward to it all week.

But as I pull out my phone during class, I see a text from him, and all my excitement begins to dissipate. My heart sinks as I unlock the screen.

ROGER

> Hey Klutz, so, we're still going but it won't be lunch. Can we change it to dinner? I have the elections today and I've been swamped.

I stare at the message, blinking a few times, hoping that somehow this is just a misunderstanding. Shaking the unease crawling through me, I type out a reply.

> We can postpone, we don't need to go—it's okay if you're busy Roger.

The weight of the silence between us feels heavier now, but as I'm about to give up on us, another text pops up.

ROGER

> That's not what I'm saying. I want us to go out, but I've got this. Will you be there?

As much as I'd like to be there and support him, I don't know if it's right. My conversation with Lexi wasn't exactly inviting and if she sees me there, I may not be able to cope.

> No, I'm heading home to take care of something. Good luck.

ROGER

> Thank you and I'm taking you out tonight, Klutz. I promised.

> Fine. You owe me a special evening.

ROGER

> Whatever you want, Davina.

And just like that, he keeps his word.

When Roger arrives at my house, I open the door. He takes my hand gently in his, leading me out to the car. The drive feels like a blur. The streets of Beirut pass by, but it's the rhythm of our conversation and the soft music playing in the car that fills my head.

We arrive at the restaurant, and I can't help but admire the charm of the place. It's a hidden gem nestled on a quiet street corner, tucked away from the noise of the city. The exterior is warm and welcoming, and as we step inside, I notice how the ambient light creates a cozy, intimate atmosphere.

The rustic wooden tables and chairs add to the inviting mood. Colorful paintings and photographs hang on the walls, giving the space a vibrant personality.

Soft Italian music plays in the background, and the dim lighting sets a romantic tone causing me to feel like we're meant to be, this life made only for us. The smile on my face remains glued on because of the beating and thumping of my excited heart. We peruse the menu. The delicious scent of fresh bread and savory spices fills the air, making my stomach growl with hunger.

Roger confidently orders, "I'll take the pasta bonsais." Turning to me with a question in his eyes, he adds, "The lady will have the lasagna?" I nod in agreement.

"Anything to drink?" the waitress asks.

"A bottle of your local red wine," Roger suggests. "What do you think, Davina?"

"Red is fine for me."

"A preference, sir?" the waitress speaks trying to get Roger to look at her.

"House wine," he tells her, sending her a quick, polite smile and immediately placing his attention back on me.

The night is off to a great start. I'm excited to learn more about him.

"So, how were the elections?" I ask, my curiosity piqued.

Roger leans back in his chair, a slight grin tugging at his lips. "Great, sad you weren't there to cheer me on."

I raise an eyebrow, teasing him, "Now, why would I cheer when I could have stood beside you?"

His eyes twinkle mischievously. "Oh, you would have liked to stand next to me?"

"Yeah, why not. I believe in you, Roger, and I believe in your campaign," I say sincerely, meeting his gaze.

He tilts his head, clearly intrigued. "You do? So, why didn't you stay behind to hear the speech?"

"I think you know why," I say, my voice tinged with frustration as I look away, unable to meet his eyes.

"No. I don't."

"It doesn't matter now," I mutter, trying to brush it off, but the tension hangs between us.

"No, tell me, what's going on, Davina." he presses.

I take a deep breath, hesitant. "It's about Lexi."

"What about her?" Roger asks, his tone sharp with concern.

My frustration bubbles up. "I don't want to be a problem for you, like, I don't want whatever this is between us to create an issue for you."

"You're not," he assures me, his eyes locking with mine. "I like you, Davina, and I want to keep seeing you. It's no one's business."

I swallow hard, doubt creeping in. "You sure about that?" I ask. "She seems convinced that you're hers."

He presses his lips into a firm, thin line, annoyed. "Forget about her. I don't want her or anyone ruining our evening. Please?"

"Well," I say, dancing on the letter l on my tongue, "Okay. So, why don't I tell you about something I'm really passionate about?"

"Go on," he says, leaning in slightly, intrigued.

"Baking is my thing. I got asked to bake a cake for my neighbor's son's birthday," I explain, happy to change the subject.

"Baking?" He raises an eyebrow. "What does the boy like?"

"He's going to be ten and he likes dinosaurs, so I'm thinking of making him a dinosaur theme park cake, with different rides and..." I trail off, excited about the possibilities.

He reaches for my hand, grinning, interrupting my flow to voice, "Your face lights up when you talk about baking. I like it."

"Does it?" I blush. "I hadn't noticed."

"It does. Besides, anything you're passionate about, your face lights up. I just wish that would be me lighting you up like that one day."

"Easy there, Cowboy."

"So, is that my nickname? Cowboy?"

"Would you like it to be?"

He chuckles. "Hell, no. I don't even have a horse or a hat, but I would like to be called Master."

"That's not happening."

We laugh, smiling at each other and continue talking, our conversation easy.

"You know it's been a while since I dined in such a nice restaurant. Our life is always go, go, go and we barely have time to sit and cherish these moments," I say, taking a sip of the savory red wine.

"I know what you mean," he replies. "Last time I had dinner at home and this is a good change."

"What is your family like?" I question, genuinely curious.

"Authoritative and strict," he replies, his tone matter of fact. "How about yours?"

"They're sweet and kind," I say with a soft smile, thinking of how supportive they've always been.

The waitress brings us our meals, and we dive in, savoring the different flavors. It's as if the world around us didn't exist, and we're the only two people left here. I love being with him, and I feel like he loves being with me too.

When we finish our meal, Roger takes my hand and looks into my eyes. "Davina, I've had such a wonderful time tonight," he says, his voice soft and sincere.

"Yeah, me too," I murmur, my heart fluttering with excitement.

"I'd love to see you again," he continues, his gaze never leaving mine.

"I'd like that. What do you have in mind?"

"How about we go to the forest this weekend?"

I grin. "That sounds fantastic. I can't wait."

Leaving the restaurant hand in hand, we walk through the quiet streets of Beirut. Talking and laughing, my heart fills with gratitude for this magical evening. My pulse quickening when I glance up at him.

"Thank you for dinner, Roger."

The warmth of his hand in mine makes me hesitate, not wanting the night to end when we reach my house. We stop in front of the door, and he looks at me with a grin that makes my heart skip a beat.

"God, you're so beautiful," he says sincere, his gaze lingering on me with admiration.

I blush, not knowing how to respond, but the way he looks at me makes me feel like I'm the only person in the world. Biting my lip, nerves flutter in my stomach. I really want to kiss him, but I don't want to be the one to make the first move. Without another word, he leans in, brushing his lips against mine. The kiss is soft and lingering, leaving me breathless. He pulls away slowly, his eyes locked on mine.

"Goodnight, Davina," he murmurs, before turning to walk away. I stand there for a moment, my lips still tingling where his had been, my breath shallow.

My heart races as I watch him disappear into the night.

Fourteen

Roger

Driving home after my date with Davina, my mind wouldn't stop racing, replaying every moment. Her smile, her laughter, the way she looked at me with such open curiosity. It all felt so right. But even in the glow of it, doubt crept in. Am I leading her on? That's the last thing I want. She's not some distraction I picked up to escape everything happening at home.

Just thinking about her makes my heart beat faster, and still, I hesitate. What if I'm falling too fast? The feelings are real, I know that, but I keep pulling back, trying to read her, trying not to push. I can't be the first to say something. It would be too much, too soon. And pretending everything's fine when it's not, that's not fair to her. She deserves honesty.

And then there's Lexi.

What the hell was that? Why did she have to go after Davina like that and make things even more complicated?

And who's been spying on us?

I can't let Lexi keep pulling the strings, not when it comes to someone who matters to me as much as Davina. As I pull into the driveway, I kill the engine and sit there, letting my thoughts settle.

My phone buzzes. Frowning, I ignore it.

Right now, I need to focus on Davina, on the possibility of a future that doesn't feel like a cage. But the moment I step inside, everything shatters. Chaos.

Nurses and police are everywhere.

My parents are on the couch. And Lexi's with them.

"What's going on?" I ask, my voice laced with confusion, glancing between my parents.

"Where were you, Roger?" my father demands, agitation evident in his tone.

"What's wrong? What happened?" I press, panic rising in my chest as I step closer to them.

"It's Jiddo," my mother says softly, her expression somber as she looks at me. "He had a heart attack."

"What?" I explode, my voice echoing through the room as fear takes hold.

"He's okay now," she assures me quickly, her voice calm but tinged with worry. "He's resting in your bedroom. As a matter of fact, he's expecting you."

Lexi looks up as I make my way to my bedroom. "I can go with you," she offers.

I shake my head. "No." I pause. "What are you doing here anyway?"

"The lights, I saw them—"

I cut her off. "Sure, you did."

Huffing, she says, "Where were you, Roger?" she asks with her hand on her hip.

"Nowhere. I'm going to check on him," I say quietly, nodding before I head to my room.

Jiddo sits in the chair beside my bed, his face pale but set with quiet authority. I walk over and sit down, clasping my hands in my lap, waiting. He doesn't say anything at first. He stares, eyes sharp, scanning me like he's trying to piece together where I've been.

"Why didn't you answer the phone when I called?"

"I didn't know it was you," I reply, keeping my tone neutral.

"Really?" he asks, his sharp gaze narrowing on me.

I saw the call earlier and pressed ignore.

"Yes, really," I lie, hoping the tone of my voice doesn't betray me.

"You know—" he starts to say, but I interrupt.

"Jiddo, I'm sorry you had to go through this," I blurt out.

"Shut up, Roger," he snaps. "Just shut up!"

There is a lecture coming my way, I know it.

"Before you were born, your parents and I decided together to plan your life. Everything was set for a perfect beginning. You were a good boy, back then, you did as you were told and you listened. Ever since you got to university, you have changed and I don't like this version you have become," Jiddo declares, his tone leaving no room for negotiation.

"What—no," I stammer. "I didn't change. I'm still the same person, Jiddo."

He laughs, a bitter, humorless sound. "You are funny, Roger."

My voice trembles with frustration. "What have I ever done to you? It's like you hate me so much and I don't know why."

"Don't be so dramatic."

Shaking my head furiously, I say, "I don't even like Lexi. Jiddo, please. Isn't there anything else I can do to please you? Anything, just please, not Lexi."

"I don't care what you want, Roger. It is the Hoards way." My voice falters as the weight of his words begins to sink in. He laughs, taunting me. "Besides, you have no say in what you want anymore."

"Jiddo, please," I plead, desperation creeping into my voice. "You don't have to do this—"

"You will do this, Roger. Or you will lose a legacy. A born legacy."

"Can I think about it?" I ask, trying to keep my voice steady. "No."

My frustration boils over. "That's a life sentence."

"A life sentence would be to deport you to the military academy and then follow in my footsteps, which sounds like a good idea, right about now, Roger," Jiddo replies, his tone final. "But the military does not have a place for you at the moment. And for everyone's sake, break it off with Davina."

My heart sinks. "What? How do you know about her?"

"I know everything, Roger. Everything you do. You're a grandson to a highly important politician," he claims, watching me close. "She's a nice girl, but she's not for you, my grandson."

"She's my girlfriend."

"Lexi is your girlfriend. Make it official. We are done here."

I beg again, trying to reason with him. "Please reconsider. I love her, Jiddo."

He gets up, walks to my door, and pauses to deliver his final blow. "If you ever see Davina again, I will ship you to the military academy in Russia."

He steps out, his footsteps fading down the hall. His words hit me like a tidal wave. I collapse onto the edge of my bed, burying my face in my hands. A sob tears from my chest. I want to scream, to throw something, but the weight in my chest keeps me frozen.

Just as the anger starts to rise, the chime of a text cuts through the fog.

I unlock the screen, bracing myself for whatever's waiting.

DAVINA

Thank you for tonight. I had fun.

Davina. My sweet Klutz.

Seeing her name light up my screen makes my chest ache in the best way. She's the one thing that still feels untouched by the chaos closing in around me, my escape, my reason to keep pretending that I'm not already broken. I can't give her up.

I let her words soothe something raw inside me. She's my last piece of something real. But how could I ever let her see the truth? How could I tell her that everything she thinks she knows about me is built on lies?

> Yes, me too, Klutz. See you soon.

DAVINA

> I seriously can't wait.

> Me too, Davina.

At least for now, everything is peaceful.

For now, Davina doesn't need to know.

For now, I can pretend.

Fifteen

❤

Davina

The weekend is finally here!

Roger and I have another date today, and I can't wait to see him again. Stepping outside, I spot him waiting with a big smile, instantly bringing one to my face.

"Hey." He pulls me into a hug, and I relax in his arms.

He leans in towards me, our eyes meeting, and our lips touch igniting a spark within them. Our heads tilt slightly, allowing for deeper contact between us.

The sun begins to dip below the horizon, radiating a warm paradisiac glow across the sky. Roger takes my hand leading me along the Corniche. The sound of the waves crashing against the shore and the gentle breeze carrying the scent of saltwater fills the air, heightening our senses.

Strolling along the promenade, we pause to take in the magnificent scenery. The breathtaking view of the Mediterranean Sea is spread out before us, shimmering in hues of blue and gold.

"This is so beautiful," I murmur with awe.

He smiles. "You are. How did I get so lucky?"

My heart skips a beat as I look into Roger's eyes. A warm, fuzzy feeling spreads throughout my body. All my doubts and fears melt away, and a rush of gratitude and happiness consumes me.

"Klutz." He hesitates, a smile tugging at his lips. "I never thought I'd ever meet someone like you. You take my breath away in the best way possible. I can be myself when I'm with you."

With every passing moment, our connection was growing stronger. I'm falling for him deeply, but with what my parents are going through, it didn't feel right to be happy while they were sad.

Why am I letting my thoughts wander to my problems when I should be enjoying this beautiful date with him?

He notices my unease and with a gentle touch, places his hand on my cheek. "What's on your mind, Klutz? Did I do something wrong?"

I shake my head. "No, it's just... my parents. They're going through something, and I wish I could help them but—"

"I'm sorry to hear that." His eyes fill with empathy. "You know you can talk to me about whatever is bothering you."

"I know Roger, but I don't know what is really going on with them. They say they can handle it. But they don't know what I'm going through when I watch them struggle."

"I get it, but you don't have to burden yourself with their problems. When the time is right, I'm sure they will tell you everything."

"You think?"

"Of course," he says, his voice reassuring.

I look at him, surprised by his words. It's like he understands me better than I understand myself. Maybe it's his gentle touch, or the way he looks at me, but I feel like I could trust him.

"You can still be happy," he emphasizes, taking me in his arms, kissing my lips.

My heart pumps, excitement overwhelming me. His hands roam my body, from my jeans to my top and my waist. He kisses me deeper and I melt into him, until he suddenly stops.

"I know. Too fast." I whack his hand playfully and we laugh.

"Shall we have a seat somewhere to eat?" I ask fidgeting with my hair, glancing around, looking for a spot.

We continue our walk along the Corniche, savoring the salty sea breeze and the warm colors of the sky. Soon, we arrive at a cozy seaside café and order a couple of drinks. We're led to a table on the patio, where we can enjoy the stunning view of the ocean. Perusing the menu, contentment brews over me. Everything feels so perfect-the warm breeze, the sound of the waves crashing against the shore, and most of all, the company.

"What looks good?" I ask, probing him to make the choices.

"You," he jokes, glancing towards the menu again.

"Funny." I giggle.

Gazing into my eyes, he suggests, "We're at the beach, so, maybe fish and anything along the lines of seafood?"

The waiter approaches our table. "Welcome to the Seaside Café, what can I get you?"

Roger takes the liberty to order for us as I'd hoped. "The fish meze for two, with the house bottle of red wine." He turns his attention back to me. "Tell me more about your hobbies?"

I chuckle as I take a sip of my glass of water. "I like hiking trails, and reading, and yourself?"

"Taking long drives and visiting the beach, it's calming."

"Yeah," I agree, as we wait for our meals to arrive. We continue chatting effortlessly. It feels like we've been friends for years, not just for a few weeks.

"So, do you have any siblings?" he asks, curious.

"Nope, I'm an only child. How about you?"

"Same. Only child. My parents had been trying so much for a child and when I came along, they didn't want to try for another."

"I'm sorry to hear that, Roger. My parents chose to have only one child, so I don't know what it feels like for your parents."

"Yeah. But it would have been nice to have a sibling."

"Maybe, yeah," I say, trying my hardest to keep my thoughts at bay. My life, everything about it was hard, even if it didn't have to be. I want to be able to talk about it with him, but maybe he's not interested in that much.

"Something seems to be bothering you."

"It's difficult to admit, if I'm being honest."

"Admit what? Talk to me. Past, present, and future. I want to know everything about you Davina. What is it?"

Chuckling, I try to push away my thoughts. "I—"

He blushes. "Please, Davina. Let me in."

Taking a deep breath, I explain to him just enough for him to understand why it's been affecting me, without ruining the moment. "My high school days were not as one would think," I begin, my voice quiet. "Are you sure you want to hear this?"

"Let me be your anchor, Klutz."

Before I tell him, I take a deep breath in; allowing the world around me to fade, so the words that come out, will be my truth and no one else's. As I let the breath go out of my lungs, I feel relaxed, at least for now. "Lexi used to torment me. She bullied me for a long time." I pause, trying to steady my breath. "I've never really gotten over it. Even now, when I see her, it's like I'm sinking into quicksand."

The weight of the words hang in the air, heavy. I don't want to go into too much detail, but the past is still there, lurking.

"I'm sorry, Davina." Clenching his fists and eyes flaring, he looks annoyed at what I admitted.

"For my entire high school experience, I was the one my classmates targeted. Every day, almost every hour, they'd throw shots at me. I never knew why, and I never asked. It was like I was their punching bag for no reason."

He places a soothing hand on mine. "And Lexi was a part of it?"

"Yeah, she practically orchestrated it all." Tears spill out.

"I can't imagine what you went through, Davina. I'm so sorry."

"You know the worst part?"

"What?"

"When you asked about my exes, well, I never had any. But I did have a crush on a boy. When he found out, he and Lexi just went around high school, hanging on each other, making me jealous. And I was, I'm not going to lie."

Placing my head in my hands, tears began to fall. The pain resurfacing from those days, and the ways Lexi tortured me came back full force. I still can't believe they dated. He got up off his chair and knelt by my side. I didn't want his pity, but it happened, and it's about time I spoke about this. It was a painful time to be bullied for being different, or when they used to call me the frigid queen.

"Is that the real reason you took a year off?" Roger asks in concern.

"Only part of it. The main reason I took a year off was..." I hesitate.

"What?"

"I tried to kill myself," I say the confession slipping out.

Freezing, I hold my breath watching his face as he pales, his eyebrows coming together in concern. My heart stops and my stomach churns. It's the first time I've admitted it to anyone out loud.

Saying it now is not exactly easy.

My eyes widen as I stare at him. It's as though the air has left the room. My chest rises, but I don't seem to breathe. He watches me grip the edge of the chair, my knuckles white, as my words sink in.

"What?" Roger's voice cracks.

"The day that happened with my crush. I felt so alone, and I was sick of being bullied. Of hurting. I went into the art room and mixed a bunch of things together, I drank them, but nothing happened. He found me on the floor, and they called the ambulance. I was told to finish my schooling after school and on the weekends. Later, my parents didn't know how to cope, so I took a year off, to travel. I visited a lot of places. I loved every moment of it. But I was missing something," I explain.

"Missing what?" Roger's voice remains soft, barely whispering.

"I missed the university experience. When I was rejected everywhere, I gave up."

"Then, you got an acceptance," Roger says a small smile forming on his lips.

"And it was the best thing that ever happened to me," I reply remembering how far I've come.

"Look at me," he utters, removing my hands from my face. "I'm sorry for whatever she did to you. And for what you went through. But know that you'll never feel like that with me. Ever. I care about you so much."

I swallow hard, the lump in my throat making it feel like I can't breathe. My eyes well up, but I nod. "Thank you."

"Stop thanking me." He laughs and so do I, feeling a little lighter. "You're going to make me blush." He takes my hand in his and lifts me up, holding me in his arms, close to his heart. I'm falling hard.

Silence calms us both. We pull back, staring into each other's eyes as we sit back in our places. He leans over, giving me a chaste kiss. I smile, taking his face in my hands, and kiss him back. We stay like that for a little while, lost in each other, until the waiter arrives, clearing his throat, "Seafood meze for two."

The waiter sets our plates down, steaming hot and fragrant. I dig into the seafood risotto, creamy Arborio rice wrapped around plump shrimp and mussels. Across from me, Roger eats with equal enthusiasm, his eyes lighting up with each bite. We don't talk much, just savor the food and the moment.

Between bites, we pause to admire the sunset and the view beyond. After dinner, we stroll along the beach. The sand is cool beneath our feet, the water still holding the sun's warmth. We walk hand in hand, stopping now and then to admire shells, the waves or simply each other.

The night ends with Roger driving me home and a sweet kiss goodbye. It feels like a dream, one I don't want to wake from. I'm already looking forward to the next time, hoping we keep moving closer, because when I look at him, my heart wants more.

I'm in love with him, badly.

Sixteen

Roger

The date was amazing.

I couldn't stop smiling, and every moment spent with Davina felt like a dream. From the way she laughed to the warmth in her eyes when she looked at me, everything felt perfect. But then, as we were sitting there, talking about life, she let something slip that twisted my stomach.

When she admitted what she'd tried to do... when she told me about the darkness she'd been through, I felt my heart break for her. I had no idea. How could someone so full of life, so strong, go through something so painful?

And to know it was Lexi...

The person who had caused so much pain in her life. It tore me apart hearing how Lexi's words and actions had driven Davina to the edge. How could someone be so cruel?

But Lexi is still cruel, now forcing me into an engagement I don't want, pushing me for marriage. I can't go through with it. Not after what she did to Davina. I won't pretend it didn't happen. Not when I know what she's capable of.

I'm falling in love with Davina, and I need her to know she means the world to me. But a gnawing feeling in my gut keeps whispering: maybe I should let her go.

I can still hear her voice: fragile and broken, confessing how close she came to ending everything.

And I'm supposed to pretend that didn't happen? Smile and nod through a future with the person who pushed her to the edge?

No. I had to try one last time.

I stormed into the living room, where my parents sat planning engagement photos and guest lists, like we weren't all walking around with blood on our hands.

"I can't do this," I said. "I won't marry Lexi."

They stared at me like I'd just cursed God.

"She hurt Davina," I added, voice shaking. "You want me to build a life with someone like that?"

They stare into my eyes and continue, not caring. "So, the caterers said they would be able to make the delivery to our house," mother said oblivious to me standing there frustrated at what I found out.

"No, but my father said to make sure they deliver at his house, not ours, since that's where the wedding will be, no?"

"You're right honey. Is there something else you need Roger?"

"No, nothing else. Just nothing."

Defeated, I attempt to push those thoughts aside, and focus on my date with Davina.

Another one.

This weekend would be engraved as the best weekend of my life and I won't let anyone ruin it for me.

Not my parents. Not Jiddo, and especially not Lexi.

We arrive at the Beirut Pine Forest, a natural reserve with hiking trails, picnic areas and scenic views of the city. I knew it would be a more relaxed and casual time together, while we enjoy the natural beauty of Beirut.

"It's so magnificent. I can't believe this place exists here," she tells me in awe. "I know what you mean."

We walk hand-in-hand through the forest, with the sun shining bright, and the air filled with the sweet scent of flowers. Our guide, a knowledgeable nature enthusiast, leads us through the trees, highlighting the different creatures and animals that live here.

"Look over there," the guide advises, pointing. "See the family of squirrels playing on that tree branch?"

When we continue to explore, my thoughts drift. Spending time like this once in a while is what I've been craving. I hope it lasts. There's something special about being in such a beautiful place surrounded by nature's wonders that makes me feel the need to express myself.

Suddenly, our guide stops and gestures towards a large cedar tree. "This is one of the oldest trees in the forest. It's said to be over 500 years old."

"Can we climb?" I ask, eagerly hoping the guide would allow us.

"At your own discretion. We don't offer guides up the tree or climbing gear."

"We'll be careful. Klutz, you with me? Would you like to see the view from the top?" Holding out my hand, she takes it. Climbing these trees was something I used to do when I was younger, almost like seeing life from up high, and glancing down.

Our laughter echoes through the forest as we climb the tree, my eyes flicking to Davina to make sure she's safe. She has a way of bringing a smile to my face. At the top, the sun catches her black ponytail, and she just glows. She's so beautiful: a woman I could see myself with for life. Wifey material, no question.

I love her. I know it.

I want to tell her, but part of me hesitates. Would it scare her off? Probably not. She's not the type to scare easy.

So why am I still overthinking?

Without further thought, I blurt out, "I love you, Klutz."

Silence wraps around me at the top, heavy and still. My thoughts start to spiral, but the cool air grounds me, I can taste its crisp edge on my tongue. The wind stirs the trees with a gentle rustle. Then her gaze pulls me back. She's watching me, eyes locked on mine. But the world seems to shrink around us.

"What?" she asks, her voice slicing through the moment.

Shit! Shit! Shit! I can't believe I said that.

Is it just me, or is it really high up here?

A gust of wind slams into my chest, and for a second, I swear I'm going to faint and maybe fall to my death. Why did I blurt that out? I tug at my shirt, trying to breathe.

"I—I love you," I mumble again, barely above a whisper.

She says nothing. Maybe she doesn't feel the same. Crap.

Great. Now the rest of the date is going to be painfully awkward. How stupid can I be?

My thoughts spiral as we start the descent from the top of the cedar tree, the forest quiet around us. We catch up to the guide and follow him with the rest of the group. Her hand stays in mine a small mercy. Still, I'm dying to know what she's thinking.

Why hasn't she said anything?

The warmth of her hand is electric, steady, grounding. Then, suddenly, she stops. I turn to her, heart thudding, waiting.

She faces me. "Roger."

"Yes?" I ask, knowing this is it, she doesn't feel the same way and I blew it with her.

"I love you, too," she shouts her voice echoing throughout the forest.

My heart stops. My chest tightens. She loves me. Davina loves me.

Without a word, I pull her into my arms, and we kiss hard. Teeth clash, lips bruise, but it doesn't matter. It's raw, urgent, and electric. All the feelings we never said aloud pour into that moment, stealing our breath.

When our eyes meet again, the air between us crackles. Time seems to hold its breath.

We cling to each other, lost in the heat of it, the world fading around us.

Then a ripple of applause breaks the spell. We pull apart, breathless, and glance around. The guide and the rest of the group are watching us, smiling.

A grin spreads across my face, and Davina blushes. I take her hand and say, "Let's just keep walking."

After a while, the guide gives us some time to explore on our own. Naturally, we return to the ancient 500-year-old cedar, drawn back like it's calling to us. We stand beneath its massive limbs, but our focus remains entirely on each other.

"This tree will symbolize our love," I whisper.

I draw Davina into my arms. She leans back against the tree, its strength cradling her as I kiss her slow at first, then deeper, hungrier. Her dress leaves room for my hand to gently wander. She doesn't stop me, but I don't push further.

My fingers trace the edge of her underwear, lightly caressing the soft skin beneath. She gasps, trying to pull at me. I kiss her again, harder this time, feeling her body melt into mine. Her hands tangle in my hair, drawing me closer, deepening the kiss until I lose myself in her warmth.

Eventually, I wrap my arms around her waist, holding her there with me, neither of us ready to let go until the guide calls the group back together.

When the day ends, I drive her home and park outside her house.

"This was so much fun, Roger," she says, taking my hand in hers.

I smile, not wanting the day to end. "Would you want to grab dinner with me tomorrow?" I ask, my heart pounding a little faster.

Her face lights up, and she squeezes my hand. "I'd love to."

Tomorrow waits just around the corner, carrying the chance for something even better.

Togetherness: a traditional Lebanese restaurant, a place where all the elite dine. The kind of place where expectations are high, where appearances matter.

But tonight, I wasn't here for that. I wasn't here to impress anyone. I was here for us.

Me and my Klutz.

I wanted this to be cozy, intimate, just the two of us, away from the pressure of the world and the noise that always seems to follow me. This dinner wasn't about the place or the food, it was about showing her that, in this moment, no one else mattered. It was just us.

The waiter comes over, his smile polite but professional. "You have a choice of the meze for two or I can get you a bunch of barbeque bites," he says, waiting for our decision.

I look at Davina, the warmth of her gaze meeting mine. I want her to feel at ease, to feel special, because she deserves it.

She speaks first, and I watch her with admiration. "I think I'd like the meze, but for one person, we can share."

She surprises me, catching me off guard. Her voice is confident. It's so different from anyone I've been with, and it excites me.

"Sure," the waiter replies with a nod. "That's fine. And to drink, ma'am?"

"White wine, house wine, please."

The waiter jots it down, and I smile as he walks away, but my focus stays on Davina. I didn't expect her to take the reins, but I like it.

"Is that okay?" she asks, and I nod, trying to hold back a smile.

"I'm sure you were going to order a big one, but I wanted something light. We didn't need to order for two, since we share."

Her words settle around me, and I realize how much I love the way she thinks, how much I love the way she sees the world. "You're right," I reply.

She leans back slightly. Her smile soft and genuine. Then, with a little more confidence than I expected, she says, "I love you."

For a moment, everything seems to pause. Her confession feels right. "Likewise, Klutz."

"So," she starts, her voice light. "What's for dessert?"

"I could think of a few things," I reply with a playful smile.

"Cheeky," she teases.

"Fine, then, what would you like?" I ask, raising an eyebrow.

"You," she says, making my heart skip.

We finish our dinner, pay, and walk out the door. Holding her hand, we walk to the shore. My mind is in a debacle. What do I do? I love this girl. I don't want this to end. But I don't want anything to happen to her either. I need her in my life. She's the right person for me, but I don't want to lead her on and my family...

I place a blanket on the sand that I brought with me from home. We lay on the cold, sandy ground, the sound of the waves in the distance. After a moment, I sit up, turn to face her, and finally speak.

"Davina..." I begin, my voice filled with confusion. "I need to talk to you."

Before I could speak, she takes my face in her hands and she kisses me. Her emotions change mine as she lays back, pulling me over her and kissing me even more. She takes my hand and moves it down into her panties. I feel her soft, slick flesh making me moan; she's already wet.

But should I do this?

"Oh." Her gasp rings in my ear like a bolt train as my heart hammers in my chest, lil Roger getting stiffer. Paying attention to the way she's reacting to my fingers inside her, I groan, her juices flowing all over my hand. Taking my fingers out, I suck them, holding her stare.

"Mm..." Crashing my lips to hers, she pulls back, whispering, "I can't wait anymore. I want you now."

"Are you sure?" I lick her ear and her neck wanting her affirmation.

We're in a quiet place, no one would bother us. I sit up and remove my shirt, leaning down to kiss her stomach. She sits up and removes her dress, my eyes widening at her beauty.

"I love you so much, Klutz," I want her to hear my words, the real meanings in them.

She unclips her bra as if she's in a hurry. Her perked nipples draw my attention, my lips brushing against her skin, I taste, my tongue twirling each one. She grabs my hair and pulls me towards her breast as I take them in my mouth, biting and kissing them one by one.

I remove a condom from my back pocket, and unzip, looking at her. "Are you sure?" I ask again, reminding her she never answered.

"Yes..." She gasps as she forces my hand inside her now soaked panties.

"I love you," I whisper to her again, as I insert another finger, fucking her with my hand.

"Roger, put it in already!" She moans, but I need to make sure this is what she really wants.

"Are you sure, Davina?"

"Yes," she reiterates, pulling me in for a kiss. "Now, do it. I can't take it anymore, Roger."

Putting on the condom, I hover over her, kissing every inch of skin I can reach, "You ready, Klutz?" I pant, licking her neck, biting her lips, easing her passageway open. She's moaning, moving her body close to mine, as if she's ready for me. Kissing me back, she looks into my eyes, urging me to keep going.

"Please," she begs. "Yes, now..."

I plunge into her as if our separate lives didn't matter. At that moment, her and I are one. Her breath catches, and I pause, my body tensing as I see her wince. "Are you okay?" I whisper, brushing her hair back.

She nods but doesn't meet my eyes, her grip on my arms tighten. I slow down, letting her adjust. The wall between us is gone and while it isn't perfect or easy, we find our rhythm, together.

My lips trail all over her body as we glide together and the silence of the environment amplified the music of the moment. Slowly, we begin picking up the pace and my final push, the final thrust, the explosion ignites in her a fire, where she exhales and her teeth show, while I feel a warmth spread through me.

"Uh, uh," she pants. "Yes, oh, yes, harder." I dig in, leaning on her, giving her my whole body. "Uh, yes. Roger, yes," she gasps.

She climaxes and so do I.

We collapse on the sand in each other's arms, kissing each other, not wanting it to end. Eventually, we break apart, breathless. "I love you, Klutz," I murmur, my eyes shining with emotion.

"I love you too." She smiles up at me.

Laying on the sand, we watch the stars sparkle above us. This is just the beginning of our journey together, but how can I avoid doing what my grandfather wants? We get dressed and head to my car when a tear rolls down my cheek, followed by another and I began to cry, sniffling. Overwhelmed with love and sadness, all at one time. Davina takes me in her arms and cries too, not asking any questions.

She kisses my face, and I kiss her lips.

Taking her hand in mine, I place it on my beating heart, tears still falling from my eyes. I glance at my phone, knowing it's time to leave, when she says, "I can't see my life with anyone else."

My chest tightens. "Oh, Klutz, I feel the exact same way." I take her in a hug, wishing there was hope for us.

She pulls away, takes my hand, and places it on her heart. "My heart goes crazy for you."

"That's because we just had sex." I smirk. "Let's get you home."

Arriving at her house, I walk her to her door where we're greeted by her dad and his suitcase. "Dad?" she asks, confused. "What are you doing?"

"Going away for a bit, honey. I'll be back in a week, and we'll talk, okay?"

She hugs him. Her mom stands in the doorway as we wave goodbye to her dad, the sadness in her eyes apparent. She wants to cry, but I guess she's holding a brave face.

"Come in," her mom urges, making way for us. We settle on the couch, with our fingers wrapping around each other.

"Mom, this is Roger."

"Hello, Mrs. Dwain," I greet her politely, shaking her hand, as I stand and sit back down next to Davina. "It's a pleasure."

Her Mom grins. "So, Davina says, you used to know Lexi."

Clearing my throat, I begin, "She's my ex."

"Ex, right, and now. What are your intentions with Davina?"

"Mom!"

I take Davina's hands in mine. "I'm in love with your daughter." It's how I feel, but with my family...maybe, I'm leading her on.

Her mom nods with a satisfied grin. "That's all I wanted to hear."

Getting up, I pull Davina into my arms, kissing her cheek. Shaking her mom's hand another time, I say, "Well, it's getting a bit late, I better be going." She sits back on the couch while Davina walks me to the front door.

"Is everything okay?" Davina asks, probing for an answer, but I can't give her one, not the one we both want.

"Everything is fine, Klutz. I love you."

"I love you too."

Leaving Davina's house, I find myself parked at my favorite spot by the beach. The sound of the waves crashing against the shore provides a soothing background noise filling the night air. Gazing out of the window of my car, the moonlight dances on the surface of the water.

The salty ocean breeze brushes against my face when I close my eyes. "What do I do now?" I ask myself aloud, the words hanging in the air.

On the one hand, there's Davina, the person I love, the one who is right for me. On the other, there's my duty to my family, and all the rules that come with it.

After a while, a phone call interrupts my thoughts. Mother is calling me. "Hey, Mom."

"It's getting late, Roger. You should come home soon."

"'Kay."

Sighing, the engine hums to life, as I pull away. But even as I leave, the quiet from the beach clings to me, a reminder that for once, I can breathe.

Seventeen

Davina

T he week Dad left, Mom became distant, throwing herself into her job and leaving the house, and me behind. I understand she's dealing with her own problems, but it would have been nice to be included in the conversations that affected me. We should have talked about how things would change moving forward.

Over the next few weeks, I found my rhythm at university. My classes grew more engaging, and I got involved with extracurricular activities, especially baking and handling customer orders for cakes and cupcakes. But Roger was nowhere around. His sudden silence bothered me.

Sitting in Calculus class, I finally decide to reach out and text him.

Can we talk?

He doesn't reply. I keep staring at the screen, willing it to light up. A message? A call? But nothing...

Did Mom scare him off? Or was it because I gave myself to him too soon? That can't be it. Not after all our dates.

The teacher calls my name, pulling my attention to the front of the class. "Davina, come here please."

Jumping up from my seat, I'm unable to focus. My mind stewing over Roger. Maybe I scared him off or what if he simply lost interest?

Approaching the front of the class, my heart races. I couldn't concentrate on the lesson. Am I in trouble?

"Davina, dear. Mrs. Elena informed us about your situation with your parents, are you alright?" The teacher watches me, noticing my distracted state.

"I'm fine," I reply, trying to keep my emotions bottled up. "Everything at home is fine too."

Frowning, she hands me my quiz with a big red ZERO marked on it. "Your quiz doesn't show me that everything is fine."

My mouth drops slightly open, stunned. When did we have a quiz? "I apologize miss. This won't happen again."

"Do you want to talk about it?"

I shake my head and walk stiffly back to my seat. The paper crumples in my hand as the tears finally spill over, blurring the red zero staring back at me. I sink into the chair, the failure, the silence, and Roger, all pressing down on me like a heavy stone.

Just as I'm about to contemplate my next move, Charlie's voice breaks through my trance. "A zero?" he asks, concern etched on his face. "Are you okay?"

Irritated by his prying, I say, "Yeah, I'm fine. Mind your own business."

Charlie lifts his hands in surrender. "Sorry, I was just trying to help," he mutters before turning his attention back to his own paper.

"Charlie," I begin, attempting to apologize, but he shrugs me off before I can even get the words out.

"Forget it, Davina," he says, dismissively, his attention fully on his work. I let out a frustrated sigh, feeling overwhelmed.

Why did everything have to be so complicated?

When the class ends, I don't move, staring at the mark on my paper. I knew all the answers. I knew every single problem, but I didn't solve anything. As the last of the students filter out of the classroom, I remain seated, lost in thought. The professor makes her way over to my desk and sits down across from me.

"Davina," she starts, her voice tinged with sadness. "I wanted to offer my assistance with tutoring, and I can allow you to retake the quiz, but I will have to deduct twenty points."

I take a deep breath, trying to keep my emotions in check. "Thank you for the offer, Professor." Gathering my things, I head out.

Walking out of the classroom, I accidentally bump into Charlie and fall to the floor. "I'm sorry," I quickly apologize, embarrassed, not even bothering to get up.

Sighing, Charlie kneels beside me and starts clearing the contents off the floor and back into my bag.

"Thanks," I mumble, grateful for his help.

"Need a ride?"

Pausing, I glance at the time, realizing I'm running late and already missed the bus. "Yeah."

"Come on." Standing, he offers me a hand, helping me up.

I hesitate, wondering if it's a good idea to accept his offer. Charlie and I have a complicated friendship. I don't want to lead him on or hurt his feelings, but I really do need a ride. Resigned, I walk out of the building with him and towards his car. As we get in, I look around. His car appears clean and organized, smelling like roses. It's a stark contrast to Mom's cluttered and messy car.

"Talk to me, Davina," Charlie prods, breaking the silence, as he places a hand on my leg.

"It's nothing. Just pretty personal stuff, and I don't think we're at that stage of friendship to talk about what I have going on," I reply shortly, not wanting to get into any details.

"Did you hear about the engagement?"

"The what?"

Glancing at my phone, I notice there's still no response from Roger, and it's worrying me. I send him another text hoping he'll answer me this time.

> Why aren't you answering me? Is it because we had sex? One moment you are talking to my Mom telling her you're serious about us, and the next, you're cold as ice.

"Roger popped the question to Lexi," Charlie claims.

I clear my throat staring outside the window when his words register. "What?" I gasp, shocked. "What do you mean?"

"What do you think I mean?"

My breath catches, but I don't get the chance to think about it. Suddenly, I realize Charlie is taking a route unfamiliar to me. We're driving along the quiet back roads, surrounded by fields and trees. My heart begins to race and my stomach churns, feeling uneasy. I try to remain calm and collected, but my increasing fear and anxiety push through.

"Charlie, where are we going?" I ask, attempting to keep my voice steady.

"Just taking a shortcut," he replies, his eyes fixed on the road ahead as he pats my leg with his hand another time, leaving it there longer. "Don't worry about it. You'll be home soon."

I move my legs further away and his hand falls, going back to the steering wheel. I'm not sure if I believe him, but I don't want to panic. I take a deep breath and try to stay alert.

We arrive at a small lake surrounded by trees. I need to get out of the car, but I'm scared. He parks the car making my heart stop. The sound of a lock, and the ensuing silence around us encompasses me. He unclips his seatbelt and sits back comfortably in his seat. My heart races, consumed with the worst thoughts.

"Davina," he begins, as he reaches over and undoes my seatbelt. "Loosen up."

His body moves back to his seat, but his hand glides over my chest, slightly touching the fabric. My heartbeat pounds against my ribcage. I'm frightened of where I am, already fearing the worst and no clue what to do.

"Why are we here?" I ask, my voice unsteady, afraid I already know the answer.

He looks into my eyes, licking his lips seductively. Taking a deep breath, he moves towards me. "To have fun," he breathes out and devours my lips without warning.

"No!" Placing my hands on his broad, muscular chest, I push with all my might, but he's too strong and eager, going after what he wants.

"Shush," he urges, kissing me. "I know you want me, Davina. Our lust for each other is evident."

He consumes my lips, impatient, eating them. I could not catch my breath, not until I feel his hand go from my face to my leg.

"Stop," I shriek again, louder, hoping he listens. But he doesn't.

He's stronger than me, and pinning me to the seat. Suddenly, his weight is on me. "Please, Charlie, you're not a bad person, please don't do this..." I beg, plead, and beg some more.

Tears begin falling from my eyes. This can't be happening! "No, please, no."

"It's going to happen. You knew that when you accepted my ride. Or have you been teasing me all this time?"

"Nooooo!" I shout. "Please, no, stop, please..."

Charlie finally has me where he wants me, and he's right, no one is going to save me, not even Roger.

Minutes after, he pushes me out of the car. He gets out and walks to where I'm slumped on the ground. Laughing, he takes his phone out of his pocket and puts it to his ear. "Hey, it's done. I want the funds wired to my offshore bank account."

Who would pay someone to do this? Who asked him to do this to me? Was it Lexi? Dear, God, was it her???

The forest around us was dark and still, except for the rustling of leaves in the wind. Charlie stands above me, his face cold and impassive, his power and dominance looming over me. Unfortunately, getting in his car might be my only way to get to a hospital or just home. Struggling to get up, my body refuses to cooperate.

There is no escape.

I close my eyes, waiting for the inevitable, my heart pounding in my chest.

Lights out...

Eighteen

♥

Roger

The following week, my family planned every possible date night with Lexi. Father kept me busy: lawyer dinners, partner meetings, appearances that made me feel like I was living someone else's life. Mother floated around planning her next soiree, barely noticing me. It was all meant to keep my mind off Davina. And, for the most part, it worked.

But not really and definitely not tonight.

I escaped to my flat to breathe, needing space to think. The question Davina's Mom asked still echoed in my head.

Do I love her? Yes. Undeniably.

But lately, it's begun to feel like a chore I have to tick off my list of things in my life. That isn't the kind of relationship she deserves.

I try calling a few friends, hoping for a drink or distraction but no one picks up. So, I just sit there, alone, surrounded by silence and my own thoughts.

Her smile.

Her laugh.

The way she makes me feel like I didn't have to perform, didn't have to pretend.

A knock sounds at my door.

I groan, dragging myself to answer it, only to stop cold. My father stands there, dressed in a sharp black-and-white suit, that usual look of disappointment settled on his face like a permanent shadow.

I blink. "Dad?"

Without a word, he steps past me and sits on the couch like he owns the place.

"Sit," he commands.

I hesitate, nerves already twisting in my gut, then follow and sit on the opposite end.

"You have questions," he says, more a statement than a guess.

I nod, unsure how to begin. "Yeah."

He leans forward, hands clasped. "We love you, Roger. Everything your mother and I do—it's for you."

"I get it," I mutter.

He gives a dry laugh. "No, you don't. You think we're just trying to control you."

I stare, unsure what to say.

He gets up and paces, picking up a photo from my desk. "I was like you, once. In love."

I freeze. "What happened?"

His eyes don't leave the photo. "I hurt her. And she left."

My mouth falls open and I sit back, stunned. "How?"

He doesn't answer at first. Just standing there, the weight of something unspoken fills the space between us. Then he looks at me, his expression softer than I'd seen in years.

"Let's go for a drive."

"Why?"

"Because I'd like to spend time with my son. No suits. No expectations. Just us."

I hesitate, then nod. "Let me grab my keys."

"No," he says. "I'll drive."

"Okay."

The car ride is quiet at first.

Then a sound slices through the stillness a phone ringing insistent, echoing in the enclosed space. My father doesn't reach for it. Doesn't flinch. He keeps hands on the wheel and his eyes on the road.

But I glance at the screen. The name Jennifer Mead glows back at me.

It hangs in the air like a question. I don't know who she is, but somehow, I know she matters. A backdrop to some other life.

Still, I'm relieved. At least it's not Jiddo. Thank God.

Strangely, though, I don't want the phone to be answered. Not now. Not in this moment. Because for the first time in a long time, I'm sitting beside my father, and it's not forced. It just is. And I want this quiet, this connection, to last a little longer.

Finally, he cuts the engine. And there it is.

Raouché Rock: majestic.

The wind is stronger here. Carrying the scent of salt, something older, ancient. I step out of the car, shoving my hands into my jacket pockets, and follow him toward the edge. The waves crash below, echoing the pressure in my chest. The air wraps around us, cold, tugging at our clothes.

We stand shoulder to shoulder but worlds apart. Behind us, the lights of Beirut flicker to life, out here, everything feels raw.

"This is where I first met her," he finally says, voice nearly lost to the wind. "I wasn't loyal to your mother. After you were born, I told her all about the fling I had. But this spot... this was where I told the other woman, I would leave my wife for her, but I lied."

I glance at him, startled by his openness.

"What happened?"

He doesn't look at me. "I walked away when she needed me the most. And by the time I wanted to make it right, it was too late. She was gone. I don't want that for you, Roger," he says, his voice raw. "But we don't have a choice. This is the country we live in where family and duties are what matter above our heart."

The wind howls, cold and fierce.

For the first time, I see not the man who commands a room, but a father who's still mourning. And for the first time in a long while, I listen knowing me and Davina are no longer something I can look forward to, crushing my heart.

I take him in a deep, genuine son-loving-father hug, and hold him. My eyes water. "I'm so sorry, son. If things were different, I'd say, go for Davina, because anyone who puts a genuine smile on your face is someone I'd love in my family, but it's politics and business. We need strong names to hold us afloat, to survive."

Sniffling, I hold him in another hug. "I understand."

He breathes out. "Thank you, son."

A few days later, I start to pull away, becoming distant. It wasn't intentional. Most of my time I'm with Lexi, even though my heart aches for Davina. While waiting outside the cafeteria, I receive a text.

My fingers dance around the reply button. I should have an explanation for Davina, but I don't know what to say. There are so many scenarios in my head, and none ending well for us.

Panic throbs inside me as I grasp the little red box in my hand. It's my mother's wedding ring, the same one my father proposed with.

Walking into the cafeteria, bouquets of roses surround Lexi. She's sitting with her headphones on. My father and hers stand to the side each holding a video camera. Our mothers stand holding the flowers, while Charlie plays the drums, badly I may add.

She glances at me in shock, or at least pretends to be. "Lexi," I begin, trudging towards her as if walking to my death. Her happiness is evident in her eyes. "Lexi Barnes. You mean the world to me," I lie. The words pour out of me like a criminal robbing a bank. "Will you marry me?"

She jumps up off her seat and runs to me, taking me in her arms. "Yes."

Everyone claps and disperses. Relief washes over me the moment I sit with our parents at the table, tuning out their excited chatter.

However, it's short-lived. I'm not sure how long we've been sitting here when my phone beeps with a message from Davina. Her words hit me like a ton of bricks, and my heart sinks.

She's hurt and confused. I don't blame her.

"It's not you, Davina," I whisper to myself. About to type out a reply, apologizing for my silence, Lexi nudges me and I freeze.

"Thank you for this Roger, you seriously surprised me."

I pocket my phone and concentrate on her. Lacking emotion, I say, "You're my family now, Lexi." No matter how much I don't want it.

My parents smile at my declaration, but my heart hammers in my chest. I cringe at my own words, but like Dad said, I have to do it after everything Jiddo did for us.

Jiddo steps up to me. "Roger, I need to speak with you." We walk to the other side of the café.

"Yes, Jiddo?"

"You have done well, son," he declares.

"Thank you."

"I would have liked better words, but those are good enough. For your vows, make sure you put more heart into them."

"We just got engaged, Jiddo," I say. "You can't expect me to write vows that quickly."

"That is true but I need you to keep practicing for your wedding. I want it to sound perfect. There will be cameras and the news crews will be there. The vows are important," he mentions, and my heart sinks.

"What? Why?"

He grabs my arm and pulls me close to his face. "Listen to me, Boy. Lexi will be your wife. You will become a politician. You will graduate with a PhD in Political Science," he demands, his voice coming out rigid, cold. I nod, saying nothing. He ushers me back to my parents and Lexi. "Set a date for the wedding."

Tears appear. I try my best to wipe them away, but I'm too late because my mother notices. "Roger," she says softly. "A word?"

"Yeah, sure." I nod, my voice is thick with emotion.

We stand outside the cafeteria. My heart breaks at the sound of applause and excitement. I should be happy because my family will

171

be safe, and my Jiddo will continue to run for office, but what will become of me and Davina?

"Honey is there something you want to tell me?" my mother asks with concern.

"No. I'm fine," I reply, trying to avoid her gaze.

"Don't lie to me, Roger. I birthed you. I know you're hiding something," she says more insistent.

Glancing around, hoping I won't be spotted, I admit, "I don't want this life Mom."

"Oh, Roger..." she says with empathy. "I'm sorry honey."

"I'm in love with someone else," I emphasize with certainty.

"Oh, that girl. I heard about her," she says, a frown tugging at her lips. "Davina, is her name?"

"Yeah. She's awesome, Mom. She's everything I'd want in a wife."

"Wife?" she repeats, a sigh escaping her.

"What do I do, Mom?" I ask, desperate.

"Oh, honey, I'm sorry," she says full of regret.

"Can't you talk to Dad?"

"I'm so sorry Roger," she says barely above a whisper. "I can't say anything to them, you know that."

Sighing in defeat, I mumble, "Yeah, I know."

The thought of being with Davina evaporates like the love in my soul.

Nineteen

♥

Davina

The morning sun announces its early entrance peering in through my bedroom shades and waking me. A sleepless night enduring the constant horror and damnation I succumbed to. Emptiness hovers in my soul as darkness creeps in and fills the void.

Memories of what Charlie did to me flood my mind. I had been drowning my sorrows in alcohol, hoping to numb the pain and forget the reality of my situation. But as the sun rises higher in the sky, I can't hide from it anymore.

Standing I stare blindly at the world outside. Hollow. I'm dead inside. I close my eyes, but Charlie is all I see, forcing himself on me...

Wait. What is the last thing I remember?

Making my way to my bed, I glance down, but it's nothing but leaves. There are so many leaves.

I never made it home.

Where am I?

My heart pounds and I struggle to breathe while reality comes crashing down.

The world comes into focus as my eyes slowly open and I take in my surroundings. I'm in pain. Every inch of me aches. My eyes roam over my body covered in bruises. Shifting, I try to sit up, but a sharp pain shoots through me.

Silent tears stream down my face. Looking towards the lake, exhaustion weighs me down, sapping my strength. Every movement is a struggle. The need for water pushes me forward, my mouth parched. The lake shimmers in the moonlight, beckoning me towards it.

Placing my hands in the icy cold water, my whole body shivers. A sound of silence collides with footsteps making their way to me. Panic engulfs me, my heart thundering with fear and dread, terrified he's back to finish me off. I tumble into the bleak, cold water and slip under.

A faint whisper urges me to open my eyes.

But... weren't they already open when I fell into the icy cold water?

"Wake up, Davina," the voice commands, sharp and electric, jolting through me.

I collapse onto the ground, slumping in the same spot where it all began.

"Wake up," the voice echoes again, drilling into my mind.

With a loud gasp, my eyes snap fully open.

Suddenly, I become aware of a machine whirring next to me on the ground, the paramedics attempting to revive me. My head spins as I look around, disoriented, and confused, but a woman looks at me with a smile on her face as she disappears into the sunlight.

"Are you okay?" the paramedic responder asks. I nod slowly, still trying to process what just happened.

"What was that?" I ask, my voice hoarse.

"A defibrillator. Your heart stopped and I had to bring you back."

A surge of relief falls on me as I glance at my phone clutched in my hand. "Did I call you?" Because if I did, I don't remember doing so.

She looks at me with a firm nod. "Yes, Ma'am." Then, she turns to her colleagues, announcing, "She's awake."

A woman hands me a bottle of water. I try to drink, but I wince. The discomfort in my neck as I struggle to swallow is too much. "I can't."

"Ma'am," the lady begins, "I'm going to help you sit up."

Pain shoots through me as she wraps her arm around me, assisting me. "Is there anyone you need us to call?"

"No, I'll do it myself but I need to talk to a nurse," I plead, my voice barely a whisper.

"Sure, Ma'am. What about?" My eyes land on my discarded underwear and bra on the ground near my bag. She gasps, and I know she understands. "We need a rape kit at the hospital."

When the ambulance pulls up to the hospital, I can't delay it any longer. I fumble for my phone, fingers shaking. It rings and rings, a wave of relief hitting me when she finally picks up.

"Mom," I rasp, my voice shaking, barely audible.

"Jesus Davina! Where have you been?"

"I'm at the hospital."

"What? What happened? Why are you there?"

"I can't explain, Mom. Please, I need you." My voice cracks. "I-I was—I can't say it. Can you come? I need you here." The worry in her voice was clear, but her questions will be better answered in person. "Please come, I need you."

"I'm on my way," she answers and hangs up.

Finally, after what felt like an eternity, Mom arrives at the hospital. I hear her talking to a nurse in search of my room, her footsteps hurrying down the hall. She bursts into my room, her eyes wild with worry.

"Davina," she gasps, rushing to my side, and embracing me tightly. "Dear God, my baby girl, what happened?"

I glance at the officer and the nurse, forcing out the words, my voice hoarse. "Can you tell her for me?"

Attempting to ignore them, I focus on trying to drink as the officer and the nurse explain quietly what happened to me. Mom stumbles on her feet, unable to stand. Dad finally arrives and enters the room. I hug him. The officer continues to ramble as my mind drifts to my last text message to Roger. Why didn't he answer me? Why wasn't he there to save me? Maybe we're not meant to be.

Dad's face pales. "Raped?"

The nurse speaks up, her voice soft and sympathetic. "I performed a rape kit on Davina, with her permission of course."

The word 'rape' echoes in the room. Mom's face crumples in shock and horror. Dad's expression changes to sorrow and heartache. Tears stream down their faces as they struggle to come to terms with the news. A pang of guilt floods me at causing both such pain.

Mom collapses onto the chair next to my bed, her hands shaking as she wipes away tears. I reach out to hold her hand, hoping to offer some small comfort. The pain and fear in her eyes is visible, mirroring my own.

Cautiously, the officer steps forward, her eyes soft, compassionate. "Ma'am, we are going to do everything we can to find the person who did this. I will be working closely with the hospital and the forensic team to gather evidence and track down the perpetrator."

The officer walks out. The nurse finally finishes her tests and quietly leaves the room, giving us some time alone. I feel their eyes on me, a silent reminder I'm not alone in this. Mom holds onto my hand tightly, her grip almost painful. "I can't believe this happened to you," she whispers. "I'm so sorry, I should have been there for you."

I squeeze her hand. "Mom, please."

She bursts into tears. "But he…"

Tears continue to fall down her face as she leans over to embrace me again. "I know Mom," I whisper, pleading. "Please don't blame yourself."

Grief engulfs my very being and I cry. My heart aches. Dad takes me in a hug, holding onto me. "You should have called me to pick you up."

I sigh, wiping my tears. "I'm sorry."

"No Davina," he says. "Don't apologize."

"Do you know who did this to you?" Mom asks, her voice breaking.

I clench my jaw, disgust and fear run through me, recalling the exact incident, seeing his face in my mind when I close my eyes. Hearing his voice as it trickles down my spine, like this gnawing feeling of overwhelming hatred for being so naïve, so nice, so forgiving. "Charlie Scimitar. He's in my Calculus class at Roadwood University."

"He'll pay for what he did to you," Dad insists, holding me. "The police will arrest him, be sure of it."

"I hope so."

Twenty

♥

Roger

I take a deep breath, reaching for my phone, feeling the weight of the day's events pressing down on me. It's time to call Davina and explain everything. To tell her that I am stuck in a nightmare with my family. But the thought of hearing her voice fills me with both longing and dread.

Before I tap her name, Dad walks in. "Morning, Son."

"Morning, Dad."

He sits by my bed with me in it and sighs, his face remaining neutral. "Thanks for the drive."

I cross my arms in front of my chest. "It was fun."

He breathes out in frustration. "I'm sorry Roger. I'm sorry for what you had to do."

"It's okay, Dad."

My heart sinks as I stare at my father. Words catch in my throat, so I just nod, not even sure if I believe what I agreed to. But right now, I have to get them all off my back. This is the only way.

Glancing at my phone, my fingers tremble above the keypad. I have to see her one last time. Maybe I could lie and tell her I cheated on her with Lexi, make her hate me the way I deserve.

After getting ready, I text Lexi to wait for me, apparently, according to everyone in my life, I'm her personal driver now. The quiet between us is heavy as I pull out of the driveway and head toward campus.

Lexi breaks the silence. "We need to talk."

A rush of anger washes over me. "I don't want to fucking talk to you, you skank ass whore. I never loved you and I will never love you, get that through your thick skull."

A wave of emotion crashes through me as I let the fury pour out. She says nothing in response. The rest of the ride remains heavy with the weight of my words.

Did I mean what I said? Absolutely.

Was I too harsh? Yeah... but after everything she put me through, she deserves it.

She studies me intently and talks again, "So, will Charlie be your best man?"

"Why are you so interested in Charlie all of a sudden, and speaking of, what was that wink you two exchanged the other day?" I ask, a bit suspicious.

"Oh, honey, are you jealous?" she teases, a playful smile tugging at her lips.

"No. I am curious."

"Charlie was going to help me with something."

"With what?" I ask not sure what she's getting at.

"He's good with numbers. You're not. So—yeah," she claims, shrugging.

"Ugh, whatever," I mutter, clearly unimpressed.

Our conversation is interrupted as I drive up to the university, greeted by a chaotic scene of flashing police cars and officers everywhere. My heart races, struggling to make sense of it all.

An accident? A shooting?

Hurrying toward the chaos, I'm desperate to find out what happened. "What's going on?" she asks.

I give her my car keys without looking at her. "Go back to the car, I'll find out and text you."

"What?" she asks, confused.

"Just, go!" I push her towards the car.

I make my way through the crowd and into the courtyard, bumping into a classmate from Politics 101.

"Hey," I say, glancing at him.

"Hey," he greets me casually.

"What happened here?" I ask, confused.

"No clue," he responds with a shrug.

We stand in the courtyard as a lady officer strides up to one of the students. "Are you Charlie Scimitar?" she asks.

"I might be." He smiles, smugly. "Who's asking?"

She smirks, removing handcuffs. "You're under arrest for the rape of Davina Dwain."

My heart stops. Did she say, Davina Dwain?

The words ring in my ears like bullets to my soul.

Davina Dwain: RAPE.

My anger rises as I rush towards him, grabbing him by his neck and holding him there. I hear the police trying to stop me from hurting him, but their words fall on deaf ears. All I can think about is getting answers.

"What the fuck did you do to her, Charlie?" My grip tightens on his neck.

Charlie struggles to breathe, but I don't let go. "What she needed from me," Charlie chokes out, laughing. "What you couldn't give her."

Anger drives me to hold him harder, but I need to know the truth. I need to understand what happened to Davina. The commotion brings Lexi closer. She stands away, staring at me as I hold Charlie, fighting for Davina.

"Get this prick off of me," Charlie shouts, barely getting the words out.

While holding him, thoughts of her race through my mind. The image of her face scared, battered, and bruised filling my mind, and a wave of anger and guilt crushes me, fueling me. The police officers begin to close in around us, their hands reaching out to pull me away from him. But I'm too strong, too determined, refusing to let go. It's only when the officer speaks to me peacefully that I begin to come to my senses.

"Sir, let him go. He's not worth the trouble. He'll get what he deserves soon enough."

I take a deep breath, try to calm down, and slowly release my grip on Charlie. He gasps for air, coughing and wheezing, as he stumbles away from me and into police custody.

"She loved me fucking her. Touching her. She gasped when my hands were on her pussy," he shouts. "Fingering her. She tasted so nice, sweet. The juices flowing on my fingers like caramel."

My head rears back, about to punch him in the face when the officer grabs my clenched fist. "Don't make me arrest you too."

My heart sinks. The thought of her being hurt and alone fills me with a sense of dread. "Where is she?"

"She's at home."

Shaking my head in disbelief, I can't imagine Davina talking to anyone but me in her condition. Turning, I make my way out. Suddenly, I remember Lexi has my keys. Frantically, I look around. She walks over to me, silently.

"Take me home, Roger," she demands, her gaze calculating.

"No. I need to go see Davina. Give me my keys."

She gapes at me, handing them to me with a disgruntled huff. "You're going to regret this."

I take them from her, and reply, "My biggest regret was you, Lexi."

Spinning on my heel, I run to my car. Driving towards Davina's house, I press down on the accelerator, the car speeding down the road while my mind races with questions. All I can think about is getting to Davina and making sure she's safe.

When I arrive at Davina's door, my heart sinks at the sight of yet more police cars outside. I push my way through the officers and shout for her, my voice desperate and cracked with emotion. "Davina. Davina." I search for any sign of her. "Davina."

Finally, I spot her sitting on the couch, wrapped in bandages, and looking utterly defeated. My heart breaks at the sight of her like this.

I rush over to her, kneeling beside her. "What did he do to you?" Davina looks up at me with tired, sluggish eyes. "Klutz," I sniffle, carefully taking her into my arms. "They arrested him."

Davina nods weakly, tears streaming down her face. "It was my fault. I never should have gotten in the car with him." Davina cries on my shoulder as I hold her close, her sobs wracking her body.

"It's not your fault," I speak, through my tears, guilt overwhelming me. "I wish I was there for you. I wish I had answered the phone when you needed me."

"Shush," she interrupts gently. "It's okay. You're here now, and that's all that matters." Davina lifts her head and looks at me with red, puffy eyes. "Can we talk?" she inquires; her body language suddenly rigid.

My body stiffens. It feels like I'm losing her. I couldn't live with the guilt.

"Of course." I take her hand and follow her to the kitchen. Away from the chaos and noise, where we can have a private conversation.

"I love you, Roger."

"I love you, too, Klutz," I blurt out, hoping, it sticks.

She smiles sadly, then sighs in defeat, making my heart drop into the pit of my stomach. "But when I needed you the most, you weren't there for me."

"Davina, I'm so sorry. I should have done something, answered you, but I let you down. I am so sorry. I'm really sorry."

She smiles again, but it's forced, as if she's trying to agree with me or make me feel better. "You're the best thing that has ever happened to me. I know the time we spent together—"

I stop her before she says anything we'll both regret, placing a gentle hand on hers. "No. Davina. Don't do this. Please. I want to be here by your side, all the way, we can get through this. Please. You can't..."

She places her fingers on my lips to stop me from talking. I kiss her fingers, but she ignores my request. "I will always care about you," Davina admits her voice heavy with pain. "But..."

My heart sinks, and a lump forms in my throat. "No," I plead, my voice barely above a whisper. "Don't tell me it's over. I'm sorry I wasn't there, but please, please, please don't give up on us, not now, I can't. Let me be here for you. I love you."

"I can't be with you anymore," Davina says firmly, kissing my cheek before stepping away from me. She places a hand on my shoulder. "I hope you understand."

The world comes crashing down around me. "I'm so sorry, Davina," I beg, kneeling on the floor, and hugging her legs. "Please don't do this. I can handle anything else, except you leaving me, Davina, please. I'm so sorry I failed you. I promise to always be there when you need me, please, Davina. Please let me help you now. We need to be okay. Say we'll be okay, please."

Tears fall from my eyes while all I catch from hers is pain, hurt and betrayal, hitting me like a punch to my chest. I wish I picked up the phone. How could I be so stupid? I wish I was there for her when she needed me. How could I do this to her? To us? I wish I never let my life, my family stop us from being together.

"Klutz," my voice comes out like an aching balloon, as it loses air. "Please."

Davina gently shrugs me off and helps me up. "It's not easy being around you. It reminds me of what I endured," she claims, delivering another punch. "I need time to myself."

"How much time?" I'm desperate for any sign that she hasn't given up on us.

"I don't know," she murmurs, her expression unreadable. She gives me a chaste kiss on my cheek and walks off.

Devastated, I sit in my car, crying. I've been stabbed a billion times by so many people, but nothing hurts more. I'm hurt. Not only because we broke up, but when she needed me, I wasn't there. I was so worried about her getting hurt because of me that I only succeeded in making that a reality.

I failed her and I hate myself for it.

Making my way to my car, I get a text on my phone.

LEXI

> We need to talk. Meet me at our spot by the church.

Driving to the church, my mind races to what happened to Davina. What if I answered, maybe this wouldn't have happened. Why did I ignore her? I should have been there for her.

I park my car next to Lexi's, and step out of my car, my eyes scanning the area around the church. Lexi stood there, waiting for me. As I approach, I can't help but feel another twinge of guilt. My heart was with Davina, the same place I should've been. I hope that one day, she will come back to me.

Lexi looks at me, her expression unreadable. "Roger, are you okay?" she asks, her voice soft and gentle.

I shake my head. "No." My voice trails off, and I take a deep breath to steady myself. "Do I look fucking okay?"

Lexi places a gentle hand on my shoulder but I shrug her off. "What happened with, Davina?" she asks.

"You know what happened," I spit out, furious. "Why am I here?"

"I want this thing between us to end," she tells me.

"End how?" I ask, my voice rising with anger.

Lexi raises her eyebrows. "I deserve better than what I am getting from you."

I roll my eyes, frustrated. "You're right. But I can't pretend I'm in love with you or that you did nothing wrong. I'm in love with Davina."

Lexi scoffs. "Why did you propose to me then?"

"Don't pretend like you had nothing to do with it, Lexi. This was all your doing from the very beginning, and you know what, I hate you for this. You went behind my back and spoke to my family about us!" I shout, feeling the weight of the last few days crashing down on me. "So just leave me alone!"

She grabs my arm and shoves me towards her. "You're right. I did that. I'm sorry Roger. But I don't want this to be an issue with us. I don't want to marry you if you don't love me. I don't want to start a life with you if you don't want that with me."

"It's easier said than done and you know that damn well, but you didn't care. Did you?"

Lexi falls on the floor utterly shocked. "Oh, Roger. I am so sorry. I never meant for it to be this way. When I saw Davina, my green-eyed monster came back to life."

I huff, her admission taking me by surprise. "I can't believe you bullied her like that in school. Who the fuck are you? That's not the person I used to know."

"I never forgave myself when I heard she tried to kill herself because of me." Lexi's voice hurt.

"And yet you pushed me and her apart, with your vendetta and now look what happened. I don't buy it."

She rolls her eyes at me. "I'm sorry. God when will you forgive me, I really am sorry."

"Stop saying sorry. Do something about it. Tell them you don't love me. You don't want to be with me. Please, tell them we're not made for each other. I need to get Davina back."

"I'll try." Lexi's voice fills with sympathy, and I can see the sadness in her eyes. "But until then, we need to keep up appearances."

"Another thing, what is going on between you and Charlie?" I ask.

"We used to date before me and you." Lexi's voice is firm. "You know that."

"That's it?" I push.

"Yes, that's it. Why don't you believe me?" She pleads, desperately.

Staring, her gaze doesn't waver. Heaving a sigh, I concede, "I do. I don't have to like it, but I do."

She sighs. "Okay, sure. Come on, let's deal with our family dearest."

We both get into our cars and drive off. One thing is certain, I want to do anything to get Davina back and cherish her like she deserves, hoping she might forgive the man I once was.

Twenty-One

Davina

The sun lights my room for the twentieth time since I broke up with Roger. It's a struggle to wake up. My nights are spent curled up in a ball, sobbing my eyes out until I pass out from exhaustion.

I'm going to visit a psychologist today. Mom and Dad blame themselves for what happened to me, but I don't; it's just hard to let them know how I feel. They haven't left my side, taking turns staying with me in bed every night until I fall asleep.

I cried in their arms telling them what I had to do with Roger. Looking at him kneeling on the floor, begging me, was a blow to my soul. But it had to be done. He reminded me of the person I counted on to save me from the monster, but he never got in touch with me until it was too late, so I left it the only way I could, breaking us both and knowing I'll heal–eventually.

The image of him with someone else fills me with anger and sadness, a bitter cocktail of emotions I struggle to swallow. Shoving the thought away, I walk to my closet. Standing, I stare at all the colorful outfits I don't deserve to wear anymore. The constant pain of that incident lingers in my mind, holding me back.

"Honey, you ready?" Mom questions as she walks in, placing a gentle hand on my shoulder. "No, I have nothing to wear."

She turns me to face her. "Would you like to wear my black sweatpants set?" I nod. "Okay, I will get them for you." She kisses me on my forehead, and I wait in my room, sitting in silence. She walks in handing me the clothes. "Here. Get dressed. I will take you."

"Where's Dad?"

"At work. Why?"

"Just asking."

"I'll wait for you outside."

The moment she exits my room, I close the door and slump onto the floor broken. I know I have to do something to take my mind off all this, but I don't know what I want to do. I get dressed quickly, without looking at myself in the mirror. I put my hair in a ponytail and depart.

"Ready." I tell Mom, finding her sitting at the breakfast table.

She smiles at me, but I can't smile back. "Do you want anything to eat?"

"No."

She sighs. "Let's go."

The psychologist lives in Ain Saadeh, only a ten-to-fifteen-minute commute, depending on the traffic. It's a village located in the Metn District of Lebanon, known for its beautiful scenery with pine forests and olive groves dotting the landscape. We drive through the village, mostly residential homes, with red-tiled roofs and stone houses.

I remember when we used to come here as kids, out on excursions with school because of the diversity of vegetation and the landscape. It has beautiful buildings and the best food. Our school used to take us to one of the open fields and have us run laps.

Those were the best days, when life was much simpler, when we didn't know the bad stuff around us...

The car ride remains quiet. Our windows are down, and I inhale deeply, smelling the fresh pinecones from the trees, the scent of pollution seeping through.

Snuggled in the lush greenery and rolling hills, sits a magnificent estate, a grand house surrounded by acres of trimmed land. We approach a long driveway, leading us through towering trees, creating seclusion.

Mom parks the car and inhales a deep breath as we get out, taking in the view. The house itself is an architectural masterpiece, radiating elegance and sophistication, its exterior featuring a blend of traditional Lebanese design elements and modern touches. The front showcases intricate stonework, large windows, and a grand entrance decorated with lavish details.

Mom and I stand speechless at the exquisite detail. The housekeeper opens the door, and we step into a spacious foyer with high ceilings and polished marble floors reflecting the natural light streaming through the windows.

"Please wait in the study," she instructs, pointing. But as we make our way there, I can't stop looking around in awe, each room more breathtaking than the last.

A few minutes later, my mom leaves me alone with Mrs. Mead. It's not long before I'm zoning out and listening to sounds around the house, but nothing keeps me aware.

She gazes at me, waiting for a response, but all I can say is, "I have no issues with my childhood. I'm only here because I'm wearing black, I don't smile anymore, and I don't do fun things anymore. I took a couple weeks off from university and I'm thinking of dropping out. I don't know why I bother when the incident that happened, happened to me and everyone around me feels hurt, when I'm breaking inside. I can't even look at Roger, my boyfriend, or ex-boyfriend, who I broke up with because when I needed him the most, he wasn't there." I take a deep breath not knowing tears were falling as I spoke.

She hands me a tissue. "Okay, Davina. Can we begin with the basics?"

I take a few deep breaths, clear the tears from my eyes, and sniffle. "Yeah, we can, but nothing too drastic. I don't want to get into many details. Apparently, from what my parents were told, you're good at your job."

"I am." She smiles. "So, Davina. I will ask you a series of questions and please answer honestly. I know you will, but sometimes people tend to embellish their truths to live them."

"I will be honest. My name is Davina Dwain."

"Thank you, that's my first question. Okay, maybe we can skip the basic ones and go into something more about you. Can you tell me a bit about yourself?"

"I was raped."

I sit nervously in the comfortable armchair, my hands tightly gripping the edges of the seat. The tension in the room feels profound, with frustration and disappointment welling up inside me.

Mrs. Mead's gentle eyes reflect empathy. "I understand why you are here, but that doesn't tell me anything about who you are. Being raped doesn't define you as a person. So, let's start again."

Taking a deep breath, I muster the courage to speak up. "I am a girl who had her heart yanked out of her body as if I was a ragdoll. Does that sound any better?" I ask as I get up and head for the door. "This was a mistake." I leave in a rush and sit in the garden by the calming trees.

I take a moment to gather myself and hold back the wave of tears threatening to overcome me. A while later, I feel Mrs. Mead approach me. "Can I give you a hug?" I nod, wiping my tears. She wraps her arms around me. "Everything will be fine, Davina. You will be happy again. I promise you. Would you like us to continue out here?"

"No. I just want to sit here and say nothing."

"Okay, I will go make a call." She walks back into her study.

Sitting there in nature, the breeze blows through, and I glance up at the sky hoping I get some sort of sign. I miss my happy life, the one I used to know...

Pulling me out of my thoughts, I get a text on my phone.

ROGER

I'm always here for you. I will never stop loving you, even if you want me to.

"I'm broken," I whisper to myself pocketing my phone and ignoring the message. It hurts to read that when he was not there when I needed him the most. "I'll never be whole again."

After an hour in the sun, I walk back into Mrs. Mead's study and sit in the armchair, exhaling.

She leans forward, her calming presence comforting me. "Davina, I appreciate your efforts. Let's reflect on the good you have in your life?"

I offer an accepting smile. "Maybe we should reschedule."

She smiles back, a hint of awkwardness lingering in her expression. "Is that what you want?"

I let out a weary sigh. "I don't know what I want."

Her lips curve up. "Why don't you try again and tell me a bit about yourself Davina."

I hesitate, but concede, starting, "I live with my parents and go to university."

"What's your major?"

"I haven't declared it yet and I don't think I want to continue anymore."

"How so?"

"I don't know. I don't think I deserve it."

"Why don't you think you deserve it?"

Tears begin to fall, the incident lingering in my mind. "Every time I close my eyes I see his face." I glance at her, silently pleading for her to give me some time to open up. "I want to believe that things can get better."

"Why wouldn't they get better, Davina?"

"I don't know." I sigh, getting fed up with the session.

"Take a deep breath for me, Davina." I do as she asked. "Now, relax."

"What was that for?"

"To help you calm yourself. Listen," she begins, leaning forward in her seat as if she's trying to tell me a secret. "I was in love a long time ago. It was amazing."

"Why are you telling me this?"

"Because I want you to understand that I have been there."

"You were raped?"

"No, but I lost something, something very dear to me. It broke me. And, ever since, I decided to use my skills to help others. To help people get better."

"What happened to you, Mrs. Mead?"

She sighs, leaning back into her chair, placing the notebook on the side table. "I was pregnant and I lost the baby."

I gasp in shock. "I'm sorry."

Taking a tissue, I hand it to her. "Thank you, Davina. The baby died and it stayed with me. The loss I mean."

"Wow. I'm sorry."

"Yeah, so—what I'm trying to say, is you'll get better. I promise you will."

"I guess." I attempt to relax in the armchair, trying to make the connection with our stories, but struggle. Still, I let it go and press on. "But what do I do? Do I stay and continue university when my heart is not in it, or do I drop out?"

"It's up to you, Davina. What do you want to do?"

Tears begin to fall from my eyes. It hurts. It's so much pain. "I don't know what I want. I'm so confused. How many sessions until I get better?"

She smiles, laughing a bit. "As long as you need."

"Okay."

"I think we should try some meditation."

The meditation session begins as her voice bounces off soft beams of sunlight. Molding a gentle glow upon the serene study, through the sheer curtains. As Mrs. Mead's gentle voice unfolds, it becomes evident the weight of the incident still rests heavily upon my conscience, echoing within my mind and heart.

I'm still broken but I want to forget.

Closing my eyes, I place my head on the pillow, carefully branching out, as Mrs. Mead guides me through the meditation. The comfort of the room and her soft voice helps me feel rested and tranquil. Delicate incense wafts through the air, carrying a scent of serenity calming my every being.

With a gentle sigh, I allow the external world to fade into the background, surrendering to the present moment. The rhythmic motion of my breath becomes the focal point, guiding me deeper into a state of inner stillness. Each inhale draws in a sense of clarity, while each exhale releases any lingering tension within.

The music plays on when Mrs. Mead's voice comes into focus. "Okay Davina, it's time to come back to me."

Her words are like an anchor, gently pulling me back to the present moment. With a deep sense of gratitude, I slowly open my eyes, greeted by the serene environment throughout the meditation.

"Better?"

"Yes. Thank you."

"Your Mom is on her way. Would you like to wait outside, until she comes?"

"Yes. Thanks again, Mrs. Mead."

Sitting in my bedroom, I contemplate my feelings for Roger. I still love him, and deep down, I believe we could work through this. I'm starting to realize what happened to me is not his fault, but I'm not ready to talk. Putting my phone on the charger, I lay my head on the pillow, and drift into a deep, relaxing sleep.

Twenty-Two

♥

Roger

It's been a couple of weeks since Davina broke up with me. My thoughts wander to the missed phone call when I failed her. The weight of my mistake presses heavily on my conscience.

I messaged her but I got nothing back.

Her words came from a place of agony. I know that, but it doesn't make it suck any less. And I wish... I wish she would let me back in. I want to mend the wounds I unintentionally inflicted as I gaze upon the last pictures of us at the cedar tree.

I grit my teeth. If it weren't for my family and their stupid fucking expectations, I would've been there. Their looming influence has always twisted my choices, and now I've lost her because of it. It's a bitter truth I have no choice but to accept.

Just as the weight of the situation threatens to suffocate me, I hear the rustling of sheets, Lexi waking up. We didn't sleep in the same room, out of respect for Davina and me. I'm not going to do anything to jeopardize that, but she is here. Deciding to distract myself, I go to the kitchen to prepare breakfast. Soon enough, she emerges from the bedroom, wearing nothing but my white T-shirt.

Ever since Davina broke up with me, I make it a priority to keep up appearances, until I find a way out of this. Lexi moved in with me. She's been planning our wedding with our mothers every chance she gets. I don't know why she's doing that, especially since we met at the church, and she told me different things.

She greets me. "Morning."

"Morning," I reply and turn to face her, emotions swirling inside me. "Slept well?"

Lexi smiles as she sprawls on the kitchen counter, the t-shirt riding up her body. "Yup, but I am famished."

Turning my attention back to the breakfast preparations, my hands move robotically through the familiar motions. The sizzling bacon and the aroma of freshly brewed coffee fills the air but fails to provide the solace I desperately need.

Lexi watches me soundlessly, her fingers playing with the hem of my shirt. The silence in the kitchen grows. Unspoken words threaten to burst through.

Taking a deep breath, I turn to face Lexi. "So, we need to talk."

Lexi's gaze meets mine. Her features soften with a glimmer of acceptance. "Yeah, I knew this was coming."

"What are you doing with our mothers?" I ask.

"I couldn't say anything. My mother, the way she looked at me, happy. I didn't want to take that from her, and I didn't know how."

"You can't be serious, Lexi."

"I'm sorry. I tried. If you want me to try again, I can."

"You tried, then what happened?"

"Then, they asked about us."

"What did you say?"

"Why don't we talk over breakfast? I'm starving."

"Fine. Sit and I'll finish up soon."

She smiles. "I need to get dressed first." She walks towards me and takes a bite of the scrambled eggs I prepared. Moaning, she walks into my bedroom. "Yummy," she calls from inside my room.

Lexi emerges from the bedroom in a mini blue dress, with blue heel pumps. Excitement dances in her eyes as she sits at the table. "So, Roger," she purrs, her words dripping with satisfaction. "Let's talk about you and Davina."

I falter. "What about me and Davina?"

"Do you love her?" Lexi asks as she takes a giant bite of the scrambled eggs. "Oh, my God, this tastes so good." She moans in excitement.

I hesitate, but know I lost this one. "There is no me and Davina."

Lexi smiles. "Who are you lying to? Me or yourself?"

Taking a deep breath, I release it, letting out all my painful frustration for how things between me and Davina ended up. "I'm serious Lexi. There's nothing—I mean, me and Davina... It never, we'll never..."

After she eats a few more bites, she gets up, makes two mugs of coffee, in sheer silence, and sits back down at the table, passing my mug to me. "Because of Charlie?"

"Among other things."

"And me?"

"Yeah, kinda."

She chuckles. "You want me to believe that?"

"I can't change her mind. I need to figure out my issues before I do anything."

She giggles again. "Oh, silly boy."

Gulping, I place my fork down and answer her, "Yes?"

Her smile is not as playful. There's something more serious behind her words. "If you believe Davina is the one, you have to fight for her. What better way than to do the opposite from what she wants."

I freeze for a moment, unsure how to respond. "Is this a trick question?"

"No." She watches me carefully, as if waiting.

My pulse quickens. I can't stop the words from spilling out. "Davina broke up with me because of what Charlie did. I can't..."

She takes a deep breath before continuing, "I've been thinking about everything."

"What about exactly?"

She looks up at me, her expression unreadable. "I love you Roger. At least, I think I still do, but I have feelings for someone else. Unfortunately, I don't think I will be with him because of something he did."

"What are you talking about Lexi? You won't even tell your parents."

"This isn't real between us. You know that. I know that." Lexi's voice trembles, her gaze avoiding mine as she speaks.

"You do this now?" I explode, frustration surging through me, even though a part of me is relieved to finally get it out. The anger isn't just at her, it's at everything. "Why now, Lexi? Why not before? When I could have protected her? Why do this now?" I stand up abruptly, hands gripping the edge of the table.

Lexi looks at me, her eyes wide, like she's struggling to hold it together. "I don't know, Roger." She sighs, slumping in her seat. "It's just too much for me. It's exhausting. I've had enough."

I sit back down in the chair, staring at her, everything pressing down on me. She looks utterly defeated, as if every effort she made had blown up in her face. A pang of sympathy for her escapes me, but it's quickly overshadowed by the cold reality of the situation.

We were friends once, back when everything was simpler, and maybe I still care for her in some way, but right now, I can't shake the feeling she ruined us. I'm not sure I can ever forgive her for this. She destroyed what could have been my best relationship for pettiness.

"Lexi, can I know why?" My voice cracks, though I try to hold it, wanting, no, needing to understand why she did this.

She looks away, her eyes distant. "I don't have an answer for you, Roger. Maybe... I was jealous that Davina was the center of attention again. I don't know." Her voice trembles.

"So, it's been about getting back at Davina more than you being with me?" I challenge.

She sighs, her shoulders slumping further. "Yeah, pretty much."

"I—I can't fucking believe it." The words come out in a near whisper. My heart is heavy, like it's sinking in my chest.

"I'm sorry, Roger. I really am." Her voice cracks, and for the first time, the true depth of her regret is visible.

I swallow hard, her apology difficult to hear.

What's the point of a sorry when everything is already destroyed?

Twenty-Three

♥

Davina

Every night, I sit and cry over what could have been and what never will be. There's no fairytale ending. Not for me. Not for us. Our love is gone and in its place there is a hollow ache I can't escape.

Staring at my university books, I pretend to care, but my heart was never in it. Only filled with emptiness. Now, I don't want this life. The hallways. The classrooms. Everything reminds me of Charlie.

I can't focus. I can't imagine graduating, doing all the things my parents hoped I would. Worse than that, I can't even walk into class without remembering how my Calculus teacher pushed Charlie on me.

I keep replaying that moment she made me feel powerless.

And the truth is, I'm angry and she deserves to hear it.

Dear Mrs. Calculus,

I literally couldn't be bothered to remember your name especially after what you put me through by forcing Charlie on me. It's like you didn't understand or even care about how uncomfortable I was.

You insisted that we work together.

You've destroyed my life! I hope you're happy.

If I hadn't been in your class, if I hadn't been paired with that ogre, none of this would have happened.

You're the reason I can't bring myself to go back to that godforsaken place.

It's you!

You, alone!

I FUCKING blame you!

Stupid bitch!

Davina

I press send on the email, refocusing on the family photo of us at the beach. I remember the happy smiles. Those moments feel so distant now. The air in the living room feels heavy.

Mom sits on one end of the couch, her gaze distant and preoccupied, while Dad occupies the other, his expression etched with a hint of resignation. It's evident their relationship has reached its breaking point, leaving me with unanswered questions.

Summoning my courage, I approach the scene and take a seat on the chair facing the couch.

"Mom, Dad, can we talk?" I ask, breaking the silence.

Dad places a warm comforting hand on my knee, as his eyes meet mine. "What is it, Davina?" he inquires, his eyebrows drawn down with concern.

A deep breath escapes my lips as I gather my thoughts, knowing the words I'm about to speak will shape the course of my future. "I want to drop out of university," I finally reveal in a rush.

"Drop out?!" Dad yells.

And then the room falls silent.

The gravity of my statement hanging like a heavy fog. Mom's eyes flicker wide open in surprise and worry, while Dad's expression softens, his brows furrowing deeper with concern. I need to explain, to convey the depth of my reasons behind my choice. "I've been doing some soul-searching, and university isn't giving me joy anymore. I feel lost."

I watch as they process my words. Dad's grip on my knee tightens. "Davina, you can't drop out now. You have to finish, at least complete your degree."

"If she wants this, then we should respect it, honey."

He shakes his head. "No, I don't want her to ruin her life."

"Dad!" I shout. "It's already ruined. Did you forget what I went through?"

He sighs. "No, I haven't but I haven't spent my entire life bringing you up for you to throw your university degree to the side because you had a hiccup."

"A hiccup?" I yell, my voice flaring. "It was more than a hiccup, Dad! You were there. You saw me! I was raped. That bastard, even though he's behind bars, he did something horrid to me. He hurt me in ways I don't think I'll ever bounce back from."

I stand up and walk out of the living room. Slumping onto my bed, I clutch my pillow in my hands.

How can he be so inconsiderate and call my ordeal a hiccup?

Mom knocks on my door before she walks in. I feel the bed shift as she sits next to me. "Honey, can we chat?"

I swallow my saliva and sit up, still holding onto my pillow. "What do you want?"

Dad comes to the door and stands there, hovering. "I'm sorry Davina. May I come in?" I nod and he sits on the bed beside Mom.

"I don't feel like I want to live anymore. Do you understand that?"

His eyes tear. "I do. And I understand where you are coming from, but what about studying from home?" he suggests. "I promise you Davina, I will do everything in my power to accommodate your needs, but I need you to know, I want you to finish your degree. It's your ticket to a better life."

I take a deep breath and request, "I'll think about it. I just need some time."

Dad takes me in a hug. "I love you."

"I love you, too."

A couple hours later, after Dad had a few chats with Mrs. Elena on the phone, they came to an agreement and I overhear snippets of their conversations. I will attend private classes with my professors and sit for exams.

"I understand," Mrs. Elena's voice comes through calm but firm. "If she's not ready to return to the university just yet, private classes might be the best option, until she feels ready."

Dad's reply was more settled. "Thank you, Elena. She needs to have the space to heal. I know this isn't ideal."

"You know I'm always happy to help," she said, and then pauses. "By the way, the calculus professor received an email from Davina, and I saw it. It's not polite but I understand why she wrote it. Whenever she's ready to chat with her, I'd be happy to set up a meeting."

He glances at me, and I shrug in my seat. "I see, okay—please apologize on our behalf to her. At the moment, Davina is not in the right state of mind to talk about anything."

"I understand, and thanks," Elena replies.

They hang up, and Dad turns to me. "Care to explain to me about the email?" he asks, raising an eyebrow.

"Erm, not really." I huff out in annoyance. "She deserved it."

"I raised you better than that." Dad presses. "What did you tell her?"

Rolling my eyes, I recall the words I said in the email. "So, am I grounded?" I ask, tilting my head.

He smiles, and Mom laughs. "Grounded," Mom spits out between chuckles. "Since when have we ever grounded you?"

"Never?" I answer, grinning sheepishly.

"Never is right." She pulls me into a hug, and Dad joins us. "Davina, what do you want to do?" she asks warmly.

Taking a deep breath in and releasing it, I express myself, truthfully. "I want to open a bakery."

"A bakery?" Dad repeats, standing and pacing up and down the room. "Okay, if that's what you want to do. We will do it. Let's sell our businesses and help you create yours."

"You'd do that for me?"

"Of course, we would. We want you to be happy. Besides, our businesses aren't doing so well. I think it's a nice time to change avenues for a bit. Who knows, you may do something better than we ever did."

Blossoming over the course of a few months, my bakery comes to life, and Besties & Cakes is born.

One busy afternoon, a group of friends enters the bakery, their excited chatter filling the air. As I listen and watch their interactions, I can't help but appreciate their enthusiasm. "Enjoy your treats and have a wonderful time together," I call out to the teens as they exit the bakery, their laughter trailing behind.

A little while later, an elderly couple enters holding hands. Their eyes sparkle with a lifetime of shared memories, squeezing my heart, but I ignore it. "Good afternoon. Welcome to Besties & Cakes."

The woman's voice carries a sense of nostalgia. "We're celebrating our anniversary, and we were hoping to find a special treat to commemorate this day."

I nod, wondering if I will ever have that, and forcing a smile, I swiftly temper my wayward thoughts, focusing on my task at hand. "Congratulations."

Each day, the bakery fills with conversations, laughter, and heartfelt interactions. Customers of all ages and backgrounds come together, united by their love for delicious treats, slowly mending my broken heart.

One evening, as the sun dips below the horizon, I find myself at home sitting on the couch.

Dad sits in his favorite armchair, lost in his own thoughts. He turns his attention towards me, his eyes filled with sadness. "Davina, we need to talk."

Taking a deep breath, I glance over at him. "Sure, what's wrong?"

His brows furrow. "I don't know how to say this. I love you, you know that, but things between your Mom and me are a bit hazy."

"How so?" I shift uncomfortably.

Dad leans forward, his expression turning thoughtful. "We need a break from each other, but we don't want you to choose." My stomach drops. He reaches out and gently places a hand on mine, his touch filled with understanding. "Davina, I want nothing more than to see you happy." Just then, Mom walks in with a suitcase. "I'm going to live with my sister for a while."

"Have you not thought about what I would want?"

Mom sighs, walking to me, taking me in her arms. "We did. Every moment we did. But with all the therapy we've been through, it didn't help. I love you and I don't want you to choose. Dad and I need some time away from each other."

"Is it because of what happened to me?" I ask, desperate for an answer.

They shake their heads, Dad replying, "No. Of course not. It's just we need some time to figure things out."

"He will be back before you know it," Mom assures me before Dad leaves.

Our once-unified home has left a trail of shattered dreams in its wake. Dad relocates to his sister's, while Mom immerses herself within the familiar walls of our home, with me.

During the early hours, before the world stirs from its slumber, I stand in the warmth of the kitchen, allowing my hands to work their magic. The fresh dough and warm chocolate embraces me. When the sun rises, painting the sky in hues of pink and gold, I transition to the front of the shop, greeting each customer.

I find myself engaged in a dialogue, not with the customers but with myself, a quiet conversation amidst the flurry of activity. "You're doing well, Davina," I whisper to myself, wiping a bead of sweat from my brow. "Each smile you bring, every satisfied customer, it's all a testament to your passion and hard work."

With my internal pep talk, I continue serving customers, every interaction a reminder of the purpose and joy baking brought into my life. I find a connection fueling my passion away from thinking about the one who got away because Mom and Dad have proven love, to me, never lasts forever.

If my parents can't make it work...

Twenty-Four

Roger

My mind drifts back to Davina, after my conversation with Lexi. Where is she? What is she doing? It can't be that easy to forget me, to forget us, or maybe it can?

Every day like clockwork, I find myself transfixed by not being there when she needed me the most. It feels as if the weight of the world has been placed on my shoulders since she left me. My heart quickens its pace, while my mind struggles to grasp the true implications hidden in my sleepless nights, knowing it's because I miss her.

I may have typed over a dozen messages trying to explain to her why I wasn't there, why I didn't try harder, but all I could do was stare blankly at the screen. Time stands still as I trace my finger over the smooth surface of my phone. The world around me fades into the background, my focus entirely consumed by Davina's words.

Days turned into nights.

Nights turned into days.

Yet, a haunting reminder remains: Davina and I are no more.

The world continues to move around me, while I remain oblivious. I ignore my university and my family duties day after day. Eventually, I'm called into Mrs. Elena's office for a chat. I fade into the chair, staring straight ahead. She talks to me, but I'm not listening. I remain caught in the devastation in my realm of chaos. Her voice cuts through the silence like a knife with a hint of concern.

"Roger," she urges, her voice gentle yet firm.

"Yes," I say with a knot tightening in my chest.

"You have to get back on track or we will have to revoke your presidential position." Her eyes, filled with sympathy, bore into mine.

A flicker of irritation sparks within me, unimpressed by her suggestion. "I don't care. Do whatever you want."

She clears her throat, her expression stubborn. "What happened to you, Roger? I'm worried about you. You've been moping around so much your grades have flaked, and your teachers are not happy."

I shrug. "Maybe I don't give a fuck anymore."

The thought of letting go felt like surrendering a piece of myself, a piece of Davina I still hold near my heart, and I'm not ready to part with it; part with her. "Roger..."

"I'm to blame because I didn't pick up the damn phone!" My voice cracks, the weight of my mistake sinking in all over again.

She interrupts, her voice softer, "No, Roger. Don't blame yourself for something Charlie did."

"I should have been there for her. I should have answered the phone."

"Roger, it's not something you could have known."

"I know but why? What did Davina do to deserve this?"

Mrs. Elena sighs.

I roll my eyes, wiping my tears, "What do I do?"

She clears her throat. "You could visit Davina. Talk to her. Tell her exactly what happened to you. She opened a bakery, you know."

My heart skips a beat, caught off guard by this unexpected revelation. "She opened a bakery?"

The mere mention of what Davina is doing now sends emotions rushing through me, memories flood my mind like a bittersweet symphony of our discussions and how she used to light up when she talked about baking.

"She did," Mrs. Elena acknowledges with a glimmer of hope in her eyes.

Leaving Mrs. Elena's office with this new information has me in a daze. Lost in my own thoughts, I get into my car and start the engine, the familiar hum providing a brief relief. Without considering where to go, my hands guide the steering wheel, leading me.

The streets pass by in a blur as I navigate through Brummana, the outside world, a mere backdrop to the internal battle I'm fighting. Nearing Davina's bakery, my pulse quickens with a hint of excitement. I had been so absorbed in my own turmoil I hadn't even considered the possibility of encountering a bustling crowd. The sight that greets me when I pull up is overwhelming.

Watching from my car, an ocean of emotions floods through me. A sense of longing wells up mingling with a twinge of disappointment. The sight of the bakery bustling with people is not the time to confront her and tell her what I want to say, to explain what happened to me all this time. But I don't have the nerve to talk to her without my confession.

I catch a glimpse of her serving people, making my chest tighten. Resigned, I put my car in drive. The moment I park my car in the apartment complex, my mind swirls with a desperate need to see Davina. I reach for my phone, my fingers trembling, and dial Lexi's number. I know this is a bad idea, but I have to try something. I'm desperate. As the phone rings, each passing second feels like an eternity, amplifying my growing anxiety.

"Hey."

"Hi Roger. What do you want?" she gasps.

"Why are you panting? What are you doing?"

"Exercising. What do you think it sounds like?"

"Not exercising."

"What is so important you had to disturb my daily yoga?"

"Well, remember when you said you could help me with Davina?"

Silence stretches. Finally, the shrill sound of her voice makes way to my ears.

"Did I say that? I don't remember saying those words," she claims, stressing on the letter s. "But, if I did, I guess, sure, whatever."

"Really?"

"Yeah, really, and by the way you always have bad timing," she retorts, irritation lacing her words. Taking a deep breath, she presses on, impatient. "Pick me up in five minutes."

"Thank you, Lexi."

I arrive at Lexi's house, my nerves in shambles. I have no idea how this will go. Lexi finally gets into my car. "You have no idea how much I'm hating missing my session but if you really need me to—" she trails off.

Moving towards her, my arms instinctively wrap around her in a genuine friendship hug. "Thank you, Lexi."

We make our way to Davina's bakery, the wheels on the road echoing through the streets of Brummana. When I park the car, Lexi glances at me in disgust. "Davina's bakery?"

I nod. "Yeah, so—got a plan?"

She scoffs, planting her hand on her hip. "I thought you had one." She mocks me as she gets out of the car.

I'm not sure what I was thinking by coming here with Lexi, but I thought it was the best way to see her. I want to do so much more than see her, I want to talk to her, hold her, and kiss her, but I can't now.

"Lexi, I have no plan. I have a broken heart that needs mending but I…"

With a brief nod, Lexi makes her way towards the entrance. I watch her disappear through the bakery doors. She waves from the window and ventures around. From what I can see, Davina offers her a couple things to try and then Lexi pays at the counter.

Suddenly, Davina was waving her hand to Lexi, and they start talking. Soon, Lexi hurries back, and I hold my breath, consumed with worry.

"What happened?" I blurt out, unable to contain my anxiety any longer.

Lexi sighs, her expression full of excitement. She takes a moment to compose herself before speaking. "She gave me all this for free. She told me this is a present for us for our wedding. Like that's going to happen."

The weight of Lexi's words hit me like a tidal wave, crashing over me with a force I can't comprehend. My heart skips a beat, my eyes widening in disbelief.

"What did she say exactly?" I ask, my voice trembling.

Lexi takes a deep, steady breath, her eyes meeting mine. "That your Jiddo asked Davina to bake our wedding cake," she reveals, leaving me breathless. "Gosh, he moves fast."

"Yeah. Very fast. Thank you for doing this, by the way."

"Well, it's the least I can do after everything. Anyway, what are you going to do about it?"

"I need to talk to my Jiddo." I state, knowing too well it will not go as I want it to, but I have to at least try.

His involvement in the wedding and the unforeseen connection with Davina washes over me as fragments of my broken life. How fucking dare he?

My hands ball into fists, and my chest tightens with heat, every nerve in my body screaming with fury. I can no longer deny the truth: Davina, the woman I love, is no longer mine.

After dropping Lexi off at her car, I drive to my parents' house, finding a line of cars, my Jiddo's among them. I walk in and see the commotion.

They're preparing for the wedding, my wedding.

"Honey, you're home!" My mother's voice rings out above the noise of the crowd. She makes her way towards me, enveloping me in a hug.

Summoning my courage, I muster the words, "Can we talk?" I direct my plea to her, silently hoping Jiddo won't be present for this conversation. "Where's Dad?" They both need to know what I'm thinking.

Her brows furrow slightly with concern, but she nods. "Of course, sweetheart. Let's find a quiet place to talk." We walk side by side and find my father. "Honey, Roger wants to talk to us."

"Sure." He nods, ushering us into his office. "What's up, Son?"

With a quick glance over my shoulder, I catch sight of my grandfather standing nearby, in the crowd. I offer him a nod, but his expression makes me uneasy.

Turning away, I close the door to the office, shutting out the noise and distractions of the surrounding environment. In the confined space, with my parents by my side, I allow the absence of external influences to sharpen my focus.

"We need to talk," I repeat, my voice carrying determination.

"Talk, Roger," my father responds.

Taking a deep breath to steady myself, I stare at my parents, searching their faces for any sign of acknowledgment or guilt. The question burns within me, demanding an answer. "Why did Jiddo order a cake for my wedding from Davina's bakery?"

Confusion clouds my mother's expression, while my father appears uncertain, grappling with the significance of my question. "When did Davina open a bakery?" Mom asks, her voice filled with genuine bewilderment.

Frustration wells up within me. The situation falls on my shoulders pushing my voice to rise in volume with each word. "Don't act confused." I shudder. "Why would he do that to me?"

My parents look at me with genuine concern on their faces. My anger makes it difficult for me to find the right words to express myself. My shout manifests, shattering the fragile peace.

"You know how much I love her. Why would he do such a thing? Why?"

My mother's eyes attempt to provide comfort. "I have no idea what you're talking about honey, but if you want to talk about it, we can." She turns to Dad. "What do you think..."

Dad opens his mouth, when suddenly, the doors fly wide open. The commanding presence of my grandfather fills the space as he enters, demanding attention and obedience.

"Sit," he orders, his voice steady. "You two can leave," he dismisses my parents with a cold dead stare. Mom opens her mouth, but he grabs her by her arm, holding tight and glaring down at her before letting go. His hand reaches high grabs a vase on the desk and smashes it on the wall. The broken shards come close, falling short of doing any other damage. "Sit down, you filthy boy!"

He settles into the business chair, assuming a position of power and control, while I stand stunned. My mother runs out of the room in tears, and my father turns to follow her. My grandfather grabs his arm, stopping him. "Set a date for the event and get back to me, in the meantime, check on your wife." My father walks out without looking at me.

"You're an asshole," I shout despite my fear.

He chuckles as he gets out of his chair walking towards me. "At least, I'm a powerful asshole, who can control your life and your parents too. This means a lot. But since you have done so much to disobey me, it's about time, I send you away."

"What?"

"You will go to military academy this weekend. They will teach you discipline among other things."

Before he could speak more, I grab my keys and leave. I don't even know where I'm headed, just away. Away from that house. From him.

It's this weight, this knowing that no matter how much I am hurting inside, it still won't be enough for them. And yet... through all of it, I see her: Davina, my Klutz.

Driving to Davina's house, thoughts race in my mind. All that matters is having her in my arms, holding her, and never ever letting go...

But when I pull up to her house, I see Davina in an elegant black dress.

Gorgeous...

A guy gets out and walks her to her door. Reality slams into me. She's moved on with someone else, shattering me in the process.

My world stops as she takes him in a hug holding on to him for a while. My heart plunges at the sight.

She's mine.

My Davina!

My Klutz. Not his!

Twenty-Five

♥

Davina

The air remains heavy as the July sun casts its warm rays on the glass windows of Besties & Cakes. Finally, I got the courage to go back to university and attend classes with everyone.

But I'm not doing well. It's not that I can't handle the pressure, no I could, but I don't want this anymore. I want to be out in the world. University is not for me and I'm okay with it because at least I graduated from high school. I don't need to get a degree, especially when I explored the biggest degree out there—life.

My parents and I agreed it was best for me to drop out completely, so I could concentrate on Besties & Cakes—where my heart lay. And, that's what I did.

During the early hours, before the world stirs from its slumber, I stand in the warmth of the kitchen, allowing my hands to work their magic. The fresh dough and warm chocolate embraces me. When the sun rises, painting the sky in hues of pink and gold, I transition to the front of the shop, greeting each customer.

I find myself engaged in a dialogue, not with the customers but with myself, a quiet conversation amidst the flurry of activity. "You're doing well, Davina," I whisper to myself, wiping a bead of sweat from my brow. "Each smile you bring, every satisfied customer, it's all a testament to your passion and hard work."

With my internal pep talk, I continue serving customers, every interaction a reminder of the purpose and joy baking brought into my life. I find a connection fueling my passion away from thinking about the one who got away because Mom and Dad have proven love, to me, never lasts forever.

Arriving at Besties & Cakes, I park my car and step out, anticipating the rest of the day ahead. The moment I look up, my eyes meet with a sight instantly making my heart skip a beat. An undeniably attractive man stands near the entrance, bathed in the warm afternoon sun.

My breath hitches taking him in as I approach. He's tall and well-built, with his sandy blond hair tousled, falling in disheveled waves, adding an air of rugged charm to his appearance.

His deep, piercing eyes meet mine and he smiles. "Hey."

"Can I help you?" I question as I make my way to my door.

I unlock it and step inside with him following right behind. He has an air of maturity adding to his natural magnetism. His well-groomed appearance hints at careful attention to detail, enhancing his undeniable handsomeness.

"I think you can." He steps to the open door. "May I come in?"

"It is a shop, and you are a customer, so, yes—you may."

He smirks again. "Thank you."

"What can I do for you, Mr.?" I ask, looking up from the counter.

"Eddy. Eddy Mead," he says, offering a polite smile.

"Mr. Mead," I repeat, nodding.

"Eddy. Please, call me Eddy," he corrects, his tone easygoing.

"Okay, Eddy. How can I help you?" I ask, leaning slightly forward.

"People have been raving about this bakery, and my Mom has a birthday coming up. I wanted to ask, do you cater?" he questions, glancing around at the displays.

"No, sorry. We don't," I reply, shaking my head apologetically.

"Oh, okay," he mutters, looking a little disappointed. "Erm—how about you tell me what you can offer me for a woman who helps everyone with their problems and is okay with surprises?"

"Hmmm, wait, Mead..." I trail off, tapping a finger on the counter. "Is your mother, Jennifer Mead?"

"Yes, she is," Eddy affirms, a fond smile creeping onto his face.

"Isn't this a conflict of interest or something..." I say thoughtfully.

"I'm sorry, I'm not following?" Eddy's tone curious but serious.

"Okay, so your mom is my psychologist." I reply, trying to sound confident.

"I see."

"Yes."

"Well, I've got to come clean then."

"Why?"

"My mom told me to come here."

"Oh, okay. Sure. I guess. When is this party?"

"In a week," he says casually.

"A week?" I repeat, blinking in surprise.

"Is that a problem?" Eddy asks, his brows knitting together.

"Usually, we ask people to book a month in advance," I explain, hesitating for a moment before adding, "but a week can be fine, I guess."

"Please," he says, almost pleading.

I nod slowly. "I'll see what I can do."

"What are you thinking?" Eddy presses, leaning slightly forward.

"How about I create a therapy themed cake. Many patients waiting outside, as your mom juggles a bunch of stuff in her office?" I suggest, my mind already whirring with ideas.

"You can do that in such a short time?" Eddy asks, his eyes wide with surprise.

"I can try," I say, smiling faintly.

Nerves grip me like a fragile cloak. An aura of confidence pulses from him, manufacturing a spell on me. Excitement swells within me, fueled by the anticipation, yet fear lurks beneath the surface, reminding me of my vulnerabilities and uncertainties.

A moment of silence hangs in the air, my heart racing. His next words, delivered with playfulness and intent, cut through the anticipation humming between us. "Well, thank you, Davina."

"You are welcome, Eddy." Warmth spreads through me, and a genuine smile escapes my lips.

"Nice to meet you," Eddy says, extending his hand with a warm smile.

"Likewise," I reply, shaking his hand and matching his smile.

The days unfold in a blur, leaving me to dive headfirst into preparing for Eddy's mom's birthday party. Mom and I work tirelessly alongside my staff, brainstorming ideas, sketching designs for the therapy-themed cake, and testing recipes late into the night.

Each day brings new challenges, perfecting the details, coordinating decorations, and ensuring everything aligns with the theme. Despite the exhaustion, there's a sense of purpose that drives us forward.

This party has to be perfect.

Finally, the big day arrives.

The cake: a stunning therapy office complete with famous therapy sessions, sits proudly as the centerpiece, surrounded by a spread of whimsical desserts. Mom gives me a reassuring nod, and I can't help but smile, knowing we've pulled it off.

"Wow," I say to myself, my eyes widening as Eddy walks into the bakery, looking impressed.

"Amazing job, guys," he says, glancing around at the setup with an approving smile.

"Thank you," I reply, feeling a swell of pride as my staff murmurs their gratitude.

"Where do I pay?" Eddy asks, reaching into his pocket.

"Never mind," I say, shaking my head.

"What do you mean?" He pauses, looking at me in confusion.

"It's on the house," I say with a grin, crossing my arms.

"You can't be serious," he says, his tone incredulous.

"Tell your mom, Happy birthday," I reply, my smile growing wider.

Eddy stares at me for a moment, then breaks into a laugh. "If that's the case, close up, and I'm inviting you all to the party. Please, I insist."

I turn to my staff, eyebrows raised in question. They exchange glances, then nod enthusiastically, grinning with excitement.

Once home, Mom sits down with a weary sigh. "I think I'll pass on the party," she says, rubbing the back of her neck. "A quiet night sounds more my speed."

I hesitate, worry flickering through me. "Are you sure? You've worked so hard."

She waves me off with a small smile. "I'm sure. You go have fun, kiddo. You've earned it."

I nod, not wanting to push. "Alright, but text me if you need anything, okay?"

She chuckles. "I'll be fine, Davina. Have fun."

Upstairs, I slip into a stunning black corset gown, its sleek design hugging me perfectly. The dress shimmers under the light, made for a night out. As I fasten the last clasp, a small thrill of excitement buzzes through me. Tonight feels like a celebration—not just for the party, but for everything we've accomplished.

When I walk out the door, Eddy is waiting for me by his car, leaning casually against it. "I thought a proper escort was in order," he says, a playful gleam in his eyes.

"Did you now?" I reply with a smirk tugging at my lips.

"Yes, Ma'am," Eddy says with a slight bow. "And, if I may say, you look stunning."

"Thank you," I blush.

We soon arrive at his mom's. Climbing out of the car smiling, he takes my hand and helps me up the steps to his house, the same one I'd been to for my sessions; until she told me I didn't need her anymore. And she was right. The soft music plays in the background, creating a smooth melody.

Later in the evening, the party starts to quiet down a bit. I slip away from the crowd, needing a moment to myself. I wander through the house, curiosity guiding my movements as I search for the bathroom. Stepping out of the bathroom the warm touch of hands send a shiver of thrill through my body, the first one since Roger and I broke up. The hands pull me into him as his arms wrap around me.

Eddy's voice breaks the silence. "You look absolutely breathtaking tonight."

A blush creeps up my cheeks as I turn to meet his gaze. "You said that already," I reply. "Why are we whispering?"

A playful smile tugs at the corners of his lips, and he leans in closer. "I really want to kiss you."

My heart flutters at his words. "I'm sorry but I'm not ready for that yet."

Pulling away from him, a hushed silence envelopes us. "It's okay, maybe another time." He smirks, taking my hand in his. Gently, Eddy squeezes my hand, reassuring.

"I'll take you home," he insists.

"You don't have to," I reply, trying to stay composed.

"I want to," he says leaving no room for argument.

Eddy drives me home. The ride remains quiet, but not uncomfortable. At my door, we hug, but I'm not ready for anything more. Not yet anyway. I release his hands and step inside without looking back.

My heart stutters, leaving me rooted to the spot as I catch Roger sitting alone in his car, hands on the wheel glaring at me.

Twenty-Six

♥

Roger

After witnessing the devastating scene between Davina and the random guy, my heart shattered. I threw myself into rebuilding my family, striving to mend the fractures I threatened myself with.

Embarking on a parallel journey, one that would bring me closer to Jiddo and his influential status in Lebanon's political world, I push forward trying to forget, trying to make my life make sense and trying to live, no matter what the cost. It was against my parents' wishes, but it's where I want to be, at least this was steady. My other focus remains on my education, winning another presidency term with no help from Charlie, but with Lexi by my side. Although, I still struggle with Lexi's actions against me and especially Davina, my anger has subsided. With our long history and being stuck in a situation neither of us want, Lexi and I moved on from our hate, even becoming friends again.

Lexi and I visit a local café in Beirut Martyr's Square, next to the big clock after weeks of planning and sending out invitations to our wedding. Lexi's voice fills with sincere affection. "It's so good to see you smiling."

A grin tugs at the corners of my lips. "Well, I'm sitting here, with my best friend sipping on the best coffee in town."

Lexi giggles. "Oh, Roger! I am no longer going to be your best friend, you know. I'm going to be your wife soon."

"Wife. Yeah." My voice echoes, hollow. "We deserve better, don't we?"

She leans back and exhales in contentment. "Well, I'm thinking of moving to the UK, or the US and start something for me. Maybe be a model or a movie star."

I laugh, mirroring her enthusiasm. "I can see you doing that."

"Yeah, but here's one important question. How do we escape our family duties?"

I pause for a moment, collecting my thoughts. There's a part of me longing to say we will find a way, but there's also another part that says, there's no point without Davina. "I'm not so sure, Lexi. But you can do one thing... The runaway bride is an option."

Lexi sighs, her eyes showing sorrow. "Maybe?"

She plants her hands on the table, her eyes locked onto mine with an intensity demanding my attention. "Do you still love Davina?"

She searches my eyes, delving into the depths of my soul. "You know I do. I never stopped."

"What are you going to do about it then?" Lexi asks, removing her hand from mine. "You need to man up and talk to her, Roger."

I take a deep breath exhaling the weight of my actions. Lexi reaches for my hand, again and slaps my head, saying, "She would never move on from you that fast, doofus."

Regret washes over me like a tidal wave. Lexi is right, Davina would never do something like that to me; her heart doesn't work that way. The ache in my chest mirrors the pain I inflicted. I look at Lexi, a tear escaping my eye.

"What have I done?" I whisper, filled with regret.

We say bye to each other with a heartfelt hug and Lexi walks away.

After talking with Lexi, I wanted to reach out to Davina and talk to her, but Jiddo sent me a message telling me about the dangers of going out in public without protection. His campaign was threatened by fanatics and with our family in the public eye, we could be in danger. Davina was better off safe, away from the perils of the world I lived in.

We had become acutely aware of the risks. My parents didn't like me always putting myself in harm's way, but it kept me grounded.

It kept me away from trying to contact Davina. It's better this way. She's safe.

At least, I hoped it would keep her that way...

My world was in chaos in nearly every way as Christmas approached. My parents organized a Christmas party for all the politicians who were on Jiddo's side. At the party I met a lot of people, and one stood out to me.

The guy from the other night.

The one Davina was with.

The one who took her home.

The joyous atmosphere fills the room, as guests mingle and exchange cheerful greetings. The guy glances in my direction as he speaks to another guest. I really want to punch him in the face, but I resist, trying to mingle with our guests. He stands by the wall near the tree, and I find myself watching him from across from the room. Rage surges through me as I recall the visual still plaguing my mind.

When the clock strikes midnight, the festivities begin to wind down, yet my encounter with the guy was still pending. Before everyone leaves, we need to chat, intent on having it out now, rather than waiting for the next time I decide to throw a punch without remorse.

"I'd say it was nice having you here, but let's face it, it's not," I say, silently seething.

He scoffs. "Have I done something to offend you?"

My eyes narrow, smirking at him. "You're funny."

The tension grows, about to consume us. "I'm sorry but do I know you?"

I laugh. "No."

"I'm Eddy," he clarifies, holding out his hand.

My eyes narrow on it, but I don't take it. "I saw you bring Davina home."

"Davina?" he repeats, dropping his hand to his side.

"Yes, her."

Eddy waits for me to say more, but I don't. He places a hand on my shoulder. "Well, my dear friend. Davina and I are just friends. She did a small favor for me for my mom and that was it. I mean, I could have, but I respect boundaries."

"You've done enough," I huff in annoyance about to grab him, but refrain. "That didn't look like friends, when you walked her to her door, had your arms around her and waited for her to get inside."

"No, you're right. I was a gentleman. That's what we men do. Being polite and all. Anyway, what's it to you?" he asks, playfully nudging my arm.

"Nothing. Thanks for your honesty."

Looking at Eddy, clarity washes over me. Maybe that was the truth. Maybe he lied. But maybe there's still a chance. I think it's time to focus on me and Davina. If there will be me and Davina ever again. He walks out, leaving me confused.

Do I call her, or do I leave it as we left things?

Twenty-Seven

♥

Davina

R oger.

A name echoing in my heart for all eternity, a haunting web of tangled emotions threatening to devour me. He consumes my every thought, every emotion, every desire to be with him but I'm still struggling to forgive him. I tried through therapy, but I can't seem to get my unanswered call out of my mind, even though I know it's irrational.

When I needed him, he wasn't there...

Bleary-eyed, I look out my window, hoping for some clarity in the chaos. But my eyes widen, landing on Roger sleeping snuggled in his car parked across the street. My heart lurches, wanting to go to him, but I can't. With a deep breath, I step away from the window and make my way to the door.

My hand hovers on the doorknob, remembering he's engaged to Lexi, squeezing the air from my lungs. Instead, I go for my phone, knowing what I have to do. With my fingers trembling, I dial Lexi's number. She answers with a hint of irritation as if my call disrupted her sleep. "Who are you and why are you calling me this early?"

I roll my eyes at her sarcasm. "Lexi. Your husband to be is parked outside my house, sleeping in his car. You need to come and get him."

"Davina? Is that you?" Her response is immediate, laced with questions. "Parked outside your house. Why?"

"I have no clue why, Lexi. Just come and get him." My voice quivers as I speak trying to be firm.

"You're joking, right?" she challenges, the sound of her sigh traveling through the phone. "I can't be bothered getting out of bed."

"Either you come and get him, or I'll call the police."

"Ugh, fine, I'm on my way."

I huff in annoyance. "That's all I wanted."

As soon as I end the call and place it on my nightstand, the memory of Roger's grandfather walking into my shop resurfaces, turning my stomach.

The aroma of freshly baked bread filled the air as I worked in Besties & Cakes. It was a typical day, filled with conversation among customers, and orders. A storm brewed within me knowing I had to fight for Roger.

An old man entered the shop, looking elegant in a Navy Blue Gatoo suit from France. He stood by the door as my customers ordered. I gave him a quick nod, before I went to talk to him.

"Hello," he greeted me extending a hand for me to shake, and I did. "You must be Davina, the owner of this establishment, correct?"

"I am, and you—"

Before I asked, he continued, "I heard a lot about your bakery and was wondering if I could do my grandson a huge honor."

"Honor?"

"Well yes," he spoke, his voice trailing off while he walked around the shop. "He's getting married and they, well, you know how weddings are... Lots of work and everything. May I try this?" He took a piece of the display cake and devoured it in one swift motion. "Hmm," he beamed as he let the flavors dance around in his mouth. "My wife, God rest her soul, would have enjoyed this. What is it?"

"Hazelnut and peanut butter flavor, sir."

"So polite." He smiled with the side of his cheek. "Right, where was I? Oh, the cake. So, they have a lot to do, and I wanted to surprise them with a cake from the best cake shop."

"How nice," I told him, taking my notebook and pen from the counter. "How many people?"

He laughed. "Quite a few I must say, but I was thinking that the bride and groom and the immediate family would have a special cake while the rest of the guests get any flavor. What do you think?"

I cleared my throat. "Well, our secret weapon for wedding cakes is the vanilla and custard cream. For a big tier cake. As for the wedding party and the immediate families of the bride and groom, we usually offer them the molten chocolate, strawberry lava cake."

He beamed. "I'd like that very much."

"I'll ring that for you. What kind of cake toppers would you like?"

He hummed for a while, until he spoke, "A man and a woman, made of fondant. If possible."

"That can be done. Anything else?"

He smiled, as if creepily trying to tell me something. "Davina, may I ask you a question?"

"Sure."

"Do you not know who I am?"

I shook my head, perplexed. "Should I?"

He placed a domineering hand on my shoulder, as if trying to intimidate me. "I'm Roger's grandfather."

"His grandfather," I repeated, clearing my throat, my heart plummeting. "I'll ring that for you right away."

He chuckled. "You are funny, dear child."

"Why?"

"Because you will not ring it. You will do this for my grandson free of charge, you will deliver the cake personally, and you will watch as he marries Lexi. Do I make myself clear?"

I turned to look away from him, tears wanting to burst out. My employees looked at my predicament and stepped forward to help me, *but with my hand I waved them away. I faced him clenching my jaw and tilting my chin up in defiance and said, "I would gladly do this for Roger and Lexi, but the invitation to his wedding, I will have to personally decline."*

"Why?"

"Because I don't want to be there," I spoke loudly, my voice echoing off the bakery walls. "Please leave and never come back again."

He smirked and walked off, but not before saying, "You will be so kind as to send it in a gold box."

Memories flood my mind, bringing back my heartache. I cried all night. After that, I gave up on Roger. On us. I had no choice.

Lexi arrives at my house in a taxi. Observing from inside, I watch as she steps out of the cab, our eyes meeting in a silent goodbye. She moves towards Roger's car, guiding him to the passenger seat with a gentle touch. He lifts his head and briefly glances at the house in defeat.

Wishing things could be different, a tear slips down my cheek as the car's engine gradually fades in the distance.

Twenty-Eight

♥

Roger

I am stuck.

Well, technically, after how Lexi expressed herself to me, and how she tried to help me with Davina, we're stuck in a situation we can't get out of. She's actually keeping up appearances as if she's really into me and wants this to happen when all I want is to break free.

I'm sentenced to life with the Barnes family.

Married to Lexi. Children with her. But, I still can't find another way...

Planning the wedding was horrible. My parents, though busy with their own preparations, noticed the quiet ache in me. The way my eyes would linger on things that reminded me of Davina, the way my smile never quite reached my eyes. Even my Jiddo, who usually kept to himself, noticed the shift in my demeanor.

One evening, after dinner, he asked to meet with me privately. At first, I didn't want to. I knew what he was going to say, how he'd ask about Davina and how I was holding up. But deep down, I knew I had to go.

"You haven't stopped loving Davina, right?" Jiddo asks as he leans in.

"Wow, so perceptive," I mutter.

"Don't mock me, Son," he responds, defensive.

"I'm doing what I'm told, what else do you expect from me?" I challenge.

"I want you to act like a man and grow up. Stop living in what could have been," he insists.

"Jiddo..."

"Roger, I admit I made a mistake. I'm sorry. Cut me some slack. I thought I was doing the right thing at the time," Jiddo says with regret.

"Really? Forcing my hand?" I ask with disbelief.

"I know now, it's wrong," he claims.

Does he mean it? "I need to see Davina. I can't go on without seeing her," I admit, choked with emotion.

He nods. "I can arrange something for you."

"Really?" I question, hoping I didn't fall into his trap—which my gut is telling me I did, from the way he is looking at me with his piercing brown eyes.

"Do you take me for a fool boy?"

Breathing out, I try to say something, but he pins me against the wall, leaning in close. "You will marry Lexi. You will keep up appearances and you will make the Hoards' name stand out in the political world."

"I'm not the only one who doesn't want this union to happen, Jiddo."

He slams his hand on the wall beside my face, daring me to defy him. I can't take it anymore, but I'm stuck, and I hate it. Wedding planning wasn't something I'd ever expected to worry about. Not yet anyway and definitely not with Lexi.

A couple of months pass, with me moving on autopilot. The morning shines its rays with the rising sun, waking me up from my tormented life I can't escape. Lexi sits at the edge of the bed, her face in her hands in tears.

"Lexi, is everything okay?" I ask, hoping she is.

Despite everything, I still care for her. Before we were boyfriend and girlfriend, she was one of my best friends.

"Lexi, talk to me." I lean closer, my brows drawn tight.

"Roger," she chokes out, tears streaking down her face as she breathes in broken sobs.

"What is it? Tell me what's wrong," I press, urgent.

Her eyes dart away, tears fall from her eyes. "I'm in love with Charlie. Even after everything, I still love him. I never stopped. And when he did what he did to Davina, it got me thinking, would he have done it to me when we were all alone?"

"What are you talking about?" I ask, my hands curling into fists on my knees.

She whispers, her gaze dropping to the floor. "I just wondered, if, like, you know..."

"You were alone with him?" My voice rises, and I shift forward in my seat.

"Yes," she concedes, barely audible.

"How many times?"

"A lot," she says, wrapping her arms around herself.

"How was he with you?"

"Gentle," she admits, shaking her head. "That's why I'm confused. I want to go see him and talk."

"I don't think that's a good idea, Lexi," I say, my voice firm.

"But I need to know. My heart aches for him," she claims, clutching at her chest, her face crumpling. "I need to know the truth. Please."

"I understand," I say, taking her hand in mine and squeezing gently. "But what if you don't get the answers you want?"

"Don't you want answers, Roger? Why did he do that?" she asks, her voice trembling.

"I do. Believe me, I do."

"There's no but," she interrupts, her eyes flashing. "I need to know."

"And then what?" I ask, tilting my head, searching her face.

"Then, then—" she stammers before breaking down in tears, her shoulders shaking. "Then, I don't know."

"Did you sleep with him?"

She says nothing, her gaze dropping to her lap.

"When?" I ask again, leaning forward.

She stays silent, her lips pressed together.

"How long were you sleeping with him?"

"It's, ah, it's more complicated," she says, her voice barely above a whisper.

"No, Lexi. It's not. It's simple," I say, standing abruptly. I start pacing the room, running a hand through my hair.

"I've been sleeping with him every so often, until he got arrested," she admits, the hurt in her voice evident.

"What?" I ask, my brow furrowing.

"Charlie was my first," she admits quietly. "And after that, we continued. When I was yours, we stopped for a bit. But one drunk night, we started up again. Up until–"

My chest tightens. "I don't know what to say to you, Lexi."

She sighs, her shoulders sagging as the memories resurface, pulling with them one of the reasons why me and Lexi never worked. She cheated...

"I'm sorry, I never meant to hurt you, Roger." Her voice breaks, as she sniffles.

I can't believe what I'm hearing. My best friend and my girlfriend. The tale as old as time. But also my best friend, a psycho maniac. Maybe Lexi is right, maybe I should know.

"Fine, let's go," I say, cutting through the tension.

"You sure?" she asks, her eyes searching mine.

"No, but I guess it's for both of us," I reply, standing straighter, hardening in my chest.

Roumieh Prison.

It's the kind of place where they lock up the worst of the worst people who have done horrible things and are sent there to pay for their sins, or whatever it is they call it. I've heard enough about it to know that it's not a place for anyone to end up. But here we are, me and Lexi on our way to face the man who changed everything for us.

When we finally arrive, we are checked in and processed. The guards give us a thorough search and make us fill out a bunch of paperwork. The whole process is cold, methodical, and it makes me feel like an outsider in a world that doesn't care about anything but rules.

I push it all aside because I know what I'm here for.

After what feels like forever, they lead us into a small, dimly lit room. The walls are bare, and the air is heavy with the smell of metal and sweat. I can feel my heart beating in my chest, fast and hard. I know who's waiting on the other side of that door.

It's him.

Someone who has caused me so much pain: Charlie.

My hands tighten into fists as I sit down across from him. Lexi sits beside me, sniffling. Her pain is mine and this time, we share the same goal. I try to keep my face calm, but inside, I'm boiling.

"Well. Well. Well. Look at what the cat dragged in." Charlie smirks, leaning back in the chair.

"Charlie, you look well," Lexi says, her voice cool.

"I do. Thanks. Unlike you and Roger. I'm living the dream." He chuckles.

I smirk, trying so hard to keep this peaceful. But he's making it tough.

"I'm shocked you're both here. I would have thought Roger would come alone, you know, to discuss Davina. My sweet Caramel Pussy. Hmmm, she tasted so good."

My fists clench at the mention of her. Lexi places a gentle hand on mine, to relax me, but I can't, I want to hit him.

Charlie leans forward, his expression turning more smug. "How is Davina doing?"

"She's fine." Lexi answers, clearly irritated with him. "We need to talk."

Charlie raises an eyebrow, amused. "Go on, I don't have all day. Well, I do, but I don't want to sit with you two all day."

I force myself to take a deep breath, remembering why I'm here. I lean in, locking eyes with him. "Charlie!"

"What?" He shrugs.

"Charlie, look at me. Me—Lexi, not Roger. I'm not here for Davina or for him, I'm here for me," Lexi declares, her voice steady as she leans forward. She tries to reach for his hand, but the guard shakes his head, signaling against it.

"You?" Charlie asks, his eyes shooting wide open, a flicker of confusion crossing his face.

"Yes, me," Lexi repeats, her tone firm.

"Speak then," Charlie says, leaning, as if he does not care, but he secretly must because it's obvious he's not comfortable slanting backwards.

"Would you have done the same to me?" Lexi asks, pressing him for answers.

"Done what?"

"You know what, Charlie. What you did to Davina," she presses, her gaze drilling into him.

"No," Charlie says flatly. "I already got what I wanted from you without taking it."

"So, you're just a creep then," Lexi snaps, her lip curling in disgust.

"If that's what you want to call me, then yes," Charlie says with a shrug. "Besides, you already know how good I am, don't you Lexi?"

"Lexi, I think Charlie answered your questions," I say, nudging her arm gently, hoping to pull her away.

She sighs, her shoulders sagging. "Not all of them."

Charlie smirks. "What more do you want to ask me, Lexi?"

"Did you ever love me?" she asks, almost trembling.

I glance at her, startled, my eyes shooting up to Charlie, waiting for his answer. He shifts in his seat, his hands fidgeting as if tied down by the weight of the question. It's simple, yet it troubles him.

"Define love," he finally says, his voice quiet but certain. "I mean, I love a lot of girls."

"So, I meant nothing to you?" Lexi questions, the words cutting through the silence like a blade. "Is that what you are telling me?"

"Yeah, you meant nothing," Charlie claims, turning to look directly at me, his expression cold and calculated. "I fucked you Lexi because Roger took you away from me. The more we fucked, the more I saw him being mad at us."

"You're an asshole Charlie."

"Yeah, and I love it."

"Fuck you!" Lexi screams loud, slapping him in the face but he doesn't flinch.

"At least I was offered a good job."

"Raping Davina?" Lexi asks. "Who paid you?"

Charlie shrugs. "I was arrested before I got paid."

"Give me a name," I demand, my voice sharp.

"I don't have a name for you Roger. I received a message on my phone with instructions," Charlie explains with a dismissive shrug. "Rape Davina, get paid."

"Really, Charlie..." Lexi's voice breaks as she bursts into tears, her face crumpling. "If they said to do that to me, would you? Would you? Answer me!" she screams, her hands shaking as she grips the edge of the table.

The guards rush toward us, trying to calm Lexi down, but it's no use. She lunges at Charlie, slapping his face and punching his stomach with wild, furious blows. He winces but doesn't fight back. The guards grab her, pinning her arms and dragging her away, but she thrashes against them, screaming, never calming.

Staying seated, I'm frozen in place, watching them force her out of the room. Charlie adjusts himself, sitting back down in the chair with a smirk that only makes my stomach churn.

"Damn it, Charlie! Give me a number." My voice comes out cold, cutting through the tension.

"I don't have my phone with me," Charlie says, shrugging like it's nothing. "Ask the warden. They took it to evidence."

Leaning forward, I narrow my eyes. "So, I'm sure Lexi would want me to get the answer from you. Would you have done that to her too?"

Charlie hesitates, his jaw clenching. "Maybe, if it was good money," he finally answers, his voice flat.

"You're disgusting," I say, standing up, my voice laced with bit-
terness. "Enjoy prison. You deserve it."

I turn and walk away, my footsteps heavy with frustration. I
came here for answers, but I'm leaving with nothing. No closure,
just more questions.

Lexi stands by my car, still sobbing, her tears falling without
pause. I walk over and take her into my arms, holding her tightly.
She leans into me, shaking, and I hold on because I know she's
mourning something deeper than today's confrontation.

She wanted Charlie not to be the man he's become, the man
who destroyed so much. She wanted him to still be the Charlie she
once fell for, but he's not. That Charlie is gone, lost forever, and
he's never coming back.

Aside from leaving without the answers I wanted, I feel like Lexi,
and I grew closer today, or at least I hope we did.

"Hey, are you okay?" I ask, brushing her hair back gently as she
pulls away slightly. "Need a ride?"

"No," she says, shaking her head, her eyes swollen. "I need a few
hours to myself. I need to think."

"You sure?"

"Yeah," she nods, her voice steady. "Thanks Roger."

"Of course, Lexi." Stepping back, I give her space. "I'm here if
you need me."

"I'm sorry for everything," she says, a faint, sad smile crossing
her lips.

"Don't," I reply, watching her as she turns away, still caught in her thoughts. "I forgive you."

I get into my car and drive off, leaving Lexi in the parking lot.

Twenty-Nine

♥

Davina

The New Year approaches.

I find myself craving the need to be alone after everything including the incident with a special visit from Roger's grandfather. It tore me a new soul. It was as if he wanted to yank me out of my body and replace me with someone of stature.

Settling in the comfort of my bedroom, I have a bottle of wine on hand and immerse myself in the pages of a romance novel I picked up on the way home. The soft glow of the bedside lamp warms the room, my eyes scanning each page as I read the story about Bree and Christian, longing for a love like theirs.

At ten minutes before midnight, a knock sounds at the front door, startling me.

A chill runs down my spine. Could it be Roger? I place the book on my nightstand and rush to the door, my pulse quickening.

But when I open it, I find Eddy standing there, holding a bottle of red wine and a bouquet of red roses.

He places everything on my table and turns to me. His hands quickly find their way to my waist, in one swift motion, pulling me closer.

Reflexively, I wrap my arms around him. We move into the living room, and he plops onto the couch, pulling me onto his lap. Five seconds, he pushes me back gently with his hands on my shoulders. I feel his heartbeat racing against mine.

Four seconds, our eyes meet, his with a question.

Three...

Two...

One...

"Happy New Year, Davina." He sighs, placing a kiss on my forehead, knowing all too well, I'm still not ready for that kind of intimacy. "I hope it's okay that I'm here."

No words escape my lips. He holds me in his arms, his fingers trailing along my arms up and down, making soothing strides. We stay in each other's arms, with me saying nothing, while his head lay on my chest, and we fall asleep.

The gentle morning sunbeams filter through the curtains, waking me up to the sight of a beautifully set breakfast tray resting on the table in front of the couch.

"Morning beautiful," Eddy murmurs.

The aroma of freshly brewed coffee mingles with the enticing smell of pancakes and crispy bacon, tickling my senses. Eddy stands beside the couch, a gentle smile gracing his lips.

I smile, taking a bite of the pancakes. "Happy New Year, Eddy. I was lost last night and couldn't say it quick enough."

He laughs. "No worries."

We savor our breakfast together, me silently hoping nothing would ruin my time with Eddy. That afternoon my parents come back home and we have a coffee together before Eddy leaves. My parents retire to their bedroom, while I take Mom's beamer and drive for a bit.

I need to think.

There's something about the new year, a wish I'd like to make, and hopefully it'd come true.

Beyond everything else in my life, Roger's absence looms over me. I need to do this, a final goodbye. An act of closure I owe to our memory, of whatever we were before he marries Lexi.

I pull up a side road, driving beyond the usual road to Roger's house, a bizarre pull guiding me further inward, deeper behind his house. Continuing along the unfamiliar path with something unknown drawing me in, I can't help but wonder what I'll find.

A gasp escapes my lips, absorbing the tranquility of the space where I could immerse myself in memories. I shift my observation upward, the sky stretching out before me, filled with twinkling stars.

Taking a moment, the cool air kisses my cheeks, mingling with the rapid beats of my heart. My fingers find their way to my chest, resting on my heart, feeling its steady rhythm.

Leaning against the car window, I allow my mind to drift: to Eddy, to our friendship and its possibilities, to Roger, to what I wish we still were.

My fingers twitch, desperate to make the call, no matter what anyone might say. I have to! I owe it to myself. To him. With a heavy heart, I reach for my phone, its cool surface contrasting with the turmoil brewing within me. Deep down, I know it's a necessary step, regardless of the potential consequences.

Taking a deep breath, I dial his number. As the call connects, my heart skips a beat. My voice trembles as I whisper my confession, "I miss you."

There's a brief pause, before he replies, "Me too, Klutz."

"I'm sorry, Roger. I never meant for any of it."

"No Davina. This is not your fault. It's mine. I'm sorry. I should have been there for you."

"Your grandfather came to visit me at my shop," I reveal, not caring about the consequences.

Silence hangs in the air once more. The weight of my words palpable.

"What did he say to you, Davina?"

"Hearing that you were getting married hurt the most, Roger. It doesn't matter what he said, but I was hurting, and I tried moving on. But I couldn't. I still love you, Roger. I always will."

"Where are you?"

"Behind your house."

"I'm on my way."

Sitting on the hood of my car waiting for Roger, makes me think about all the moments we shared. The sound of a car approaching doesn't faze me.

"I have missed you so much," he declares the moment he steps out of the car.

"Not as much as I have, Roger."

I scramble to come down off the hood, when Roger reaches for me and waits until I drop to the ground, into his arms. His hands hold onto me as my heartbeat drums in my chest. He stares into my eyes, digging for clarity. I want to hold onto him forever and never let go, feeling like I'm where I was meant to be.

"God, you're so beautiful, Klutz."

I smirk. "You're not too bad yourself."

He clears his throat. "Are you making fun of me?" he asks, as he leans forward. "It's hard not to kiss you."

"Well, get on with it."

"What about the other guy?" he asks, winking at me.

"What other guy?" I pause and then it clicks. "Oh, you mean, Eddy? He's nothing. We're nothing. He's just a friend."

"Friend?"

"I promise. There's nothing there."

Grinning, he moves closer, blowing his breath on my neck. I moan, hoping he'll make his move already. "Wait, what about Lexi?" I ask.

"What about her?" he says, placing his hand on my stomach and slips it inside my shirt.

"Your fiancé?" Goosebumps erupt on my skin as he glides his hand up to my thin bra and over my breast. He pinches my nipple, making me gasp.

"Forget about her, Klutz." He whispers, brushing against me, "She's nothing. It's you, always you. You've always been the one."

My head falls back, and my body arcs on the hood of my car. "Yes," I gasp.

He smiles, watching me breathlessly. "Come here," he urges, taking me into his arms. I hold onto him, desperate for him. He plants a passionate kiss on my lips. "Bask in this silence as we sit together. I just want to sit here with you."

I smile faintly, leaning back as he suggested, letting the quiet surround us like a warm blanket. For a moment, it feels like we've stepped out of time, away from everything.

But then reality intrudes. His phone buzzes, cutting through the stillness. He sighs, taking it out. "Hello," he answers. "I'm coming soon, Jiddo. Why, what's wrong?"

I sit up, sensing the shift in his voice. "What happened? Is everything okay? Roger?"

His demeanor changes, the calmness slipping away as he drops his phone to his side. Sadness clouds his features, pulling him into a place I can't reach. Something happened, but he doesn't speak right away.

"Roger, what's wrong?" I ask again.

He tries again, but this time, he falls to the ground. Tears spill down his face, his shoulders trembling as sobs rack his body. I reach for him, pulling him up, to stand, to hold onto him. "Shall I take you home?"

He nods, unable to speak, as we shuffle to my car. When we settle in, I place a hand on his lap, a small gesture meant to anchor him. "Roger," I whisper. "What happened?"

He turns to me, his bloodshot eyes locked onto mine. "It's Lexi."

"What happened?" I ask, my heart pounding, fear creeping in.

"Take me home, Davina. Please," Roger says, his voice breaking as he looks at me, his eyes desperate.

I nod silently, putting the car in drive. The tension thick in the air. When we pull up to his house, my heart sinks. Police cars and ambulances fill the driveway with their lights flashing.

Roger doesn't hesitate. He leans over, kissing me briefly before he runs out of the car, heading straight for the chaos inside. I watch him go, taking my heart with him.

Staying in the car for a moment, breathing deeply, I know this is it: this is a definite goodbye.

Thirty

♥

Roger

Stepping through the doors of my house, the scene before me hits like a punch to the gut. Everyone is sitting around the table, their faces a mix of shock and devastation. Lexi's parents broken, their eyes red from crying. Jiddo and my parents silent, their gazes distant, unable to find the words.

On the table, in the midst of the sorrow, lies a letter Lexi left.

I hesitate for a moment, the weight of everything pressing down on me. Then, I step forward, my heart heavy with the pain she left behind.

Jiddo pulls me into a hug, holding me like he hasn't in years. It's deep, real and something I haven't felt in forever. I bury my face in his chest, letting the comfort of his embrace hold me together, even for a minute.

"Do you want to talk?" he asks, soft and concerned, like he thinks I want to hide from this.

"No, Jiddo," I pull back just enough to look him in the eyes. "We need to be here with everyone."

"You're right, Roger." He nods, his hand heavy on my shoulder.

I take a deep breath and look around the room. "Did anyone read the letter?" My voice cracks as the need for answers claws at me.

"No honey. There's a letter for you and one addressed to her parents," my mother says, her voice barely there. "You can go into your room if you like."

I nod, swallowing back a lump in my throat. "Okay. Thanks Mom. Mrs. Barnes, I'm sorry. Mr. Barnes, I have no words."

"We don't blame you, Roger," Mrs. Barnes says, getting up and walking toward me. She pulls me into a tight hug, then sits down next to her husband. Her eyes are full of a sorrow I can't even put into words.

I take a deep breath, tears starting to sting as I look at everyone. Nodding, I make my way to my bedroom and sit on my bed. Soon, I start reading...

Dear Roger,

I came into this life thinking I would make something of myself. I really thought I would. I wanted to believe I could help people, but I wasn't nice. Not even close.

It's hard admitting it. It's a pain I've carried far too long.

Roger, this will be hard to admit, but Davina is amazing. You deserve each other. I'm sorry I ever made it hard for you two. I mean, I wish I had even half of what she has, and maybe I would've been the perfect girl for you. But I never loved you, Roger. I lied to everyone, even to myself. I'm sorry...

Tears fall, blurring the words in front of me.

I sob quietly, not wanting anyone to hear, because saying it out loud is too hard to admit.

Lexi wasn't someone I ever thought would do this.

We were trying to escape our parents' expectations.

We went to see Charlie, even though I told her it was a mistake.

But maybe that's what pushed her over the edge.

Maybe that's what broke her.

In high school, I made Davina's life a living hell. I was jealous. I hated everyone giving her attention because she was actually a good person. She didn't know how to fake it, never pretended to be something she wasn't. It was tiring being compared to her in school. All the teachers loved her, so I thought, what better than to destroy her?

I had to tear her down to make myself look good.

Let's fast-forward to us, Roger.

I loved you because you were a convenience, but I was never in love with you. I was never faithful. I always cheated. With him.

Charlie was the one I loved. He took me to places I never thought would be possible.

He stole my heart, Roger.

When I heard Davina tried to kill herself because of what I did, I broke. I wanted to apologize, wanted to reach out to her, but she was gone. I never understood until now.

Then she came back, started at Roadwood, and I knew you fell for her. It hurt, Roger. It hurt because I felt like she took you away from me, even though we were no longer together. I told her something I regret. Please apologize to her for me.

I'm sorry for what I did. I never meant it.

I keep reading. The weight in my chest presses down harder, stealing the air from my lungs. The words blur, but if I stop reading it will hurt more, so I keep going.

Writing this, hurts, Roger.

I could've stopped Davina but I didn't. I should've said something that day. I knew something was wrong, but I stayed quiet. And now, I carry that guilt, and I will, until my last breath.

Roger, I need you to do something for me.

Tell Charlie that I loved him. So much.

But when we visited him in prison, he tore me apart. His words broke something in me, and I'm not able to put myself back together.

This... what I did... it's because he killed who I was.

I'm sorry for everything, Roger.

I made you part of my game, and for that, I'm sorry. You didn't deserve any of it.

I loved Charlie, even the unhinged side of him. The sex with Charlie was better. More passionate. More real than it ever was with you. I'm sorry, Roger, but that's the truth.

I went looking for closure, and I got it. He never loved me. I was just another girl to him.

And that broke me.

It destroyed me.

Crushed me.

You couldn't have stopped me, Roger.

I was going to do this: with or without that visit.

I've felt trapped for so long.

But I'll be with you, always. I'm sorry.

And please... tell Davina I'm sorry too.

Love,

Lexi

I read her name, the last word, and it tears me apart.

I keep wishing this was just a nightmare.

That Lexi will step out from behind the curtain and say, "Gotcha..."

But she doesn't.

She's really gone.

And she took my heart with her.

Everything shifts from wedding preparations to funeral arrangements. Jiddo takes a leave from politics. My parents said nothing to me. And even though I need Davina beside me, to hold me, to ground me, I keep her away. Out of respect for Lexi and her parents, I make sure she's not anywhere near me or my family.

In the days that follow, I throw myself into the one thing I could control: giving Lexi the farewell she deserves. Not just as my fiancée, or my girlfriend, but as my best friend.

Despite everything that happened between us, I had to make sure she was laid to rest with dignity. It wasn't easy. There were so many loose ends, things I had to do alone, with no one else to rely on. Her parents were too broken to do anything and I offered, knowing it was the last thing I could do for her.

Before the funeral, I visit Roumieh Prison one last time. I didn't have to, but I need him to know what he'd done. What he caused. The pain he left behind in all of us. Especially in Lexi and show him what Lexi wrote in the letter.

He could have saved her.

"You're back," Charlie sneers, his tone laced with mockery. "Where's that firecracker?"

I can't hold it in anymore. Tears slip out of the corners of my eyes, the rage and grief overwhelming me. "She's dead, you fucking asshole! She killed herself!"

"No," Charlie shakes his head, tears welling up. "You're lying."

"I'm not." My voice breaks. I take the letter out of my pocket and hand it to him. "Read it. She hung herself. You did this to her. You!"

"No," he shouts, his face contorting with pain. "No, she wouldn't... she's not." He takes the letter and scans through it. Tears fall from his eyes and for once a soft side of him shows. Charlie's voice cracks, his eyes flooded with tears. "I don't know what to say. I never meant any of it. I loved her..."

Snatching the letter back, I pocket it. "Not enough. You killed her Charlie, and now, you have to live with what you caused. Nothing can bring her back."

"But..."

"There's no but, Charlie. Lexi left us. If only you didn't open your fucking mouth, she'd still be with us." My voice continues to break and tears continue to fall. My eyes scan him. Rage cripples my bones, I want to hit him, to hurt him, but I can't. I don't have the strength anymore to fight. "She loved you. She was in love with you. And you broke her heart."

My last words make an impact. He gets up and thrashes at the table, throws the chair and shouts so loud, guards rush in to hold him down. He falls to the floor in utter defeat. Glancing at him, we meet in a final goodbye and I depart from the prison with my heart shattered.

Arriving at the gravesite, I spot Davina standing with her parents. Everyone is present ready for the funeral, but I have no energy to stand, instead I crouch, my body trembling with emotion.

I cry, my hands clutching at the earth. "Lexi! Why did you leave me?"

The priest's voice blurs on... My gaze drops to the ground, then drifts to the casket, and suddenly, without warning, a memory bubbles up from when Lexi and I were kids.

"Lexi, it's too high," I said, clutching the rough bark of the tree trunk, staring up at the dizzying height above us.

Lexi grinned from a branch just above, one leg swinging freely in the air. "Don't be a scaredy cat, Roger. We're not climbing a mountain. It's just a tree."

"A tall tree," I muttered, my arms tightening around the trunk.

"Yes, tall. But you're strong." She leaned forward, eyes sparkling with mischief. "Come on, you have to see the view."

I glanced down at my shoes. "Can't we see it from down here?"

She laughed, that carefree, stubborn laugh. "Nope. Come on!" She reached down with her hand, daring me to take it.

My eyes open slowly, the sting of tears catching me off guard. She was always like that, pulling me up, challenging me, making me braver than I ever thought I could be.

And now she's gone.

The funeral reception finally winds down, and silence settles like dust. A deep breath escapes with the ache in my heart while my gaze lingers on the gravestone: Lexi's name carved in marble, a final reminder that she will never be around for the rest of my life.

There's an emptiness where she used to be.

Thirty-One

♥

Davina

It's been six months since Lexi's funeral.

Watching Roger unravel under the weight of his grief was a stark reminder that even in death, someone's presence can linger, reshaping the lives they leave behind.

I never liked her. Never pretended to. But I didn't think she'd take her own life, not like that.

Not after everything.

Especially considering what I went through in high school... what she forced me into.

Roger told me about the letter. She said she was sorry. I understand, in a way.

But it still felt sudden. And no matter how I try to process it, I never thought she'd be the one to do this.

No one should have to carry that kind of pain, not even an enemy.

And yet, I often caught myself wondering: why? Why did she do it? What finally broke her? I had questions, but Roger and I never spoke about it.

The funeral is still vivid in my mind: the scent of incense thick in the air, Arabic prayers echoing gently between quiet sobs. I hadn't wanted to go. I never saw her as a friend. To me, she was an enemy, someone who tormented me. But I went for Roger. Because I cared about him. Still do.

My parents came with me; I couldn't face it alone. Standing among people who knew and loved her was disorienting. And Roger... he barely looked at me. A quick, hollow, "Thank you for coming." Then, he turned away, back to her family.

The service was held in the small, sunlit courtyard of Our Lady of Lebanon, tucked in the heart of the city. The air was crisp. The sky, a pale grey, as if even the weather mourned her. Lexi's tombstone stood out from the rest: polished black granite, her name etched in elegant Arabic script, with the English translation just beneath.

LEXI ALEXANDRA BARNES
"RESTING IN THE PEACE OF CHRIST."
DAUGHTER AND FIANCÉ

The grave was adorned with yellow lilies and roses: her favorite color, we were told. A tall cross stood behind the headstone, a quiet symbol of her faith. My parents and I stood off to the side, near a group of unfamiliar faces, mostly older people: aunts, uncles, distant relatives, family friends.

"God have mercy on her soul," Dad murmured, gently taking my hand.

As the final prayers ended, the crowd began to disperse.

Dad touched my arm, his voice low but firm. "We should go. I don't think Roger's ready to talk."

Mom nodded, adding softly, "He needs time, honey. Give him that."

They led me away, my legs unsteady, my thoughts spinning. But just before reaching the car, I turned back for one last look.

Six months later, and it still feels like yesterday. Roger, shoulders slumped, head bowed, fingers tracing the edge of her tombstone like he was trying to hold on to whatever was left of her.

But he never reached out. No calls. No texts. Nothing.

Maybe after how we left things, he assumed I moved on. Maybe he believes I did. Every day, I thought about messaging him, and every day, I stopped myself.

Now, there's silence.

I've written and rewritten a hundred versions of a message. Some short. Others raw. But I always delete them. Because the truth is I don't know what to say.

Instead, I sit on my bed, eyes fixed on the cluttered surface of my dresser, pretending to plan for my date with Eddy. My heart's not in it. Not the planning. Not the date.

Still, I go through the motions. Pulling out a simple dress, tossing it on the bed beside me. It feels more like checking off a task than getting ready for something meaningful.

Eddy and I have been seeing each other for months as friends. Light moments, cheek kisses, lingering hugs, laughter over late-night coffee runs. Nothing serious. But tonight feels... different. It feels like he wants something more because he is taking me to dinner. With his mother.

I can't tell what unsettles me more: dinner with his mom or that I know I only want him as a friend.

And it's not just any mother. It's Jennifer Mead: my former psychologist. The woman who knows everything about me. Who once handed me tissues while I unraveled in her office. And now, she'll be sitting across from me at dinner.

And Eddy...

And whatever this is.

I can't help spiraling.

Why does she want to join us? Is it some kind of twisted approval? Did she push him toward me? Is this dinner some strange form of therapy?

The truth is I still love Roger.

Looking at the dress, thinking about tonight, I know I'm being unfair to Eddy. He deserves more than I can give. But I already told him where we stand, and we are ONLY friends.

I've tried convincing myself I'm ready to move on. But I'm not. Tonight, before it goes any further, I need him to understand and realize my true intentions with him. I already told Mrs. Mead I'm still in love with Roger but she dismissed my comment. I think the real reason I stopped therapy with her was because she was trying to convince me to end it with Roger and concentrate on her son.

I take a shaky breath, glancing at my reflection in the mirror. I'm not looking forward to this dinner. Just as I'm about to walk out the door, my phone rings.

Roger's name flashes across the screen, and my heart stumbles.

Freezing mid-step, my fingers tighten around the doorknob. Without thinking, I swipe to answer.

"Hello," I say, catching my breath, heart pounding.

"Hey, Klutz. I'm so happy you picked up." His voice carries relief, maybe, or longing. "How are you?"

I swallow, forcing calm into my tone. "Good. You?"

"I've been better."

There's a pause. His words land like a ton of bricks dropped in still water, impossible to ignore.

"I miss you, Klutz."

A lump swells in my throat. "I'm sorry," I murmur.

"No, Davina. I'm sorry for not being there. I'm sorry for not reaching out," he says, voice tight. "I just... needed time. To adjust. It was too much and I—I pushed you away and I'm sorry."

I lean against the doorframe, nodding even though he can't see me. "It's okay. I understand," I reply gently.

"No, it's not okay," he says quickly. "I love you, Klutz. It's always been you."

My knees nearly give out, blinking back the rush of tears. "I love you too," I whisper.

A pause stretches between us.

"So... you're not with anyone?" he asks.

"No," I say without hesitation.

"Good," he breathes. "I'd like us to talk. If that's okay?"

"Sure."

I glance down at the dress crumpled in my hand, guilt twisting in my gut.

"But I've got a dinner."

The lie forms easily. An out. A delay.

I stop myself. No. Not with him.

"Maybe after?"

"A dinner?" he asks slowly. "Is it serious?"

"No," I blurt. "It's nothing like that. I'm just being polite." I pause, pressing a hand to my forehead. "I'd rather see you, to be honest. Eddy and I are friends. He knows that. I know that. It's...

it's his mother. She thinks something else is going on. She's been pushing it."

I hear his soft exhale, maybe even a smile in it.

"Okay," Roger says. "If that's the case, call me after dinner?"

"Of course," I agree, a small smile pulling at my lips. "I can't wait."

He breathes out, like he's been holding it in this whole time. "Davina, I have missed you so much, and my life, no matter how hectic, with you in it, is better. I never stopped loving you, Klutz."

"As much as I love hearing those words, and by God I do, it's a bit hard. We're not just a passerby relationship, we're a forever match. Our love will outlast life itself. And, I know, you in my life, is all I ever wanted..."

"I can't wait to see you."

Hanging up the phone, everything inside me shifts. In just a few minutes, my world feels different: lighter, clearer. I believe now, more than ever, Roger and I are meant to be. That we could be happy. Truly happy. Gently, I sling my bag over my shoulder, and head for the door, content at our future together.

Stepping outside, I spot Eddy waiting in his car. He sees me and gives a quick honk of the horn. That's new. Caught off guard, I freeze. Eddy used to get out of the car and greet me with a smile, always, maybe even offer his hand to help me in.

But not tonight. Tonight, he's different.

I shake it off, brushing the unease aside.

Maybe he's distracted.

Maybe he's in a rush.

Maybe we're late for dinner with his mother.

Deep down, though, I know it doesn't matter. Whatever the reason, it only confirms what I already feel in my gut. Tonight, will be the last time I see him and his mother.

I'm certain of it.

Thirty-Two

♥

Roger

Drowning myself in my university obligations, is easier than facing the gaping hole Lexi left behind. My parents watch me with sadness etched into their faces. Their grief not just for Lexi, but for me too.

After the funeral, Jiddo never spoke to me about family obligations and the elections or a possible new wedding venture. He left us, went back to his mansion, and closed himself off for a while before he moved out.

I kind of condemn him for Lexi's death. He was adamant about our marriage. He didn't stop to think what this would mean for us, or the impact it would have on us.

Six months passed.

My parents finally decided to get away. They said it was to clear their minds, to step away from the suffocating settling over the house since the funeral. I don't blame them. They deserve some kind of peace, even if I can't find it myself.

Losing Lexi the way we did made me think about Davina. It's not easy to stay away from her, especially since she's the best thing that ever happened to me and I never stopped loving her no matter how hard my parents and Jiddo pushed me to be with Lexi.

Jiddo and I need to talk. It's the right time, before I lose Davina forever. I will certainly not forgive myself if that happens.

I make my way down a long hallway toward Jiddo's study. His voice echoes faintly in the distance, and as I walk, guards specially trained by the military patrol the halls. Their sharp eyes follow me, but they nod in recognition, knowing who I am.

Jiddo has transformed his study into a refuge, a secure home for any disaster. The door opens, revealing him seated at a large desk cluttered with maps, documents, and monitors.

His eyes meet mine. "Roger, nice of you to come!"

"Jiddo," I reciprocate. We embrace, the hug warm but brief.

"It's been a while. How are you?" he asks, his hands still on my shoulders as if to steady me.

"Good, you?" I answer.

"Good."

We sit next to each other on the couch in the study. Glancing around, it looks different from the time I was here last and I'm not sure why. And as much as I've been drowning, it's good to see him too.

"Jiddo, what is all this? Why are there more security guards than before?"

He sighs, unsure how to put into words what's been gnawing at him. "We have some increased threats, more urgent and dangerous. I've been targeted, shot at, money stolen from my accounts and more pressing matters, threats against you. I wanted to wait for your parents to come so we could talk about this, but it's okay. I'll tell you now."

He doesn't flinch, his expression unreadable. "What's going on?"

"Has your father ever spoken about his past? About another woman?"

"No, Jiddo." Then I remember our chat about a woman. "I mean, yeah, he told me about an important woman in his life... another woman, a previous relationship."

He doesn't say anything right away. Instead, he leans back in his chair, studying me for a moment. "She was important to him."

The words hit harder than I expect. I open my mouth to respond, but nothing comes out. "How—"

He cuts me off. "She was pregnant."

I hesitate. "I have a sibling?"

He sighs. "You had."

"I don't understand, Jiddo," I say, my voice quieter than intended. "What are you trying to tell me?"

He breathes out slowly, his eyes filled with pain. "What I'm about to share... it could break your world and everything you hold dear. But with how dangerous things are, it's time to tell you." He pauses, his voice tight, like he's fighting to get the words out. "I was really hoping your parents would be here to help me tell you the story about your sibling, but I can't seem to get them on the phone."

"What the hell's going on, Jiddo?" I ask, frustrated.

"Oh, God, dear boy..." He sighs heavily. "Ever since Jennifer came into our lives, she's been a plague."

"Who?" My stomach sinks.

"Jennifer Mead," he reveals, strained.

"The woman who called Dad recently?"

"What do you mean recently?"

I pause, trying to piece it all together. "Dad came to see me. We took a drive to talk about family duties and whatever. Then, some woman called him but he never answered. I saw her name on his phone, but never asked. Who the hell is she?"

"Your father had an affair with her," Jiddo informs me, dropping the news like a bombshell.

"What?" I whisper, shocked. "Does Mom know?"

"She never knew," Jiddo replies, shaking his head.

"What happened to her, to my sibling?"

Jiddo breathes out, his chest rising and falling with each troubled breath. He gets up from the bed and starts pacing back and forth across the room. Every step he takes, every movement, feels like it's shaping the very core of my life, and I can't escape the sinking feeling that whatever he says next will change everything.

"My boy," Jiddo says with regret. "When your father had an affair with Jennifer, it was a time when he and your mother were having problems. And, when your mother was unable to conceive. He loved your mother, but he wasn't happy without children. He wanted someone to carry the Hoards legacy, like I always taught him. He met Jennifer at the Roache Rock, and soon they were spending every waking hour together."

He turns to face me and steps into my space. "He thought I never knew about his extracurricular activities, but I had him followed because he was my son and I wanted him safe."

"Oh, God," I mutter, my mind racing.

Jiddo sits back down in his chair. "He told me about her. The bombshell she dropped on him about being pregnant. I never knew or believed it was true. I mean, anyone would say anything for money."

"Okay, so, was she?" I asked, not sure if I wanted to know the answer.

He gulps, his face tense, trying to keep his emotions in check. "We forced her to abort the baby."

"Why?"

"Because of you," he says, his eyes meeting mine.

"Me?" I can barely breathe.

"Yes, habibi, you." Jiddo's voice is heavy with regret.

"Why, Jiddo? Why would you do that?" My heart pounds anger in me.

"Because we didn't want you to grow up knowing you have a sibling from another mother," he admits. "It's not something we ever wanted or planned. And, your father was never going to leave you and your mother, no matter how much he liked Jennifer."

"Oh my God!" My voice trails off, panic rising in my chest. "Charlie said someone paid him... Please, tell me that has nothing to do with..."

"It was her," Jiddo confirms with regret. "I had my people investigate."

"Why do that to Davina?" I cry out, my breath catching in my throat. "She has nothing to do with us, with our family."

"But she loves you, doesn't she?" Jiddo presses with a knowing sadness.

"Oh, my God! Davina is at dinner with her now!" I gasp, the realization hitting me like a punch to the gut.

His eyes widen. "You need to go. She's evil. I don't trust this dinner is innocent. Nothing with her ever is. And, Roger, find your parents. She knows where they are, I'm sure of it."

"Do I go with the police?" I ask urgent.

"I'll tell them. Just go, and they will follow you. Go!"

I don't waste another second. I rush out of Jiddo's house, my heart racing, knowing I have to save Davina, my family, and everything that's still left of us.

Arriving at Jennifer's house, I see a bunch of people outside. Without fear, I storm inside, my heart racing.

"Where is she?" I shout.

Thirty-Three

♥

Davina

We finally arrive at his Mom's house. I glance over at Eddy, my stomach tight with unease. "Is everything okay?" I ask, but he doesn't respond.

He walks ahead of me, not even acknowledging me with a glance, like we're not here together at all. There's something so off about his behavior, and my mind starts to spin with questions. But I try my best to shove those thoughts away, pushing them aside for now.

"Davina," Mrs. Jennifer calls warmly, breaking my focus. "It's so nice to have you here with us. Please, have a seat. Dinner will be served shortly. We have a few more guests coming, but they'll need a bit of time to get here."

I nod, taking a seat as she motions for me to sit. Despite her warm welcome, a small knot of worry still lingers in my chest. Eddy's coldness is impossible to ignore, and I can't help but wonder what's going on with him.

"Thanks for the invite," I say as I sit at the table, trying to push away the unease that's building in my chest.

Suddenly, the door opens, and I see Roger's mother and father being dragged in by two big men. They're placed roughly in the chairs at the table. The two beefy men tie both their hands and legs to the chair and Roger's parents' expressions are a mix of confusion and fear. My heart skips a beat, and a rush of terror floods my thoughts.

What is happening?

Before I can react, I grab for my phone from my bag, needing to call someone, anyone, but in a swift movement, Eddy snatches it from my hands.

"Hey! Give it back!" I demand panic rising in my voice.

He doesn't say a word. Instead, he hands my bag over to Mrs. Jennifer, a calm look on his face as if nothing is wrong. But everything feels wrong. What the actual fuck is going on here?

"Who were you going to call, my dear?" Mrs. Jennifer asks, mocking me. But I don't answer. I don't know who I was going to call, but I knew what my heart wanted. "You were going to call Roger?" she continues arching her eyebrows. "No need. I'll text him from your phone shortly. But for now, we're all going to have dinner. Then, I will tell you a story."

My mind races, my heart pounding in my chest. "What's going on? Why are they tied up? What is this?" I demand, panic slipping through my voice.

"Eddy, be a doll and slap her," Mrs. Jennifer commands.

Eddy moves toward me, his expression unreadable, and I freeze. The sound of his hand striking my face rings through the room. The tears on Roger's parents' faces are impossible to ignore.

We're not getting out of here alive, that much is certain.

"So, where was I?" Mrs. Jennifer muses. "Ah, yes. The story. Eddy, have a seat beside Davina. We don't want her acting up, now, do we?"

"No, babe, we don't," Eddy responds, flat.

"Babe? Ew!" I recoil, horrified.

"Oh, right." Jennifer laughs. "You think you're dating my son?"

"He's not your son?" I ask, a knot of confusion forms in my stomach.

"I'm not even related to her," Eddy replies, calm but bored. "I'm an actor. I was hired by Jennifer to play a part."

Tears begin to well up in my eyes. "So, what—what does that mean?" I choke out.

"That means you were a game," Jennifer answers, cold.

"You're sick. You're supposed to be a psychologist!" I shout, my voice trembling with disbelief.

Jennifer smirks. "Right, that's a lie, too. Well, I studied to be that, but I never qualified. And when your parents were desperate, I lied."

"This can't be happening!" I yell, my voice breaking. "This is not supposed to be this way."

"Oh, honey, it's happening," Jennifer replies, her voice thick with venom.

"Let them go! They have nothing to do with this," I plead desperately.

She laughs, an evil, chilling laugh echoes through the room like the sound of death. "They're the reason this is happening. He actually is the reason," she emphasizes, her finger pointing at Roger's father with hatred.

"What did he do to you?" I ask, my voice shaking with confusion.

"What didn't he do?" Jennifer snarls with rage.

"I don't understand. What are you talking about?" I cry, the tears finally spilling over, blurring my vision. I can't keep it together anymore. I need answers.

"This started the year they got married. He wasn't very happy at home when he met me. We were at each other's houses for a long time. Every time he told her he was working late, we were fucking—like wild animals," Jennifer spits.

Mrs. Hoards turns to Mr. Hoards, her eyes narrowing. He nods, saying nothing, but the weight of guilt in his silence is visible. His heart is breaking, and I can see it clearly on his face.

"Well, one night, I found out I was pregnant. And guess what? She was pregnant with Roger too," Jennifer continues, a bitter smirk forming on her lips.

Mr. Hoards tries to speak, but before he can get a word out, Jennifer slaps him hard, the sound echoing in the room. "Say nothing, honey. Because the next part is the best," she says, unforgiving.

"Oh, the baby you told me about," I say instinctively, trying to offer some comfort.

"Yes," she retorts, coldly.

"I'm sorry, Jennifer. I am. No one should go through that."

She rolls her eyes dismissively. "Whatever. Roger's Jiddo murdered my baby. He murdered it before I could even find out if I had a girl or a boy. He took the one thing away from me, the baby I wanted to hold, touch, kiss, and raise. They took my baby from me and what hurts the most, is that I really wanted to have a baby, even if he didn't want to be in the baby's life. I wanted it."

My heart breaks at her story. I want to help her, to tell her it's okay, but the next few words out of her mouth shatter my soul.

"And Davina, after that, I declared revenge on their family and everyone and everything they care about."

I can barely breathe, my chest tightening. Her words cut so deep, they feel like they're sinking into my skin, into my bones.

"But you don't get to hurt me because of what they did to you," I insist, the words barely leaving my throat.

Jennifer scoffs.

"Oh, and Davina," Eddy says, his voice too close, too intimate as he leans into me, whispering in my ear. "You taste like sweet caramel."

My blood runs cold, and I freeze, remembering the incident with Charlie. "What did you just say to me?" I ask, trembling.

Eddy smirks. "I think you heard me, my sweet caramel." He stands up, walking over to Jennifer with an unsettling confidence. I can't even process the words that leave his lips next. "Who do you think paid Charlie to destroy you, so you wouldn't be with Roger anymore?"

My heart stops. It feels like my entire world is crumbling beneath me. My breath catches, and I can barely hold it together. The news hits me like a ton of bricks.

"You paid him?" I ask, a faint whisper escaping my lips.

Jennifer locks eyes with me. "Of course, I did. He broke you, didn't he? You didn't let another guy touch you, not even Eddy. But tonight... tonight, Eddy will finish you off so that Roger will never be able to come near you again."

The words sting, cutting through everything I thought I knew. I can't breathe. I can't think. This isn't just about revenge anymore. This is about destroying everything I am. I'm not tied like the

Hoards are, so I get up and bolt for the door, desperate to escape this nightmare.

But just as my fingers brush the handle, I'm slammed into the door, my body jerking painfully against it. The impact rattles through me, sending sharp waves of pain through my bones. My head spins with the force of it.

A wave of dizziness washes over me. My vision blurs as I stumble back. I try to steady myself, but it's no use—my body betrays me, crashing down onto the cold floor. Strong hands are on me, lifting me up, their grip rough. The world spins, fading in and out of focus.

I hear Mr. Hoards shout. "Let her go, Jennifer, she's not part of this. She's innocent." He pleads.

"My baby was innocent, too," Jennifer spits out.

My eyelids feel heavy. I slip into unconsciousness and everything goes black.

Thirty-Four

♥

Davina

A while later, consciousness creeps back in. My head throbs. My eyes flutter open. I realize I'm not where I was before. Panic sets in when I notice my hands and legs are tied firmly to the corners of a bed. The cold air prickles my skin. I feel exposed, dressed in nothing but my bra and underwear.

I turn my head, my breath hitching, and see Eddy sitting at the edge of the bed. His face is a mask, his expression cold, detached. It's not the face of the man I met at the bakery, the one who gave me shy smiles, who made me believe I meant something to him. That man doesn't exist anymore, or maybe he never did.

This Eddy is someone else entirely. He's dark. Sinister. He's not his own person; he's Jennifer's pawn, her puppet. I pull at the restraints, struggling, testing their strength, but they don't budge. My heart pounds in my chest.

Is this it for me? Will I never see Roger again?

Eddy just sits there, watching me with empty eyes. "Glad you're awake for the next part," he says, calculated.

Fear grips my chest. "What are you talking about? What part, Eddy?"

"The part where I shatter you." His words are deliberate.

"No, please, don't..." I plead, my voice cracking. "Why are you doing this?"

He leans forward, his eyes devoid of anything. "Because I like it. The way Charlie liked it. I like it too."

"No, Eddy. Please, don't do this. Please." Tears stream down my face, my pleas coming out in sobs.

"You know what, Davina?" he questions with malice. "I thought it was going to be easy enough to destroy you and then dump you, but you never gave yourself to me. So, we're going to have to resort to this."

"This?" I choke out. "What's this?"

He stands, his shadow looming over me. "You'll see..." The threat roars in my ears.

Eddy walks up to me and sits by my face. He caresses my cheek, but there's no tenderness in his touch. He leans down, planting an aggressive kiss on my lips. The force of it steals my breath, and I struggle.

"Yummy," he sneers, licking his lips. "Caramel tears."

"Stop," I gasp, my voice breaking as I glare at him. "You're not this evil."

A sharp clank of heels echoes through the hallway, coming closer. Jennifer steps into the room, with a wicked grin.

"Isn't he?" she taunts, her voice dripping with venom. "He so is, honey bun."

Without hesitation, she grabs Eddy by the collar, pulling him to her. Their lips crash together in an intimate, grotesque display, devouring each other. I turn my face away, nausea roiling in my stomach. My heart pounds violently.

"Why are you doing this?" I beg, my voice cracking. I try to keep my breathing steady, but panic threatens me. My eyes dart between Jennifer and Eddy.

Jennifer's expression shifts into a mocking smirk. "Because, darling, I want to hurt Roger. He doesn't deserve a happy ending, and neither do you."

Tears sting my eyes at her words. "What did I ever do to you?"

"Nothing," Jennifer replies coolly. "Nothing honey. You're involved with the son of the family who took my baby from me, is all. You're a means to an end, and you will enjoy yourself."

I can't hold back the sobs anymore. "No, please. I'll leave. I'll never see Roger again. I swear it. You don't have to do this."

Jennifer lets out a dark, throaty laugh. "I'm not going to do it to you. Eddy will. He deserves this after how you strung him along."

My head snaps toward Eddy. "But I didn't!" I cry out.

"Yes, you did," Eddy spits out.

My heart shatters into pieces. There's no way out. Hopelessness crushes me as I realize what's coming. If I don't submit, if I don't just let this happen, the aftermath will consume me. The fear that Roger, the one person I desperately need right now will never be able to touch me again, to hold me without this memory tainting every moment, takes root in my mind.

"Okay," I gasp out. "Okay, I'll do it."

Eddy narrows his eyes, confusion shadowing his face. "You'll do what?" he asks.

"I'll sleep with you," I say, barely holding myself together. "If that's what you want me to do."

"What?" He steps back slightly. Jennifer, on the other hand, erupts into a sharp, gleeful laugh. Jennifer's voice cuts through the air like a blade.

I steady my breathing, meeting Eddy's bewildered gaze. "Jennifer said she wants to break me, and you do too," I say, forcing my voice to sound genuine. "I accept, I might as well. I don't know if Roger and I will ever come together and I liked you, I really did, I still do, so—okay. Let's do this."

Jennifer's eyes narrow at me with suspicion. "Is this a trick?" she asks.

Shaking my head, slowly, I whisper, "No trick. I'm done fighting. You win."

I squeeze my eyes shut, a desperate attempt to block out Eddy's cold gaze, and Jennifer's venomous smirk. I tell myself I need to get this over with and trick myself into believing it's what I want.

Letting go of hoping this will end any other way, I bury my dignity. Maybe then, I can move on.

"Great," Jennifer exclaims. "I'll leave you to it, kids." She strides out of the room without another glance, as the door closes behind her.

The silence that follows is deafening. I glance at Eddy, expecting him to leap into action, but his expression is no longer filled with the sinister delight he'd shown earlier. Instead, his face is etched with something unexpected, sadness.

He stands there, frozen, as if he doesn't know what to do next. He's avoiding my eyes entirely.

"What are you waiting for?" I ask.

Eddy doesn't speak. The room feels heavier now. I can't read him, but his demeanor is different as if he now understands what he has been doing all along.

Suddenly, the silence shatters as a loud commotion erupts from outside the room. My heart races, and then I hear it, a voice I'd been aching to hear, filled with raw anger.

"WHERE IS SHE?!" Roger shouts, his voice bellowing through the house.

My savior has come for me. Thank God!

Eddy glances at me, his face unreadable. Without a word, he moves toward me, his hands working swiftly to untie the restraints around my wrists and ankles.

Soon I'm free, scrambling to my feet, my heart pounding. He hands me my dress, and I pull it on quickly. I don't know why he's doing this, why he's helping me, but I can't afford to question it now.

I move toward him, my arms trembling as I wrap him in a tight hug, whispering, "Thank you."

He glares at me, and climbs out of the window, running away. My heart aches at his act of kindness but I'm worried I'll see him again.

Here's hoping I won't...

Thirty-Five

♥

Roger

My words barely leave my mouth before my eyes lock onto the scene before me. My heart stops taking in the horrifying sight. Both of my parents are tied to chairs at the dinner table, their faces exhausted.

But Davina...

Davina's nowhere to be seen. "Where is she?!" I shout, my voice raging with anger, because all that matters is to have Davina in my arms.

"Roger, nice of you to join us," Jennifer belches out with mockery. "Your parents are a bit tied up, and Davina is a bit busy."

My fists clench with rage. "Let my parents go!"

"I would," Jennifer says with a smirk. "But I don't want to."

She throws a mocking glance at my parents, lips curling in a glorifying successful smile. "And you're going to pay for what you did to me."

"What about what you did to Davina?" I snap. My fury boils over. "This ends now." My parents' eyes widen. "Charlie told me. You paid him."

She smirks. "No, he didn't. But you figured it out, didn't you, Roger?"

"Where is Davina?"

"Oh, she's with Eddy. She's servicing his every need," she claims, taunting me, aiming to hurt me, but I stay grounded because I can't let her get to me. I need her to understand, she's got no hold on us anymore.

"Jennifer, look at me," I prod, trying to get her attention.

She turns, expression flat. "What do you want?"

"I'm sorry for what Jiddo did to you," I say, telling her what she wants to hear. Not because I mean it, I don't but I want my family safe. "Even for what my father put you through—but your fight is with them, not with me. Not with Davina. And not with my mother. Please... just stop."

She giggles and turns back to my father. "Why don't you tell your son what happened between us? Go on tell your wife too. You would've left her for me... if she hadn't gotten pregnant with Roger."

My father looks away, unable to meet my eyes. He knows I see the guilt. I let her think she's won, playing along with her twisted game buying time until the police arrive. Assuming Jiddo actually called them.

"Dad, is this true? What she's saying, is it real?" I ask, trying to mask the hesitation in my voice. I might not sound convincing.

Whatever he did, I won't hate him for it. He had his reasons.

He glares at me, silent, until she rips the tape from his mouth. He groans in pain.

"Yes, Roger. Son... it's true."

My mother's face crumples with betrayal.

A message pops up on my phone. Thank God I silenced it before coming here. The last thing I need is for her to take it. I glance down pretending to look at the floor.

JIDDO

Police on the way. ETA 2 min.

I don't reply. She can't know I have it.

"Dad... how could you?" My voice breaks through the quiet, sharp and unforgiving even though I already knew about it from my chat with dad the other day.

My pulse quickens. The seconds pound like drums in my head. I pray they show up before anything spirals further.

She opens her mouth to speak, but nothing comes.

The door slams open.

Chaos explodes into the room as police officers pour in, shouting commands. She spins around, stunned, but it's too late. They're on her in seconds. Her protests are lost in the noise.

Then, through the anarchy, I see her, my Klutz, running toward me, her eyes wide with relief. My heart swells.

Without hesitation, I wrap her in my arms as if letting go would mean losing her all over again. She trembles against me, and I tighten my hold. "God, I thought I lost you," I whisper, my voice cracking, kissing her passionately. "I love you, Klutz."

She kisses me back, murmuring, "I love you too, Roger. I can't believe you came for me."

"Of course, I would. You're the love of my life, Davina. You're all that matters to me."

She whimpers, tears falling from her eyes. "God, I love you so much!"

My heart is whole again as I hold Davina close, realizing how much I've missed her. For the first time in what feels like forever, I let myself breathe her in; the warmth, the comfort, and the relief.

While holding onto her, we see Jennifer being dragged off by the officers. The reality of everything sets in like a weight on my chest.

It's over.

It's finally over and we can be us again.

My parents' faces are pale from what they've endured. Their hands still shake slightly, even though they're free. Their eyes meet mine, but there's a distance. Like something's been broken beyond repair. But we can mend it. However long it takes, we'll be able to mend it now that we have a chance.

Grabbing onto Davina tighter, I pull her into me, not knowing if it's for her or for me. "Are we okay?" I whisper, mostly to myself.

She looks up at me, eyes wide, searching for the same answer. Maybe that's enough, for now because we made it together. "More than you know."

Thirty-Six

♥

Davina

My eyes flutter open, and I turn to see Roger beside me, still asleep. Calm washes over me, despite everything. Notwithstanding the chaos of the past few days, here we are.
Together.
Safe.

"Good morning," I greet him with a smile as he sits up in bed.

"Morning," he replies, returning my smile, holding onto me, cuddling me close.

"I can't believe everything that happened, can you?" I ask full of disbelief, still trying to process everything that happened to us until now.

"No, I can't, but that goes to show—love conquers all," he claims, squeezing me gently.

"It does." I grin, holding his gaze. "You know, before Jennifer, I wanted to talk..."

"Before you say anything, Davina. I would like to say something first," he says, and I give him my full attention. "I love you, Klutz, more than you know. I always have, and I always will," he confesses and my heart pounds in my chest.

I giggle, a teasing glint in my eye. "I hadn't noticed."

He laughs and tickles me. I squirm, diving under the covers in a playful escape.

"No, I'm serious," he says, as I catch my breath from the laughter. Reaching out, he takes my hand in his. "I want to spend the rest of my life with you."

My eyes widen and face lights up. "Me too," I murmur.

"No matter where I am, I will always love you," he tells me, pouring his heart out. "You are my life, Klutz. My one. My everything." He looks into my eyes. "Klutz, from the moment I met you, my life transformed in the most amazing way. I've made mistakes, but you have shown me the true meaning of love, and I thank you for saving me."

I'm stunned by his declaration, not because it's entirely unexpected, but because I hadn't anticipated it. I kiss him, passionately. My eyes shimmering, squeezing his hand, giving him the encouragement he needs.

"I can't imagine my future without you," he confesses, holding me close.

My breath catches in my throat. "What's going on, Roger?" He bites his lip.

Slipping out of bed, he retrieves something from the inside of his jacket. Glancing at it, I see a white box. He kneels and my heart races as he opens the box.

I gaze at it as if it's the only thing shining in the room. Time pauses. Sunlight filters gently through the window, and a soft breeze dances with the curtains. Looking around, I imagine our future: children laughing, happiness shared, hands entwined in quiet companionship. I see us as a married couple, side by side, living a peaceful life.

Then he looks into my eyes and asks, "Will you marry me?"

A radiant smile spreads across my face, and tears of joy well up in my eyes. I love him, deeply. He's the best thing that's ever happened to me.

But I'm not ready. Not yet.

It's all so sudden, especially after everything we've been through. I still need time to understand myself, to understand him as my boyfriend, and us as a couple.

And what about his parents? His Jiddo? I don't even know how they feel about me.

With my face still, I quietly respond, "No."

His mouth falls open in shock. He forces himself to meet my eyes, searching, pleading for an explanation. Slowly, he sinks back onto the edge of the bed and slips the ring box into his pocket.

It's like a punch to the gut, knocking the air from his lungs. I can feel it. I understand. But this isn't about love, it's about what we've been through to get here. Marriage feels so final, almost like an ending, when it should feel like a beginning.

"What... what do you mean 'no'?" he whispers, barely audible.

I inhale deeply. "I'm not ready for such a big commitment, Roger. We've only just found our way back to each other."

"You can't be serious." His voice cracks. "After everything we've been through, you're saying no. Are you... are you breaking up with me?"

"No, Roger," I try to explain. "I love you. But do we need to be married, to have a title between us, can't we just be together?"

He nods with unspoken words. "I can't believe this is happening, but I understand." He takes me in an intimate embrace. "I get it."

"Wait." I shake my head. "I don't think you understand what I'm saying."

He reaches out to take my hand, his fingers intertwining with mine. Tears well up in our eyes. He went through a lot, and so did I. "Goodbye, Klutz."

I grab his arm and pull him close, my eyes searching his. "Don't go."

"Why not? You don't want to marry me."

"I don't want to marry you *now*," I emphasize, steady. "But I want to be with you, Roger. I love you."

"So, not married, but together? What life is that?"

My gaze is steady on his. "Do we have to label it?"

He looks at me, and for the first time, realizes labels don't matter. "I still want us, Roger. I never stopped wanting us. I am not ready for marriage, but I still love you and I always will."

Without a second thought, he pulls me closer to him, our bodies colliding, and our lips meeting in a tender kiss as we surrender to each other. "I've missed you so much, Klutz." He holds me in his arms.

"Roger, you're the best thing that has ever happened to me," I gasp. "I love you."

Our kiss lingers, a dance of desire. He gently lowers his mouth to my body. He puts my hands up above my head as he tickles me with his tongue. He presses his mouth firmly to mine.

With hunger in our eyes, he trails aggressive hands all over my body, making me squirm at his touch, begging him, egging him on to take me on my bed. Within moments, our clothes are off and his hands possess an innate understanding of my every curve as he slowly fingers me, heightening my arousal with every touch.

"The only fingers you'll ever have inside you, penetrating you, touching you, feeling you, Klutz, are mine."

His lips find their way to my erect nipples, his tongue and teeth teasing and taunting them. My gasps transform into moans of pleasure, escaping from the depths with his mouth enveloping me.

"Oh. God. Yes. Roger, yes," I cry out, unable to contain the ecstasy of my desire.

I grab ahold of him allowing him to press into me, our bodies one, as his hard cock sinks into me. Pumping harder and faster, a moment of joy with the momentum of forever in our veins. When we finally reach our maximum passion for pleasure, he explodes inside me, both of us realizing too late, we forgot the condom, in the heat of the moment.

He presses his lips to mine. "Klutz, that was fucking amazing."

"Yes, it was, Roger."

"We belong together, Davina. I have missed you so fucking much." He plays with my swollen nipples and I continue to gasp.

Looking up at him playful, I ask, "Another round?"

He laughs softly, shaking his head. "I wouldn't mind, but we have to visit my Jiddo. He wants to talk to you, officially."

I nod in understanding. "Okay. Let's get ready to go."

Thirty-Seven

♥

Roger

On our drive over to see my Jiddo, the memory of when I spoke to Davina's parents about her hand in marriage popped into my head. I should have known what they meant, technically what her Dad meant, but it didn't cross my mind.

In order to pull this off, I have to do the one thing I've been terrified to do: talk to Davina's parents. I want to spend the rest of my life with Davina. Gripping the steering wheel a little tighter, the decision grinds at my soul.

The closer I get to her house, the more my nerves kick in. I try to push the anxiety aside, but it's hard. I've never been good at these kinds of conversations. But this time feels different, I'm in love with Davina.

Pulling into the driveway, the house stands in the distance, glancing at me, as if mocking me, like everything hinges on what I'm about to do.

"Roger, what a surprise," her father says, placing a gentle hand on my back.

"Hi," I breathe out, shaking both of their hands as we make our way to the couch in the living room.

"Davina's not here," her mother informs me, her voice warm and inviting.

"I know. She told me about her... dinner," I say, glancing at her father.

"Okay," her father responds. "Why are you here?"

Her mother shoots him a look. "Honey, that's rude. Would you like a drink, Roger?"

"No, that's fine," I say, taking a deep breath, trying to steady myself. "I'm here to ask you something."

Her father leans back in the couch, folding his arms. "Ask us what, Roger?"

I feel the moment press against me. This is it. This is the point where I can either step forward or let everything slip away. I focus only on the words I need to say.

"I want to marry your daughter," I declare, full of emotion. "I love her. I'm in love with her. I never stopped loving her. She's the one for me. She's all I think about. She's all I want."

I pause, looking at them, searching for any sign of hesitation. But I don't see it.

"I know she's the best thing that has ever happened to me," I continue, my confidence growing.

Her mother places a hand on mine, a soft smile forming on her lips. "It's about time," she says.

There's still more to say, no matter how I feel. "I'm sorry I've been distant. Ever since Lexi's suicide, it's been hard to bounce back. But I love Davina. It's always been her. I don't want to lose her again."

Her father's face is troubling me. Maybe he doesn't believe me. Maybe he doesn't want us together, thinking Eddy is better for her. The silence between us is heavy, and his fixed gaze gives me no sign of whether he's considering my words or not. "So, you love Davina?" he asks, almost like an interrogation.

I nod, trying to steady my nerves. "Yes, I do. With all my heart."

His eyes never leave mine. "Does she love you?"

The question presses down, but before I can answer, her mother reaches for his arm, her expression confused. "What are you saying, honey?" she asks, clearly taken back by his words.

Her father doesn't break his stare. "I didn't say she doesn't love you, Roger. She does. But did you ask yourself what Davina wants? Maybe she's not ready for that kind of commitment, not yet anyway. I am giving you my blessing, and my wife will too, but think about her. Besides, when she needed you most, you weren't there. She went through so much before—how can we be sure you'll be there for her now, that you won't let her down again?"

The words hit me like a punch to the gut. The memory of it, how I failed her when she needed me most shatters me, breaking my heart all over again. But I can't let that show. I need him to know how much I love her. I need him to believe it.

"I—I know I wasn't there before and I've never regretted anything more in my life," I say, thick with emotion, "but I'm here now. I'm not going anywhere. I love her. She's the one for me."

She's, my Klutz.

"Well," he says, taking a deep breath and letting it go. I shove all my worries aside, focusing on him, but my nerves are still tight. My heart feels like it's about to break. The moment is crushing, will he say no? Will he tell me he doesn't approve? Or worse, will he tell me to fuck off?

The silence hangs in the air.

Then, finally, he speaks. "If that's what she wants..."

A wave of relief washes over me. All the tension that's been gripping me releases. I can hardly believe it.

I stand up, quickly pulling both of them into a hug, with the realization that Davina and I, my Klutz and I, are finally going to have our happily ever after.

"So, do I have your blessings?" I ask him again, hoping it's what I heard.

He chuckles, "Yes, Roger. You have our blessings. Welcome to the family, son."

Thirty-Eight

♥

Davina

We survived the war conducted against us, albeit a hectic, chaotic ride. My ordeal with Charlie, Roger's family secrets, and most surprisingly, Mrs. Jennifer Mead, our real life villain. It's about time her crimes were exposed for all to see.

From paying Charlie to sexually assault me, to her affair with Roger's father, and even orchestrating every little manipulation that tore us apart, Jennifer's crimes ran deep.

At the time, I thought I was never getting out. I felt trapped. But when I heard Roger's voice, my heart welled up, and my soul felt whole again.

"Where is she?!" he shouted, his voice laced with panic and fury. Struggling against the restraints, I stared at Eddy, silently begging, pleading with him to let me go. Deep down, I knew he was just another pawn in Jennifer's twisted game.

"Where is Davina?" Roger shouted again, his voice carrying through the house. It was desperate and loud enough for me to hear.

Eddy stumbled toward me, his hesitation clear, until he finally untied me. As he set me free, I turned to him and said, "I know why you did what you did, but haven't you thought that maybe she was using you? That maybe you weren't the one for her?"

He stayed silent, and I bolted while he climbed out the window.

I ran out of the room searching for the man I loved. Roger stood ready to fight. The police raided the house as I reached him, and I sprinted into his embrace.

That night, we retired from my house, finally safe. We survived. It was over. We could breathe, live, love, and just be together.

But even as peace settled in, a small part of me regretted his proposal. It wasn't that I didn't want to say yes, I did.

But the timing felt wrong, like it was forced by the chaos.

We're on our way to see his Jiddo. The tension is light in the car, letting me know there's something bothering him.

"What's wrong?" I ask gently.

Roger parks the car one street before the hospital entrance. His hands gripping the steering wheel tighter than usual. He turns to face me, his eyes glistening with a kind of emotion I have seen only once before.

"I thought I lost you, Davina."

"But you didn't."

"With everything we went through—I just, I couldn't live if you..."

"Hey, hey, hey," I interrupt, squeezing his hand. "Stop. Don't even say it. I'm right here. I'm here."

His chest rises and falls as he breathes deeply, trying to steady himself. "You are."

He sniffles, and I can see the pain lingering behind his eyes. The same pain I saw when I broke up with him after the Charlie incident making my chest tight.

"I love you, Klutz," he says, tender. "When this year began, I never thought I'd meet someone like you."

"When my university journey began, I wouldn't have thought we'd be together by the end, you goof," I reply, my voice barely above a whisper.

"Yeah, but you dropped out, I'm still there."

"That's true, I may come back one day to continue my studies, but for now, I'm happy."

He laughs, taking my hand in his. "You don't get it, Davina." He shakes his head, leaning closer. "You make me whole. You're the reason my heart is full again. You're the reason I can breathe, the reason I want to live."

Tears spill from my eyes as his words sink in. "Oh, Roger."

"I love you so much," he says, his voice cracking.

"You mean everything to me, Roger." Letting the tears flow, I pull him close, our hands tightly clasped together.

We kiss, holding onto each other.

He pulls back, looking down at me, hesitant. "So, erm, can you wear the ring?"

I blink, confused for a moment. "What? I thought we made things clear?"

"We did." He nods quickly, running a hand through his hair, his eyes not meeting mine for a second. "Jiddo sort of thinks you're already part of the family." He shrugs, shy.

I stare at him for a moment, trying to process what he's saying. He's nervous, I can see it in the way he's avoiding eye contact.

Rolling my eyes, I finally agree. Not that I'm thrilled about it. I mean, maybe a grand gesture would've been nice.

Something more than just, "please, put the ring on."

But, hell, I love him, and fuck it. "Hmmm, fine. If it's for your Jiddo, I'll wear it."

"Really?" He arches his eyebrows in disbelief.

"Yes." I give him a soft smile. "I will, for you, because I love you, Roger."

"Good to know, Klutz." A smirk tugs at his lips.

Arriving at his Jiddo's house, my heart skips a beat. It's huge. Nothing close to Roger's house. He parks and hands me the box. It's beautiful. The same box he proposed to me with. I take the ring and slip it on my finger. Roger takes my hand gently as we make our way.

"Roger!" his Jiddo exclaims, his face lighting up with joy. "Davina, how nice of you to come."

"Hi, Mr. Hoards," I say politely, though a bit nervous.

"Nonsense!" He gives me a wave of his hand. "Call me Jiddo. That's what Roger calls me." He pulls me into a firm but kind hug, catching me off guard.

"Sure, Jiddo," I manage with a small smile.

He looks between Roger and me. "Roger, do you mind if I have a word with Davina alone?"

Roger looks at me and I give him a nod of reassurance. "Sure, Jiddo," Roger replies. Leaning in, he plants a soft kiss on my lips before leaving us in his study, closing the door behind him on the way out.

"Have a seat." He gestures to the chair. "I won't be long, but I want you comfortable."

"Sure," I agree, as I settle into the seat.

"I want to first start by apologizing for everything you went through," he begins. "I never thought you'd be subjected to such madness. There was so much, we don't need to recall them all."

"Thank you."

"And I want to personally apologize," he continues with regret. "I judged you before getting to know you, and that was never my intention. But when it comes to family reputation... I wanted my grandson, I wanted Roger, to have the best."

"I understand and I love your grandson. A lot."

"He loves you too. I must say, I'm pleased to see you're wearing my late wife's wedding ring." He smiles. "She would have loved to meet you. And in a way, by wearing this ring, you're close to her."

I beam with joy, not realizing the significance until now. "Thank you, Jiddo."

"Roger's told me so much about you, Davina, and I truly believe you two are made for each other. Thank you for being so understanding."

I rise from my chair and hug him, holding him tight. "I'm always going to be understanding, no matter what the situation. My parents brought me up this way."

"Your parents raised you right. I believe you're both going to have a happy life," Jiddo tells me with warmth.

Roger walks in, a confident smile on his face. "Yes, we will, Jiddo. But for now, I'm going to take my fiancée to Feraya for a bit so we can have a small vacation."

I turn to him, eyebrows raised. "Vacation?"

"Oh, yeah," his Jiddo says. "The vacation."

"Yeah." He nods, grinning. "It's a surprise."

"A surprise?" I repeat, tilting my head skeptically.

"It is."

And it was... what can I say? A surprise I'll never forget.

Epilogue

♥

Roger

Our trip to Feraya was not because I needed to discover it. I already knew the place well. It's a favorite spot for us locals to ski, and unwind with friends and family. This time, though, it's about something more, it is about celebrating us: Davina and me.

Even though she's comfortable wearing the ring, it still doesn't feel official. Not yet.

Our parents came with us at first, hers and mine. But after a couple of days, they gave us space. My Klutz and I needed that. A break from the chaos that's been swirling around our families.

We explored the mountains, the hotel, and everything in between. I was surprised to learn that her mother had a house in her hometown. Before she left, she handed us the keys and we stayed there. The place still carried that familiar warmth, like it had been quietly waiting for us all along.

One evening, we take a quiet stroll through the village. The air is crisp, and the stars above twinkle like they are in on our secret. I turn to her, my boyish grin making her melt or at least that's what her expression tells me.

"Hey," I say. "Want to find a bookshop? We could grab some books and read together."

My words light her face up with joy and questions. "Books? You read now?" she asks, smiling at me.

"No, you read, and I want to be part of the things you enjoy," I say, playful. "Tomorrow, we can hit a bookstore in the city, if you like."

The truth? Something big is in motion. With her parents' help, I found out who her favorite author is. The best part? That author is coming to Feraya for her new series which has made splashes everywhere and it is a major event in Lebanon.

"Hmmm, what are you up to?" she asks, raising an eyebrow.

"Me? Nothing. Just making conversation with you, Klutz," I say with a grin. Hopefully, she doesn't catch on, though something in her look tells me she already has. "You don't trust me?"

"You're definitely up to something, mister."

"Nope," I say, hands raised in mock surrender. "I promise."

"Hmmm, okay, but I still have my doubts," she replies, eyeing me with suspicion and making me laugh.

From all the things happening in my life, this is the one I want to get right. It's not just about the surprise. It's about creating a moment that's hers and ours.

The next morning, I woke up early, made a few calls, and arranged for everything to be ready. I invited our parents to join us, even Jiddo would be there. Though he already knows we're together, I want this moment to be unforgettable for both of us.

Entering the bedroom, I find her still sound asleep, her chest rising and falling with each breath. Nerves tighten in my chest, I'm unsure how she'll respond. She returned the ring to me when we arrived to Feraya. Not out of a lack of love, but to remind me where we stood. But now, more than ever, it's clear: she's the one I want to spend my life with.

She slowly opens her eyes, trying to make sense of what's happening. Meanwhile, I'm rushing around like I'm about to win a marathon, or maybe a treasure hunt. Whatever it is, the chaos must be hilarious to watch. She starts laughing as I dart around the room, grabbing random things off the counter, clearly in a hurry but with no idea where I'm actually going.

"Are you really that excited to see the bookshop?" she teases, yawning as she lounges in bed.

"Get dressed. Or better yet—just throw something on. We're going to be late," I say, urgency buzzing through me.

"Late for what?" she asks, eyebrows knitting in confusion.

"Just... late," I insist, tugging gently at her arm. "Come on, Klutz. Please."

"Roger, it's just a bookshop," she says, rolling her eyes.

Panic rises in my chest. The bookstore manager had been clear to be on time. The author would only be there for an hour before heading off to her next stop. I couldn't risk missing her. Especially since she's Davina's favorite author.

"Please, Davina," I plead, my voice desperate.

"Fine," she sighs dramatically, rolling out of bed.

She grabs her bag, and I practically drag her out the door. She barely has time for coffee or breakfast as I race toward the bookstore. Pulling up, I can hardly stay still, bouncing in my seat with excitement. When we finally arrive and she steps out of the car, her jaw drops in shock.

"How the hell—what, wha—"

She's speechless, staring up at the massive banner hanging above the entrance, bold letters reading: WELCOME TO LEBANON MS. NIKKI A. LAMERS.

Davina pulls me into her arms, holding on tightly, tears shimmering in her eyes. Gazing into mine, she leans in and kisses me deep, full of feeling.

"I love you, Roger," she whispers. "This is the nicest thing anyone's ever done for me."

A broad smile pulls at my lips, brushing a strand of hair from her face. "There's more to come, Klutz."

I take her hand. "Let's go, we've got front row seats waiting for us."

As we make our way inside, an usher leads us to our seats. The place is packed, so many faces, so much energy. Then I spot our family behind the podium, holding flowers and cameras, all beaming. My heart starts to race, nerves flooding back. For a moment, I feel like I might actually faint.

"It's time to meet acclaimed author, Ms. Nikki Lamers," the host shouts. "Who's ready?"

Everyone waits until we hear the crowd go wild for Nikki's grand entrance. She holds her head high in grace. Davina cheers as Nikki walks, making her way to the platform. Nikki stands in the spotlight with a book stand and a massive banner show-casing her latest work. Her hair cascades down her shoulders, framing her face. Adding a touch of charm, she wears silver ear-rings inscribed with the word, summer and a necklace bearing the word, unforgettable.

"It's been wonderful being here. Thank you all for having me," Nikki proclaims.

The applause reverberates throughout the venue. Davina turns to me, her eyes widen with admiration and excitement. "She's amazing," she whispers.

I respond with a small chuckle, my eyes shining with af-fection as I reach for her hand, interlacing our fingers in a supportive grip. "Yeah. And, here, let's go meet her."

She nods. "Are you serious? Ok." A radiant smile lights up her face.

Returning our focus to the book stand where Nikki is waiting for her fans, Davina walks in her direction. It's now or never. Approaching, she takes a deep breath.

"Hi," she greets Nikki, beaming. "I'm such a huge fan. I have read all of your books, and this series is my favorite. I never felt such emotions until I stumbled on your books. My favorite is book 1, but that is because it is the book that started your series."

"Aww, thank you so much. Who shall I make this out to?"

A smile plasters her face as she answers, "Davina."

Nikki turns to her publicist, and music begins to play softly in the background. For a moment, I am no longer beside Davina. With my racing heart and our family appearing from behind the people, I step forward, standing next to Nikki, a soft smile on my face. I tap her shoulder.

"Davina Dwain," I begin, taking a knee. My palms are sweating like crazy. My heart is thumping uncontrollably. I feel like the room is spinning but she is my one and I focus on her. "I called in advance and asked for permission. Nikki here said sure, why not—if she got to hear my speech."

Nikki laughs.

I continue with emotion. "I love you, Klutz. You are my life. I know you said before that you didn't want us to go through this, but I love you. I love you. I love you. I'm in love with you. It's always been you. There was no one else for me, not even when you believed otherwise. You were the one then, you are the one now, and you will always be the one."

Breathing out, I calm my nerves. "I love you, and I know I tried this once before, but you were right; it was the wrong time. But now—now is the right time. Here. What could be more romantic? Will you marry me, Klutz?"

The room goes silent. Everyone is waiting, hanging on her every word. Even Nikki's gaze is lingering on her, eager to hear what she'll say.

And in a way, I had pulled her back from the edge, even when she didn't realize she was on the brink. My heart is finally full because Davina saved me.

Everything that happened between us brought us here, to this moment. It's always been us against the world. The two of us. Me and my Klutz.

She tilts her head down towards me, looking into my eyes. We make sense, we always make sense. It was us against life.

"Yes," she says, my heart bursting with emotion. "I love you. Yes, I will marry you, Roger."

The room erupts into applause, and Nikki claps along with everyone else. I pull Davina into my arms. Our lips kiss so full of love that the world seems to blur in the background.

Our parents set off the sparks. We break apart, smiling at each other. Still beaming, we turn to Nikki. We shake her hand, and she smiles warmly, handing Davina a signed copy of her book.

"I can't believe you did this," she whispers, her voice thick with emotion.

"I adore you, Davina. You're my Klutz. I'd do anything for you," I say swelling with affection. "I love you."

With that, everything settles into place.

And no matter where we go or what we do, it will always be me and my Klutz as our destiny unfolds...

THE END

Acknowledgements

I start this by thanking the most important people in my life, the people who stood by me and the ones who never let me feel anything than what I deserve. Mom and Dad, your light in this darkness, in this period is what shines brighter than the sun. My brother. You're my best friend. Thank you for your kindness. Our dogs, sadly both Max and Nitzy are no longer with us, but Hercules, always sitting by my side when I write and so much more. Thank you, family.

Thank you to Nicole Mullaney for your guidance, help, patience and so much more. Without you, this version of Davina and Roger's story would never have been created or written. I appreciate you as a mentor, an editor and a friend, someone who I would call family, because family isn't only by blood, but by bond. Thank you so much for all the amazing things you taught me and are still teaching me till this day. I really am so blessed to have someone like you in my life.

To my beta readers: George, Nour, Valeria, Annie and AJ Campbell. I cherish every single one of you! You're the reason I can share this book with more people. Thank you for reading and sharing your thoughts on the book.

To my influencer group, and the team who inspired, helped put it together, thank you.

To my ARC readers and everyone else who read, you know who you are, I value you. Thank you.

And thank you, dear reader, for buying my book and keeping my dream alive, because without you, none of this would be possible!

Novel Playlist

1. Ruelle – Slip Away

2. Ruelle – Take it All

3. Fleurie – Breathe

4. Fleurie – Hurricane

5. MJ Cole & Freya Ridings – Waking Up

6. Freya Ridings – You Mean the World to Me

7. Freya Ridings – Lost Without You

8. I'm No Chessman – Crocodile Tears

9. Katy Perry – Thinking of You

10. Jessica Mauboy – Little Things

11. Daughtry – It's Not Over

12. Galaxy Thief – Come Alive

13. Justin Bieber – All That Matters

14. Missy Higgins – Where I Stood

15. Archie Ray – The Queen of Hearts

16. Jesse McCartney – It's Over

17. Jojo – Say Love

18. N Sync – Gone

19. Five – It's the Things You Do

20. Backstreet Boys – I'll Never Break Your Heart

About the Author

Fiction author Constandina was born in Cyprus and raised in Lebanon, where sun-drenched coastlines meet the shadows of old secrets. She writes thrillers, suspense, and contemporary romance, with a special love for unpredictable, haunting twists that linger long after the last page.

A person using a computer and drinking coffee with Author name, Constandina, written underneath.

Guided by a deep curiosity about human nature and emotion, Constandina explores the gray areas of morality, revealing how love, fear, and desire intertwine when pushed to their limits. Her goal is simple yet striking—to craft stories that leave readers breathless, wrecked, or both.

When she's not plotting her next twist, Constandina mentors fellow authors and writers, edits other people's books, and works on creating her next mysterious, suspense-filled shocker.

https://constandina.kit.com/

www.ingramcontent.com/pod-product-compliance
Lightning Source LLC
Chambersburg PA
CBHW061306170626
46817CB00001B/78